TO POKE A THIRD EYE

CORSAC FOX
BOOK 6

BLAZE WARD

KNOTTED ROAD PRESS

To Poke A Third Eye
Corsac Fox, Book 6
Blaze Ward
Copyright © 2025 Blaze Ward
All rights reserved
Published by Knotted Road Press
www.KnottedRoadPress.com

ISBNs:
Paperback: 978-1-64470-488-2
Hardback: 978-1-64470-489-9

Cover art:
Jay O'Connell https://www.jayoconnell.com/
Illustration 108050035 © Raffaele1 | Dreamstime.com
Illustration 22850687 © Seamartini | Dreamstime.com

Cover and interior design copyright © 2025 Knotted Road Press

Reviews
It's true. Reviews help. Even a short one, such as, "Loved it!" So please consider reviewing
this book (and all of the ones you've read) on your favorite retailer site.

Never miss a release!
If you'd like to be notified of new releases, sign up for my newsletter.

http://www.blazeward.com/newsletter/

Buy More!
Did you know that you can buy directly from the Knotted Road Press website?

https://www.knottedroadpress.com/shop/

ALSO BY BLAZE WARD

The Science Officer Series

Start with: The Science Officer

The Jessica Keller Chronicles

Start with: Auberon

CS-405 (Command Centurion Kosnett, part of Jessica)

Start with: Queen Anne's Revenge

First Centurion Kosnett (sequel to Jessica)

Start with: Encounter at Vilahana

Additional Alexandria Station Stories

Alexandria Station Collection

Handsome Rob (Alexandria Station Universe)

Start with: Can't Shoot Straight Gang

====================

Corsac Fox

Start with: Flight of the Corsac Fox

Operation Marrakesh

Start with: Trial by Leviathan

Captain Daring

Start with: Revoked

The Hunter Bureau

Start with: Mirrors

Fairchild

Start with: Fairchild

Last Stand

Start with: Lost Dreams

The Lazarus Alliance

Start with: Escape

Shadow of the Dominion

Start with: Longshot Hypothesis

Star Dragon

Start with: Birth of the Star Dragon

Kincaide's War

Start with: The Eden Package

Star Tribes

Start with: Winterstar

Blaze also writes Action-Adventure Here

CONTENTS

PART I
Hunter   1

PART II
Home   31

PART III
Saari   57

PART IV
Bastion   117

PART V
Vauquelin   147

PART VI
Raiders   177

PART VII
Warlord   211

PART VIII
Stradosha   229

PART IX
Rayzian   317

PART X
Free Trader Polat   333

Read More   349
About the Author   351
About Knotted Road Press   353

PART ONE
HUNTER

ONE

"All hands to action stations," the call came over the speaker.

Vanguard Ulysses Fortier—Uly—was already at his station, listening to his own words echo back out of the speakers with a snarl on his face that he supposed would frighten some people.

The ones who didn't know him. Didn't appreciate what was about to happen today.

Or how long it had taken him to track those people down so he could handle the job himself.

"Drew, what's the countdown?" Uly asked, mostly to make sure that everyone else was as locked in and focused as he was.

He wasn't worried about someone threatening *Nubia*. After all, his flagship generally qualified as a Light Devastator by mass and a Heavy one for firepower.

It was the thought that someone might get away from him again.

Not today.

"Two minutes to drop, Uly," Drew replied evenly.

Uly nodded and looked down from the command throne he had inherited with the ship. Not how he would have organized things, but easier to accept it than trying to rebuild the space.

Maybe later, when he got around to building himself a bigger and badder ship.

From left to right, down a level in front of him and facing forward: Astrogator, Sensor, Archer, and Speaker. Those were the titles that had come with the ship. Drew Roscoe, Del Blakeslee, Yaqub Zobo, and Haydar Ramezani as his first team. Two Humans, a Khet, and a Mazhin, which kind of said everything that needed saying about the crew he'd built, with Emro, Thogin, Ononguli, and many others serving somewhere.

"Haydar?" Uly asked.

"I'll be jamming everything as soon as we drop," the Mazhin gentleman pirate nodded at him with head and tentacles. "We're really not taking prisoners?"

"They have had years to surrender, Haydar," Uly growled back. "Instead, they fled as deep into the darkness as they thought would protect them from me, without realizing that if they stopped running long enough, someone would be delighted to collect the bounty I put on that ship."

Haydar nodded again, then went back to his boards, same as the others.

Uly didn't blame him. He was pretty certain that his friends were seeing him at his absolute worst right now, which was saying something, considering the situations he'd faced with them over the years.

But most of those events had been calmer. A moment of peace that turned into pitched battle when pirates suddenly unmasked and attacked somewhere. As opposed to thinking that they could raid Isann, kill innocent sailors, and then get away from him.

The only nice thing Uly could say about the current situation was that their long and merry chase had led him to discover an entirely new subset of pirates, holed up in a system just inside Imperial Sector Thirty-Two. Out beyond the Sector Twenty-One that was a good chunk of the Ononguli Sphere. Middle of nowhere. Reminded him of Daicia in many ways.

More importantly, it had reminded Haydar of Daicia, and that man had been born a pirate, before reforming himself into a scholar.

Or whatever term he was using these days.

"Yaqub?" Uly asked.

"Loaded, locked, and all wavebolt launchers set to fist for the moment, Vanguard," Yaqub replied without glancing up.

Unlike every other crew member, Yaqub had a stripe of purple cloth sewn across his shoulder blades. His surname, Zobo, was derived from a plant with purple flowers, and it had become something of a superstition with the Khet sailor, to the point that he'd always had a stripe of purple tape on the back of his boarding armor in the old days, so you could recognize him from behind.

Not a lot had changed, save that he had become Uly's permanent Gunner on *Nubia*. And convinced Uly to let him keep the purple intact.

Wavebolts came in two flavors on launch. Fist or Lance. Soft option: Knock down all your electroshields. Hard option: Punch starlight through, on the way to doing the same to the hull behind them.

Without knowing how many ships they might encounter, or how heavy they were, Yaqub was defaulting to knocking people down and potentially unconscious with the first salvo, instead of annihilating them.

Most of the ships they would encounter today were guilty of being pirates, as well as harboring a known and wanted fugitive vessel.

The Zuath crew of *Kulakhaov*, however, were forfeit. They had attacked Isann, knowing that those folks lacked the firepower to stop them. Had stripped a dozen ships and killed several hundred Isann sailors whose only fault had been their lack of sufficient technology to resist.

Isann hearts were as good as any Uly had known. His new fleet contained hundreds more such sailors, sailing beyond the darkness, as was their cultural touchstone.

Today was revenge. Nothing more than that. No fancy title. No literary aspirations. Murder.

Kulakhaov had been found, finally. Tracked down. And he was going to see it destroyed as a statement to anybody who still wasn't listening when Uly stated that he was ending piracy in this region of space.

However he had to do it. Whoever he had to do it to.

"All hands, this is Drew," the man said into the intercom. "Drop in five."

Uly nodded and willed his soul to battle.

TWO

Yaqub had been trained by Commander Huff to what that Human considered acceptable standards of Gunnery, which were three long strides better than anything Yaqub had ever encountered anywhere in Khet service.

Nubia had the normal triple/triple firepower configuration that you usually got with big ships, though Huff had mentioned that comparable Human warships might have four or even five turrets with three barrels apiece.

Here, nine wavebolt barrels, each 14.7dm at the bore, when NOBODY else mounted anything bigger than 12s. Just calling them 15s occasionally caused him to shudder, knowing what he could do with that much devastation at his fintips.

Uly wanted a political statement today. The Warlord of the Spinward Reaches had come for your souls and was going to fin you, skin you, and grill you personally, because you could have surrendered at any point along the way, or abandoned ship and gone on to live quiet, meditative lives in a monastery somewhere.

Dumbasses hadn't listened. Hadn't believed.

And today, Purple-boy was the sword of the gods themselves. A little mind-boggling, but kinda awesome at the same time.

"And DROP!" Drew called, but Yaqub already had ship-sign appearing on his scanners as fast as those ancient supercomputers could process data.

And as fast as Haydar could type.

Yaqub didn't try to identify any target. He simply assigned each scanner image a priority number and let his gun teams fire. Reload. Fire again.

A metronomic death by 15dm wavebolt.

Yucky. For you.

"Haydar, is that a station?" Yaqub asked, highlighting the biggest scanner return on his screen.

"Stand by," the Mazhin next to him muttered. "Negative. Big freighter built on a scale with *Watchtower* back home. Possibly the same ship model, or an earlier edition, decommissioned and sold or stolen."

Yaqub nodded. Made sense. Instead of trying to build any sort of permanent base, your slightly wiser pirate might just set up a floating hotel, warehouse, and R&R facility that folks could meet up with if they were trusted enough for those coordinates.

Or had been smart enough to sell Uly the location then run like hell the other direction.

"Uly, you want me to kill that freighter?" Yaqub asked over his shoulder.

Right now, he was shooting anything that moved. Anything that might move. Anybody that got his attention. Everybody.

But Uly had a rep for stealing big cargo vessels and using them better than the bad guys ever did. Plus, they had brought a LOT of extra crew and boarding parties with them on this mission, because nobody had been certain what to expect and Uly had decided to carry the biggest hammer he could.

Moment of pause, but Yaqub wasn't surprised there, either. Sterling Huff would already have a plan, but it would probably involve switching to lance and annihilating that freighter like a torch. Uly usually came up with wickedly more fun plans. And had all the political stuff, too.

"Put one across his bow, Mr. Zobo," Uly ordered sternly.

By now, that term even made sense, but it had taken some getting used to Humanisms. Not even a fin kill. Uly wanted a warning harpoon waved under their nose as a statement.

"Coming up," Yaqub said. "Drew, he might try to run anyway."

"He might *try*," Drew offered in that mad, cackling tone he did when that boy could sail a ship this size through a gap with less than four meters total clearance, not touching anywhere.

Yaqub nodded and targeted a special shot for his A-turret, then went back to killing pirate ships.

One wavebolt, sailing through a mass of about twenty ships, passed like an errant harpoon in front of the freighter and detonated right off the bow. Yaqub was rather pleased with that. Took a bit of programming to get that timing right, but Mr. Huff demanded the best.

"Yaqub, I have *Kulakhaov* located," Haydar said quietly, highlighting a small dot over on the far side of things. "Drew, I think we need to dive in a bit deeper, just in case."

"Coming up," Drew replied.

Yaqub still had to pause occasionally and compare how this bridge worked to the average pirate he'd been, once upon a stupidity ago. Uly had given them orders, then expected his officers to think for themselves when executing them, rather than him having to micromanage everything.

So, Yaqub lined up *Kulakhaov* and sent two wavebolts after it. Everybody else got one. And one 15 was usually enough to splatter anything down in the Seeker scale if they didn't have shields up, Neutron Omnipulsars live, and maybe a handful of 1 and 2dm wavebolts to fire defensively.

Two 'bolts was just being mean.

Or making a statement, which was what Uly was up to.

The Warlord of the Spinward Reaches was done with your shit.

Kulakhaov had been caught asleep. Or something. Yaqub watched them finally open with a pair of 1dm turrets defensively. And a single Omnipulsar turret.

Wasn't going to be nearly enough.

And Uly wasn't about to show any kind of mercy. Not that Yaqub minded. He had a lot of new Isann friends these days.

Uly had had to thin crews down again to staff *Serene Naddoddur* after they'd captured it at Zhoralong. The Chief of Chiefs had recruited a lot of willing Isann sailors to step in and serve on all of Uly's warships. Some of them were here with him in spirit as Yaqub brought them a measure of revenge for friends and family lost.

Yaqub glanced over at Haydar next to him as the wavebolts got close to impacting.

"Anybody trying to surrender?" Yaqub asked, mostly idle curiosity.

"I wouldn't know," Haydar smiled back. "Busy jamming all possible communications with as much overload and random signal as the generators aft can give me."

Knowing how much power *Nubia* generated, Yaqub whistled. Nodded. Shrugged. Nobody was punching a signal through that mess.

Kulakhaov imploded. One/Two. Done.

Squished entirely. Retribution executed. Float to the top of the tank, belly-up.

Yaqub studied his plot. *Nubia* had come out right on top of everyone, then left their Variable Pulse Spatial Generator on, so anybody wanting to run had to get far enough away from them to get outside of range.

And Drew was herding them. No other way to describe it, unless the image of a shark circling a school of tuna translated into Human.

Yaqub wanted to look back and see if Uly had had enough, but the man hadn't said anything, so he went back to his targeting list and updated it. Six not hit so far. Given what Haydar had been doing with available signals intelligence, the six least dangerous of the mess. Farthest away. Least likely to be able to do something defensively, ninety-nine times out of one hundred.

Nubia really was a one-percent outcome.

And Uly was making a point.

"Mr. Zobo, what is your status?" Uly finally asked.

"Last round of targets to engage, sir," he replied, face and fins forward, headcrest down, gills as flat as he could hold them.

Uly could read the same board. Probably better than Yaqub did, but Humans were a far more militantly dangerous species, as a rule. At least according to the Humans he knew.

And he could testify to that.

Yaqub kept up the firing sequence, lacking orders to the contrary.

"I think they've had enough," Uly finally announced. "Mr. Zobo, detonate this round of wavebolts early. Mr. Ramezani, ask the moorage if the rest of them wish to die in battle today."

Haydar's tentacles didn't flinch when Yaqub glanced over, but they'd flown this mission knowing that Uly was angry. Almost as angry as Mr. Huff had been.

Almost.

Sterling would have blown every hull to hell, then sailed off and let the survivors perish when their life support failed, but that one took his job seriously.

And had taught a reformed Khet pirate what it meant to protect the innocent from predators.

Yaqub confirmed that all wavebolts ceased tracking and imploded, then secured the turrets, with one barrel dead centered on that big whale in the middle, just in case he needed to be properly harpooned anyway.

"All weapons secured, Vanguard," Yaqub announced.

He'd done his part. Now, Uly got to deal with the survivors.

Or maybe Dan, since Haydar was indicating that folks were now happy to surrender once they realized that the Corsac Fox had arrived.

He sat back and smiled.

THREE

Dan figured that she'd have to give up these sorts of operations, one of these days. The Chief of Staff to the Corsac Fox and Speaker for the Congress of Wives really shouldn't be boarding pirate warships in armor. At the same time, Uly should have sent Sterling or Aibek to handle this mission, rather than doing it himself.

This one had, however, needed the personal touch. And she'd watched on screens from the flight bay with her reinforced assault battalion as Uly had crushed his target, while hammering the others.

Normally, she had one hundred and fifty troopers, the best she'd been able to recruit from five hundred candidates, with most of the rest available as security troops under Solomon Wyndham or simply crew in various capacities. It was always useful when someone from the quartermaster's office or a barber could sudden throw on boarding armor and charge into battle.

Today, she had everybody. And had brought more from Bastion when she was certain where they were going. What they were doing.

"Dan, it's Uly," he said in her helmet comm. "I think they've had enough. There is another *Watchtower*-sized ship here that I want you to take. The little ones are about half destroyed and half wounded. I'll need you to sort those out later. Blow the ones not worth repairing, then let me know what you need for crews to get the rest to Saari from here. Daicia might be closer, but I'd rather not put temptation in front of newly reformed pirates. Plus, Eskil needs better firepower more than Kadyr does at the moment."

"Understood," Dan replied, turning to take in her Combat Team.

Even Halyna had grown into the role over the last six months, much more confident that her martial skills were comparable to her impressive political ones. It let Dan keep eight combat groups, but pull herself out and let her focus on overall command, instead of shooting things. For this mission, though, they'd let Anari stay home with Sterling while Dan had taken over her group.

"Mount up!" she called, watching the group pivot in lockstep and jog to the various shuttles with a sound like a dinosaur-sized wood-pecker hunting bugs. Bang. Bang. Bang.

They didn't board quickly, but that was all the extra bodies today. She would need that to capture everything. Somebody might decide to run, but if she had more troopers than any ship over there had crew, she doubted they would get far in such thinking.

Nasrin joined her last, her tentacles expressing a seriousness today that was usually at odds with the youngest of Dan's Combat Team. Longest with her, still youngest relative to overall lifespan, even compared to Yanouk.

"We stealing another Wren?" Nasrin asked as they closed up the lock and found seats.

Dan smiled.

"The easiest way to defeat piracy is to eliminate the network supplying them with consumables and buyers for stolen goods," she replied. "I've got more than decade expertise at that sort of thing, all the way back to *Batyr*. Without those folks, you have a junkyard and a lot of desperation."

Nasrin nodded. Young, she might be, but she'd been the daughter of Mazhin merchant/pirates before *Danumash* had captured her. Then assigned to a Mazhin research project as a *Social*, which was the polite term *Danumash* used for prostitutes, because they had no other under-standing of what else a young, pretty, *female* Mazhin might be. None of the Mazhin men had touched her. Ever. Considered her a niece or daughter, but *Danumash* were punks. Specists.

Dumbasses.

And Uly had taken his time with all of his new wives, letting them set whatever pace they were comfortable with. Dan had been First Wife there, and Den Mother to the rest. It had been her idea in the first place, with Uly accepting her *fait accompli* when presented.

She trusted Uly as she did nobody else in the galaxy.

"Commander, we're cleared to launch," came over the speaker. "Free flight in ten seconds."

Dan ignored the woman. They were just as expert at their facet of things as the rest of her force, or they wouldn't be here.

She settled in as gravity fell away and the shuttle rocketed across the void to their first target.

FOUR

Nasrin felt like a grizzled veteran, a point that her various uncles and cousins took great pleasure in teasing her about, whenever they thought they could get away with it.

Today was not that day. All the Mazhin on this shuttle had their mouths shut and their tentacles still.

She might be younger than any of them. Nasrin Monfared was still in charge.

Shit, any time they encountered a roaming Mazhin trader, *those* folks expected her or Omid to *Speak*. Omid was too shy and introverted, most of the time. Nasrin had Uly to *Speak* for everyone.

Usually took strangers a few days to climb down off their high horses and understand. About the time Uly turned on the charm.

Around them, the sounds of the shuttle docking with the large freighter. Gravity faintly reaching out and establishing a down.

Dan rose first, with Nasrin immediately after her, one hand back to bring her Omnibow into position, the other hand pulling a Firesphere from her bandoleer and loading it.

Anybody giving her grief today wasn't getting politely knocked down to nausea and unconsciousness. That bright red ball on the end was nature's way of telling you to shut up and listen.

Or else.

Scout One went through the airlock at close to a dead run when it opened. Hard, fast, ugly, terminal. Nasrin had been listening to various chatter on channels as the other shuttles got close to their respective targets, but nobody had suggested that the pirates they found would be anything less than helpful when Dan's teams arrived to take charge.

And they were taking command.

Nasrin led Team One through a few seconds later, into a cargo bay about half empty and feeling like a dance hall where someone had pushed the tables and chairs back against the wall to free up space.

Couple dozen Ugotha and Zuath lined up over there, being covered by Nasrin's killers. Some had hands and stubby wings in the air. Others were frozen. A few rocked back and forth a bit mindlessly.

Nobody was a threat. And every one of them flinched when the Firesphere came around and centered on them.

"Who was in command yesterday?" she called angrily, smelling and tasting their fear and apprehension as she walked across the space.

"Team Two, nail down Engineering and the Bridge. NOW!" Dan called behind her.

Nasrin tracked bodies peeling away and heading both directions at a lethal run. The ship was enormous, but most of it would be storage. Possibly a few bays converted to things like bars and brothels, based on what she'd researched.

Who knew that she would become such an expert on piracy operations and administration?

An Ugotha stepped forward, then flinched a second time when Nasrin centered her Omnibow on the woman. The species was insectile, with a chitin shell over an endoskeleton. Two big compound eyes. Four antenna around the mouth, two up and two down. Still followed the basic erect biped with bilateral symmetry that seemed to be evolution's answer to tool use.

The shell was a muted orange she'd once heard called burnt umber, dressed in dark blue pants and jacket. Female, but that didn't mean as much as it might elsewhere, as they tended to be as matriarchal as Mazhin.

Experts at chemistry, with a sense of smell comparable to her tentacles.

"Captain Izaro Ubiña," the Ugotha woman said. "You really are from the Corsac Fox?"

"He's out there in command of *Nubia*," Nasrin nodded her head back, watching the men and women behind Ubiña flinch yet again. "Your vessel is engaged in piracy and is forfeit. You have provided aid and comfort to the pirate vessel *Kulakhaov*, but Vanguard Fortier has decided to show mercy and capture this ship instead of destroying it and killing all of you out of hand. His mercy extends to allowing you to reform yourselves, once you are..."

Squawks of outrage interrupted her speech, but Team One had a lot of weapons lined up and ready to kill everyone over there if anybody moved. Including a Firesphere.

People calmed down quickly when they realized that Uly's people would be fine killing them all and demanding that whatever deities they worshiped take responsibility for them after that.

Nasrin snarled them to silence.

"Your crew will be removed from this vessel and transported aboard *Nubia* to our next destination," Nasrin growled at them, a tone intended to grind down any edges they thought might cut someone. "You may be allowed to enlist with friendly forces, once you have been identified. Others will be turned over to the Ononguli for imprisonment to serve out your sentences. Questions?"

Firesphere. Centered. Probably looked as big as your head from that perspective. The safety was off on her Omnibow, and her finger was inside the trigger well, needing only about two kilograms of pressure to fire.

She'd already woken up this morning in a bad enough mood to kill random strangers.

Captain Ubiña considered her words carefully from the way all four antennae flickered.

"Enlist with the Corsac Fox?" she asked delicately, then turned and snarled at a larger Zuath male behind her who had started to say something. "SHUT UP!"

"The Corsac Fox is ending piracy in this entire region," Nasrin replied. "The *Vatazhko* of the Ononguli has ordered all Ononguli vessels to prepare for war with the Auga. The Corsac Fox has come this far to eliminate the vessel and crew of *Kulakhaov* for their crimes at the moorage of Isann. You may choose your destiny from here, mistress."

Nasrin could taste Dan's surprise at the tone and words, but Nasrin understood that dropping a ton of bricks on trouble up front would go a long ways to eliminating more later.

Captain Ubiña actually turned her back on Nasrin to glare at the mob behind her.

"He'll kill you if you give him any reason," she yelled at them. "So don't think you can surrender today and then do something stupid tomorrow, because I will disown every one of you who does."

Nasrin was impressed. However, Uly's reputation was starting to seep out across the entire galaxy. Mercy in one hand and a sledge-hammer in the other.

Captain Ubiña completed her circle.

"Some of the pimps might prove difficult," she said carefully.

"As long as they have employees and not slaves," Nasrin replied ambiguously. Or not so ambiguously.

Even compound eyes can get big, but Captain Ubiña nodded.

"Contractors," she said. "How they are treated might be complicated, but I lease out sections of the ship and charge them rent."

"As long as we understand one another," Nasrin said. "Let's go have a chat with them."

Sex for money between consenting adults? Lovely. Capitalistic, even, though Nasrin understood from her uncles and aunt that a proper society didn't need such things, when all you had to do was ask politely.

But then, they were pirates, and Uly made it clear that such things represented a myriad swath of socioeconomic failures. Ones he didn't think he'd live long enough to fix, but that wasn't going to stop him from trying.

Or her.

FIVE

Haydar walked into Uly's day office with perhaps a more jaunty stride than was entirely necessary, but at the same time, he was more than willing to admit that he was a first-class data nerd.

And this scenario had provided him with SO MANY NEW THINGS TO EXPLORE.

Uly caught his mood and smiled as Haydar sat.

"What trouble have you caused this time?" Uly asked innocently.

Haydar had to suppress his jolt, and remind himself that Uly could read semaphore in ways that just about no other species in the galaxy could.

"Technically, I'm just First Officer here," he replied. "You started it."

"Uh huh," Uly replied in a disbelieving tone.

"Well, we get to be heroes," Haydar said. "Over and above all the things we've already done here."

"Oh?"

"That freighter at the center of things," Haydar nodded. "The name translates out of Ugotha as *Crimson Crazy*, or at least close enough with a whole series of historical and cultural idioms that lose some of the flavor. Dance Hall. Hotel. Fence. Mobile chandlery. Kind of a one-stop shopping mall space station for pirates to take a vacation."

"Past tense," Uly said in that way that indicated a point of honor with the man.

Not that Haydar disagreed. The crazy shit he'd done in his youth still flavored a whole bunch of things in his life.

"Past tense," Haydar agreed. "Nasrin and Dan cleared it. All the usuals. Crew split down the middle in thinking that they could be reformed. Handful of them got themselves killed by the boarding teams, though I have no idea where they thought they might run to."

"Probably saved us the trouble of hanging them later," Uly shrugged.

It was the calm, assured way that Humans took deadly violence like that for granted that frightened everybody. Haydar had seen the species at first hand for more than a decade at this point, and no other species automatically defaulted to killing. Others could get themselves there, but nobody started as close.

"Anyway," Haydar stepped over that jolt, "one of the brothels contained a large group of Ancyn females who convinced Dan and Nasrin that they had been..."

Uly had perked up. Killing glare was there.

"Not slaves," Haydar deflected quickly. "Maybe stuck in an impossible situation by some asshole who had them over a barrel, if I have the Humanism correct. Trapped and working off a debt because they preferred to stay together as a group rather than anybody departing."

"Ancyn?" Uly asked. "I don't think I know the species."

"I had to look them up," Haydar said. "Erect biped, evolved from land-based avians in a manner distantly similar to Zuath. Proportions are a bit weird compared to you and me, but similar enough. Feathers everywhere but the face, with browns and grays predominant."

"And they are interesting because?"

"They once ruled a great empire that spanned a couple of solar systems, but were utterly conquered by the Auga, Uly," Haydar replied. "Long, freaking time ago. Their origin is entirely a mystery these days, as even their supposed world of origin doesn't seem to be their home-world. There are hints that the Auga relocated all of the survivors from said homeworld, early in the Imperial Era, so they might have been a close neighbor to the Imperial capital at Ajorn. Near as I can tell, they are only found in Imperial Sectors One and Three today, in spite of the elapsed time, when most imperial subjects have some freedom to move about."

"How the hell did they end up in Thirty-Two?" Uly asked.

"I haven't had a chance to interview anyone for that information," Haydar grinned. "Dan and Nasrin are too busy policing that vessel, while rounding up all the others. I wouldn't have thought it possible to find them this far from home, but apparently it is. Better, I'm given to understand that the group is over thirty such individuals aboard *Crimson Crazy*. That alone is enough mystery for me."

"Any of the other ships causing troubles?" Uly asked, eyes pensive now.

"Negative," Haydar stated. "Yaqub did an excellent job pounding snouts. Sadeq thinks that about half will be flightworthy in a few days. I presume we're abandoning the rest?"

"I might ask the Paramount of the Samuur to send out repair crews," Uly shrugged. "Or ask Maks to help them with the task, since he's in the process of building them a modern shipyard and repairing *Vauquelin* for me."

"Do we know what we're doing with the former *Serene Naddoddur* when it comes out of drydock?" Haydar asked carefully, wondering if he was about to find his tentacles in a trap.

"It will need a commanding officer, once they finish the rehabilitation," Uly smiled wickedly. "You haven't changed your mind?"

"I work better as a Science and Data Officer, Uly," Haydar shook his head. "You know that. Plus, I need to be close to the center of wherever you are, and that ship is likely to be off doing things. Putting Sterling in command is probably safest, unless you intended to move him here."

He watched Uly lean back, eyes focused on some distant point.

"I'm still a few years from being able to simply build a palace and rule this thing we're creating," the young Human mused. "And *Batyr* is a lovely ship, but a Heavy Striker like *Vauquelin* will be so much more, so yes, probably Sterling will need to transfer over with about half of his people. I'll need to take a closer look, but Yuriy Kovalchuk might be ready to be Conductor and take *Batyr*."

"I tend to agree," Haydar offered. "Your immediate staff will need to remain together. And here aboard *Nubia* with you, because this will be where decisions are made. What about Bastion?"

"Everything I've heard suggests that Maks's mom is another one that people vastly underestimate," Uly laughed. "I can see where he got it. Appointing her Governor has caused a lot of Ononguli to pay closer attention to what we're building. And the Khet Trade Factors seem a bit disturbed that Maks is willing to challenge them on their own ground, so they've extended tentacles over to investigate. That means more people. More trade. More development."

"Turning the Spinward Reaches into a place," Haydar nodded.

Uly's smile was one of those things that made getting out of bed in the morning worthwhile.

"So what about your Ancyn?" Uly abruptly changed directions. Like he did.

"I was about to take a shuttle over and interview them," Haydar replied. "Thought you might be interested in coming along, since they are entirely new, a long ways from home, and a possible source of social intelligence about what's happening deeper inside the *Auga Empire*."

"Yes," Uly said, rising. "Let's do that."

Haydar rose with him. The information hadn't seemed too good to be true, but it might represent one hell of a coup anyway.

He just needed to figure out how to exploit it.

SIX

Suka Kuri had been *explicitly* threatened not to join Dan and the Combat Team in assaulting the enemy fleet. Not that she'd really given it much thought.

Honest.

Moss School, after all, was so much easier on the knees than Sabre School.

Still, when Uly had asked her to join him on his little excursion, she'd been in motion so fast that she would have to ask someone to deal with half a pot of tea she'd left behind in her quarters. Or she'd just clean the pot herself when she got back.

The ride across had been mundane. Dan required that her shuttle pilots be absolutely amazing, every time they flew. And *Nubia* utterly commanded the immediate vicinity, a new junkyard of old ships that might end up being stripped for parts by locusts, from what tidbits Uly and Haydar had mentioned.

But then, Uly's opinions on anti-social behavior were rather well known.

They docked and were met by Ciah Dambe, the young Khet woman who was the smallest member of Dan's Combat Team. Possibly the fastest, too. The *Troublesome Warrior Child*.

"Any news?" Uly asked as Suka Kuri followed him deeper into the enormous vessel.

"Couple of hard cases," Ciah offered. "Dan wasn't playing around and Nasrin's in a bit of a mood."

Suka Kuri cringed at that term. Must have been ugly. Nasrin was usually the calmest and most rational of the team.

However, if you got *her* tentacles up…

Eventually, they found the brothels, mostly walking in silence only broken by Haydar's boots on the deck, as the rest of them moved quieter.

Looking around, the space had been decorated with an eye towards making it feel cheery, though she'd have to inquire with her Mazhin friends as to the overall taste of the paintwork. Visually exciting, which Suka Kuri supposed you wanted in a brothel. Lots of couches, chairs, and a pair of bars facing one another. For liquid courage, she supposed.

All of Dan's people that she could see in the space were female, which made a bit of sense, if you were rescuing indentured prisoners forced to prostitute themselves to survive. The crowd of civilians ran about nine to one female as well, but the males she could see weren't bouncers or bartenders.

More victims, though she paused and considered that for some people this might be the ultimately perfect occupation. It took all kinds, and this galaxy certainly experimented with just about every form of socially acceptable behavior.

She followed Uly and Haydar to where Dan and Nasrin sat with a pair of Ononguli, an Emro woman, and two Ancyn.

Suku Kuri had never met the species, but she had traveled a great deal in her decades, and studied an even wider swath. The older of the two was mostly gray in plumage with gold and black highlights in her headcrest, while the one she took as younger tended to brown.

All the other rescued victims were seated or standing around the back of the room. Watching. They even had Emro-sized chairs, so Suka Kuri dragged one over and sat next to Nasrin where hers and Haydar's tentacles were visible to watch.

She didn't speak the language, but could follow reasonably well when they weren't limiting themselves purely to scent.

"Galli, this is Uly Fortier," Dan introduced the older Ancyn woman. The most interesting one in this group. "Uly, Galli Fyodon and her kinswoman, Loh-An Huang. The others are Riko Okazaki, Nina Borysov, and Kseniya Shevchenko. Ladies, Haydar Ramezani and Suka Kuri, who is Exemplar of the Arts, Moss School."

Suka Kuri wondered how closely related the one Ononguli woman was to Anna Shevchenko, the *Vatazhko* of the Ononguli, but she also knew that Ononguli clans tended to be huge.

It was Galli Fyodon that caught her eye. Sharp. Smart. Self-contained, like a woman who could will herself to suffer just about any torture without making a noise, if necessary.

Suka Kuri leaned in and drew all the eyes to her. It was obvious that her femininity would be useful here, when Uly and Haydar were male, and thus possibly accidentally brought bad karma into the room with them.

And Exemplar of the Arts caused all five women to recoil a bit, which it normally did. She smiled to put them at ease.

"While I am a great distance from my homeworld," she began, eyes locked on Galli Fyodon, "I would believe you have come a further distance, at least socially and mentally."

Fyodon nodded. It was a compact thing. Big eyes compared to the size of her skull. Short beak that was basically Suka Kuri's mouth reversed, with the teeth on the outside.

"Given the situation, I presume that we might be rescuing you from your indenture contract," Suka Kuri continued, because if they were slaves, Dan and Nasrin might have already executed everybody on this ship.

Certain evils were no longer going to be allowed. Anywhere.

"So I understand, Elder," Fyodon replied in a musical voice, the kind that wanted to range tonally over at least one octave.

Suka Kuri wondered what a trained Ancyn vocalist might sound like.

"May I be so bold as to inquire how your group came to be here?" she asked, nodding to the large group of Ancyn women off to one side, socially distinct from the others by the way they organized themselves into a single cluster.

Fyodon opened her beak, then closed it. Eyed Suka Kuri, but focused more on Uly, which was probably to be expected.

The Warlord of the Spinward Reaches added a certain gravity to the room—to any room—though she could tell he was keeping his charisma under tight wraps right now. Letting his women talk to the other women, understanding that his maleness might prove troublesome.

Yet another reason she loved the man so much, as most people didn't reach that level of mature self-assurance until much later in life.

If ever.

"It is a long and involved tale, Elder," Fyodon finally offered. "Should I summarize initially?"

Ah, someone who understood what Moss School was, even if she didn't appear to belong. The need to study. To learn. To dive deep, when perhaps the executive summary might be more appropriate today.

"Let us stay shallow for now," Suka Kuri answered. "We are not pressed for time, but I suspect that most of your comrades would appreciate being able to pack and transfer over to *Nubia* for transport."

Almost everyone reacted to that. Shock. Awe. Fear. Surprise.

Suka Kuri understood *denial*.

"Your indenture is fulfilled," she announced to the room. "You will all be free to go, once we arrive at a place from which travel is easy."

She didn't need to look at Uly for permission. His nod was sufficient.

She focused on Fyodon. That one hadn't woken up this morning expecting to be freed from all her past troubles, but was adapting reasonably quickly. She still required a few breaths to organize it in her head.

"We were prisoners of the Empire," Fyodon began, referring to the Auga by the way she stressed that term. "Political prisoners. Rounded up for various petty infractions, separated from our mates and put into work camps. When we escaped, we stole a ship and fled. Later, we were captured by pirates when our ship broke down. We were given the option of indenture, one presumes from our exoticness in Imperial Sector Nine. And our demand to stay together as a single group, rather than being separated. That was four years ago. Some of us worked in the brothel, while a few had paid off debts and graduated to other jobs on this vessel. Barmaids. Cleaning. None of us had the technical skills to accumulate enough funds to buy out the rest, but none was willing to leave individually."

Suka Kuri could practically taste the rage boiling off Uly. And Dan. And Nasrin. And pretty much everybody else in here, so she didn't need to speak on the topic.

"The pirates that took you originally," Suka Kuri said simply. "They brought you to Fifteen? Then headed inward towards the galactic core, through Fourteen into what I am given to understand is Imperial Sector Thirty-Two?"

Fyodon paused, doing math.

"That sounds roughly correct, Elder," she replied. "Our original captors were Emro, such as yourself, then our contract was sold on to a group of Zuath and Khet investors. I would say all very businesslike, but it is not the business I would have preferred to undertake."

"Khet?" Uly asked. Quiet but sharp. Like a knife unsheathing in the darkness.

"So I was told," Fyodon nodded. "That was many years past, and only gossip. Does it matter? They sold us on."

"Four years ago, I was turning the Khet into my allies," Uly said. "If they withheld this sort of thing from me, knowing my opinions on the topic, it may be necessary to have a deeper discussion with certain folks, the next time I visit Z'Gosza. Nothing that matters to you, mistress, as we'll be departing from here back into realms I control and you will be given assistance in moving on to wherever your group decides to travel next."

Suka Kuri caught the look between Fyodon and Huang, sitting next to her.

"You are the Corsac Fox," Fyodon said simply.

"I am also the Corsac Fox, yes," Uly agreed. "Warlord of the Spin-ward Reaches. This, however, is a rescue operation. Or rather, I came here to destroy the pirate vessel *Kulakhaov*, and remind the other pirates in the region that their time is done. They will behave, or they will be ended. Innocents such as yourselves will be freed, that you can live the sorts of fulfilling lives that were obviously interrupted by the Auga initially, and a long chain of fools since."

Fyodon blinked at the raw vehemence in his voice. Suka Kuri did as well, and she'd known Uly for far longer.

"Where can we go?" Fyodon asked, eyes dancing back and forth between Suka Kuri and Uly.

Haydar, wisely, hadn't made even a sound, nor had the others. This was a much higher level negotiation.

"Rimward from here is the Ononguli Sphere in Sector Twenty-One," Uly offered. "To the right from that as you go is Sector Fourteen, which I have claimed. You are in Thirty-Two, but it is not an area that I have scouted or surveyed, and we do not intend to stay long. My immediate plans involve traveling to Saari, the homeworld of my Samuur allies. You are welcome to depart there, or travel with us to my base at Bastion. And you are not required to decide today. Today, you can travel to my flagship and leave this vessel behind, though I will be taking it with me when I leave, along with those pirate ships that can sail."

Suka Kuri leaned in and shifted the gravity of the room again.

"I would be greatly interested in learning more about your people, Galli Fyodon," she said. "How you came to be here. And how we might help you get where you need to be."

"Thank you," the Ancyn woman said simply, her beak and head-crest bobbing. "I will have many questions for you, but that represents a vast ignorance we have inherited."

"We are here to learn from one another," Suka Kuri smiled. "That is the promise of the Corsac Fox."

Uly leaned back, then, as Galli Fyodon began talking about her past. And that of this group of Ancyn women she had assembled. Had escaped from the Auga.

Had gotten here.

Suka Kuri wasn't certain where they would go next, but she would help them get there.

PART TWO
HOME

SEVEN

Sterling normally commanded *Batyr*, but he understood that being promoted to Commander meant that he had political duties to attend to. At least he hadn't had to act as Governor of the system for all that long.

Lyra Sobol was handling that. Maks's Mom and Uly's aunt by marriage. Bondarenko by birth. Her and Voldomir had come out with a whole shipful of Ononguli folks. Some members of the Bondarenko, the Sobol, and the Shevchenko clans, or at least allies. Others looking to get rich in a new system.

Looking around the meeting room, Sterling was more excited at the wide range of faces he saw. The incredible number of species represented, which was even more of a shock whenever he paused to think how he might have turned out had he remained in *Danumash* service.

Those people had a very narrow view of social acceptability, and it didn't extend to aliens of any kind. Here, he sat with Ononguli, Emro, Thogin, Khet, Mazhin, Isann, Samuur, and Yarikh, though that last might still be close enough to Human to count. They had been Human at one point, he'd been given to understand, before Standardizing and Upgrading themselves with genetic engineering.

Governor Sobol smiled back at him and rapped her coffee mug on the table, looking around the rest of the group.

"Sterling, what news do you have?" she asked.

Sterling wanted to defer. He glanced over at Anari, his research partner. And other things, though they were both a little nervous approaching certain topics. She was the one who could best translate old texts and tease out the little details. Sterling just built maps.

But this was a mapping discussion, at the end of the day.

"With the help of most of the people here at the table, I have been able to greatly extend my astrogation records," he said simply, nodding to Engineer Melpomeni Michelakos, the Yarikh woman who had provided much of the most recent data. And to Rabiu Khadijan, who had apparently blackmailed someone back home on Z'Gosza into providing a whole series of old sailing and navigational records that stretched up and inward from Khet Space, including places Sterling didn't think had ever been officially discussed. Possibly never formally surveyed.

Pirate haven sorts of things, but the Khet of Z'Gosza were beginning to understand that Uly was capable of thwarting the most egregious pirate activities by virtue of simply killing people if they refused to behave. Smugglers, Uly didn't mind, considering that to reflect a social failure. Sterling wasn't sure he understood the distinction, but Uly drew a hard line and enforced it, and that was good enough.

He nodded and clicked on the projector, bringing up a greatly expanded 3D image of Imperial Sector Fourteen, along with about half of each of the various sectors that it touched. Then he flipped a switch and started adding colors.

"All the white stars remaining are known solely from astronomical observation," Sterling continued. "The Yarikh records are the most detailed, but their interest tended to fade with distance, so I have this group best. Over this direction, Khet records have been added to show several ancient trade roads that appear to have largely fizzled out over the last eight or ten centuries, indicating that this region of the galaxy was once much more robust, but has fallen into something of a local dark age, from which folks like the Isann and Samuur are today only slowly emerging. Ononguli records taken at Daicia allowed us to peer into

Sector Thirty-Two and add a few cultures that are colonies of other folks deeper in, possibly including species we do not, at present, have records for."

He paused and drew a breath, smiling.

"But you didn't come here today to hear me talk astrogation," he nodded. "We have been able to identify a couple of places where we should be able to establish new trade routes, largely by building trade stations that will provide the necessary warehousing and resupply that folks would need. They will be centered on Bastion itself, but also running back into the darkness beyond Traiffe, where the Yarikh previously retired to. Thank you for letting us have that data, by the way."

"You are welcome, Sterling," Engineer Michelakos replied. "We took much of it from folks who were unwilling to simply leave us alone when warned off. There are others out there that were bright enough to immediately flee and not look back. Those might and might not appear in other records."

"Mostly, I think I got that covered," he told her. "At present, with Anari's help I have synthesized at least eleven different data systems into the one I've been maintaining here, along with cultural and historical notes as we've been able to extract them from any records we've come across."

He glanced at Anari and caught her grin. He did the math. She did the people. They made a great team.

And old Sterling would have been way too stupid to look at her and see anything beyond big and green. But he'd been a dumbass, and hopefully Commander Huff was smart enough to make entirely different mistakes than let a woman like Anari Supasei get away from him.

"So where's that leave us?" Ethir Ewin asked.

Head of the Thogin cousins. Founding member of Uly's Legal Department™. Dangerous guy in any boardroom.

"I remember sitting on the bridge of *Batyr*, when Uly asked us what was out there," Sterling replied. "Before he had us sail into this darkness looking for places where we might put down roots. Everyone called it the Spinward Reaches, and considered it an empty desert. Now we know that it's full of people, but they haven't climbed out to the level of the rest of the galaxy. Instead, they will be getting there as quickly as Uly and Maks can get them the technology they need. Most importantly, other than raw numbers, there does not appear to be anyone, anywhere, who is a serious threat, if we set up patrols with our allies. You have the Khet out to the far edge of Fifteen at Z'Gosza. The Ononguli Sphere in Twenty-One. The Auga along the inner third of Fifteen and approaching the edges of Fourteen, but mostly dug in as they have focused most of their efforts in Twenty-One to dislodge the Horde, a process they expect to take another millennia, as I am given to understand."

"More trade, less war?" Piruz asked. The Mazhin was commonly teased as the *Used Camel Salesman* for his ability to do deals with anyone.

"Less regional war," Sterling corrected him. "The *Auga Empire* remains an implacable foe and the Corsac Fox has declared war on them. At some point, they may even strike at Bastion, though the range is excessive and I would doubt that they could easily assemble the necessary force to project that distance. Assassins might be a threat."

"One I have been giving much thought to," Governor Sobol interjected, drawing the conversation back to her. "Uly is safe while he has Dan and the Combat Team close, but we need to start a process of much more closely scouting folks at Bastion to root out spies. Maks had a few tools at his disposal. I have added more. What can the Legal Department add?"

Sterling sat back and listened now. He was the youngest person in the room, with Anari next, then a pretty big step up to Ethir and Piruz, to say nothing of the Governor or especially the Engineer.

"I have had a few chats with Uly and Dan about how the Humans of the *Institutional Republic of Batyr* handle these things," Rabiu spoke up. "And conferred with both Anari and Suka Kuri. Citizenship appears to be a powerful token that we can take advantage of."

"Citizenship?" the Governor asked.

"The Sphere is exclusively an Ononguli place," Rabiu nodded. "Z'Gosza is equally dominated by Khet. Uly will have everyone who is willing to behave. The Legal Department, since we're something of an Administrative State until such time as the Congress of Wives and Conclave of the Species gets actively ramped up, are largely responsible for writing the first draft of laws that will apply to everyone and then be edited to need as we go. To date, we have generously mixed Khet Mercantile Law with Horde procedures, throwing in a dash of *Batyr*'s single-party system, focused on a dual hegemony of Uly and Dan."

Sterling had to pause to dissect that into something he could understand. The day he'd met Dan—and more importantly, Uly—he'd been a lowly midshipman, relegated to the Secondary Bridge on the day when the Primary Bridge had been destroyed, killing all the senior officers.

And the *Combined Crowns of Danumash* did things aristocratically. Blood and marriage got you ahead. Like the Ononguli were all about the clan, while the Khet did the corporate entity.

However, Uly and Dan would run things as long as they were around. They also expected Bastion to run itself when they were elsewhere. That meant this group.

"You folks still with us?" Ethir asked.

Sterling nodded with the rest.

"What Fish-boy here is saying is that you can apply for citizenship, which comes with certain legal advantages, but also invokes taxation and cultural costs," Ethir grinned. "You get better protection under the law, but you gotta pay for it in the process. Folks who don't plan to stay longer than a few years pay less in taxes, but don't get as much support if things go wrong and they are suddenly out of luck. We think it will inspire folks to give up whatever species loyalties might have held them in the past, to belong here instead. Turning to spies, we're going to need a process to ferret out folks lying in order to burrow into the body politic and become pests or threats."

"Ethir, are you suggesting some sort of secret police, intended to augment the fleet?" Sterling asked, flashing back to some of the things *Danumash* did quietly in the shadows.

"Something like that, yes," Ethir agreed. "We expect a lot of people to be drawn here. Uly needs bodies to build an economy that ends up being larger or more durable than a traditional space-based thalassocracy. Sure, you can create a pure trade empire that ends up being little more than merchant stations in orbit, without exploiting the planets below, but you trade off a lot of manpower and raw materials options in doing so. Think of the Mazhin Convocation. They are almost a perfect example, living permanently aboard ships that sail around, and hardly having any footprint on a planetary surface. We're going to need civilian gendarme forces because we will have planets."

"Beat cops we already deploy," Governor Sobol noted. "We're augmenting and expanding that?"

"A necessary evil, Governor," Piruz nodded. "There will be bad apples. They must be located and removed as fast as possible. Even the Auga will eventually try to kill Uly and Dan. Massed fleets are one thing. An assassin in the night is something entirely different, and must be addressed. With you exercising supreme local authority, as advised by this group, we think you will need to move sooner, rather than later, because we can create something now and then grow it as the population expands. Remember, we're still talking only a few hundred thousand colonists on the surface of the planet as yet, with a roughly equal amount in orbit at any given time. That will grow when we put down a capital city and start build pretty things that become the backbone of Uly's kingdom."

"How do we vet them?" she asked.

"I have some ideas," Ethir said grimly, a tone that caused Sterling's hackles to rise.

Ethir and his cousins had talked about their various stints in local jails for whatever the Auga authorities could make stick. He probably was an expert on that sort of thing, though many of the Ononguli had done their time as pirates, either in private service or working directly for the Horde itself.

Then Ethir turned to face Engineer Michelakos, face hard and cold.

"You got any advanced, technological tools that might be the equivalent to magic to us poor primitives, such as would let us read minds when we want to find our potential spies?" Ethir asked bluntly.

Sterling was a bit surprised, but supposed that it was the sort of question that needed to be asked. And someone in the Legal Department should be best at asking it.

Michelakos pursed her lips as she figured out which set of lies to tell. It surprised Sterling that he could read that in her face, but they were both Human that way, and he'd had to learn to understand body language across more than a dozen species as he'd turned from a dumb kid into an adult.

And the Engineer wasn't about to tell Ethir the truth. Or much of it, maybe.

"I will need to give it some thought," she finally said diplomatically. "There are probably devices that can be built, but I'm not sure how we would go about measuring such things."

Sterling considered calling her out, but she caught his eye and there was something there. Yes, they had such tools, but the Yarikh also considered the rest of the galaxy starkly primitive, both biologically as well as technologically.

And he didn't think that they had, as a culture, figured out yet how much help they were going to provide to everyone else, when the Engineer might still be alive on the day Uly died of old age.

How much did they want to destabilize things around them, in the process of protecting themselves?

He gave her a tiny nod of acknowledgment. Nobody else here could read the woman as well as he could. Because she really was Human in all the ways that generally mattered to him.

Kit Simonson had other issues, but those were personal and Sterling hadn't been asked to get involved, so all he had was the rumor mill to go on.

Governor Sobol looked around the group.

"Any other major issues to discuss, before we break and circle back to the mundane things?" she asked.

"The prisoner," Anari offered. "Conductor Székely from *Serene Naddoddur*."

"Is there an issue?" Sobol asked.

"No, but if we're talking about potential Auga spies, perhaps he might be a source of useful information?" Anari pressed.

"He has given his parole," Sobol said bluntly. "That does not extend to pressing him such."

"Understood, Governor," Anari noted. "Until recently, he and I shared a culture, but he would have a much different perspective on many things. Perhaps in merely talking, we can learn how the Auga might approach such topics."

Sterling nodded. Made perfect sense. She'd been an engineer on *Iron Wasp*, helping get it ready for auction in a police impound yard, when Uly had broken out of jail and stolen it. Anari had demanded that she be captured and taken with the vessel, and Suka Kuri had agreed.

Here she thrived, more Moss than Sabre these days, even as Yanouk was more Sabre than Moss, but hadn't Suka Kuri herself said that those distinctions tended to be artificial? The eternal student was the key element, forever learning new things.

Sobol also nodded.

"Yes, Anari," she said. "You take charge of that and keep me in the loop."

She paused there.

"Now, anything before we move on to construction timelines and budgets?"

Sterling sat back and listened as folks had their opinions on new stations, new cities on the ground, and all the other things Uly would need to make this a homeworld.

What could they learn from an Auga conductor who had made it clear that he was unlikely to ever be welcomed home as anything less than a traitor to the Empire who should be executed for his failures?

And how did they take advantage of that?

EIGHT

Anari took a deep breath in the corridor, then approached the wardroom where Conductor Székely was currently at lunch. His two aides—the Auga Jochen Dohman and the Emro woman Taki Izun—had also chosen exile with him. Both had recently found jobs they could do locally on the ground while serving their parole, so the Conductor was often alone and perhaps a bit isolated, though nothing prevented anybody from befriending him.

Nothing, save that he represented the *Auga Empire* that just about everyone in this solar system considered a terrible evil to be overthrown before his people could conquer the galaxy. And most of the people she knew had extremely bad memories or associations with the Auga, both as people and an Empire.

Anari was Sabre. And Moss. Like Yanouk, a Seeker, just as Hiko had risen to Adept and taught art in many incarnations to any student interested in learning, even as he created masterpieces.

Today was the sort of task that let her stay back at Bastion, even as all her sisters went with Uly to finally chase down those pirates.

Research. And diplomacy.

She moved through the line quickly and nodded to the Auga when she caught his eye. His surprise was obvious, but he lingered over his meal and watched her.

Anari grabbed a chair and wedged it into space across from him. Auga were shorter than most, though broad and solid. Built like Khet that way. Or Emro.

Utterly beautiful. And in Székely's case, handsome as well, though many Auga men never grew into a ruggedness that conveyed gravity.

The species had standardized for beauty, health, and long-life. Not as long as the Yarikh, but exceptional. The men could grow a beard, but he kept his face clean. Hair military short, a dark bronze only showing hints of gray above the ears. Wide, tall forehead where the Third Eye was currently mostly lidded, rather than turning the Auga's fabled mental powers on her.

Suka Kuri had suggested that those famed powers were much more limited than popular vids would have you believe. Ranges measured in meters rather than light-seconds. Expansive empathy instead of mind-rifling telepathic links.

Still, it generally gave them something of an advantage in interpersonal communications. Anari focused on *helpfulness* and scholarly interest as she smiled.

"Madame?" Székely asked as she settled.

"In my role as an Ambassador for the Corsac Fox, I have also been tasked with seeing to your needs and welfare, Conductor," she began.

"Conductor no more," he broke her off sharply, but without any fire. "That ended when I chose to save most of my crew rather than seeing them killed for hardly any benefit. Your Corsac Fox and his other women showed me how close they came to annihilating my vessel and crew, at the point where there was little I could have done to prevent it."

Anari nodded. Hard man, but there was a core of compassion there that she'd found rare among Auga officers.

Any Imperial officers, really, but the other species all had upper limits to how far they could rise. Limits well below any Auga rank.

"And you have honored your parole and acted honorably, sir," Anari reminded him. "You are, however, somewhat isolated, socially as well as physically, and we grow concerned that such deprivation might itself form a measure of torture, however unintended, at odds with your status."

That Third Eye opened, but it looked more like an autonomous reflex than a calculated move. His other eyes betrayed shock. Possibly at her words. Possibly at her emotional intent.

Uly had accepted Székely's parole, once Halyna had explained it to everyone. And ordered him treated according to the strictest tenets of such behavior as the Auga and Ononguli kept on their better days.

Even when these were not better days.

She let him study her, aware that she was probably at the optimal range for his powers. The Third Eye lidded some. The other two did the same. Emphatic focus on her.

Anari didn't feel anything, but focused on remaining calm.

Moss School. And Sabre.

"You come with questions?" he pressed. Uncertainty in tone, so he couldn't see *what*. Merely *that*.

"As you are aware, I was once an enlisted member of the Auga Fleet, sir," she replied. "Before becoming a personal student of Suka Kuri."

That got his attention. Székely understood what an Exemplar of the Arts implied. And what it suggested that she trained directly under such a person. He might have heard those words before, but not really grasped what it implied.

He nodded now, about as compactly as one might imagine, so small that she almost imagined it.

"The Corsac Fox intends to build an entirely new stellar nation, centered on Imperial Sector Fourteen, the so-called Spinward Reaches," she continued. "If you feel that you are unable to return to Imperial space, that implies that you will likely remain with us for an extended period. Perhaps the rest of your life, though I cannot imagine that Uly would hold you here against your will."

"I cannot foresee my ransom ever being executed," he said, more of a growl than anything.

Another one of those tools Halyna had primed them all with. Here was a man of honor, with a strict personal code. Sooner or later, he was going to admit to himself that the Empire had betrayed him instead.

Székely had chosen the honorable course to protect his crew. The Emperor would order him executed as a failure for it.

How did one square that circle?

"Thus, sir, it behooves us to start a conversation today about how the former-Conductor Székely sees his future unfolding," Anari pointed out. "If he cannot ever go home, what does he do with his remaining years? Where does he envision spending them? How can we serve honor and your parole in the process?"

Third Eye was open again. Utter shock. It felt good to be able to do that to one of the overlords.

Rude, but good.

Idly, she reflected on how far she'd come from that silly punk who had been drafted, forbidden Sabre School because she was supposedly too smart, and forced to be an engineer in a police motor pool.

But for Uly, Dan, and Suka Kuri, it would have all turned out so much differently. She'd had to grab that chance when it came, then fight for it subsequently.

Anari let him read that about her. They shared many similarities, when you got right down to it, just as he and Uly did. Neither were going home any time soon, so both were going to have to make something new where they lived.

Auga blink rapidly, just like Humans, when hit with an emotional overload. She'd seen it with Uly and Dan. And Sterling. She watched Székely process her words and hit a hard reset in his brain. Like scramming a reactor.

Thunk.

She pasted a smile on her face and waited for him to finish rebooting. Took a moment.

"What are my options, Ambassador Supasei?" he finally asked.

"Almost limitless, sir," she said quietly. "We did not intend to take you prisoner. You demanded it, and we honored such. Uly's interest was in capturing and impressing your vessel into his service, given the abrupt option. Now, you have joined us at Bastion, and stated emphatically that a return to Imperial space is impossible. Personally, I would expect boredom to weigh heavily on my soul at some point, were our situations reversed."

She left it at that. Lyra had suggested that it would be easier to lead the man somewhere than to push him. Hand him a blank piece of paper and shrug. Let him decide how to fill it out.

"Dohman and Izun have both taken up employment?" he confirmed, eyes and head turned a little sideways now. Tone a little uncertain.

"That is correct," Anari nodded. "This is a growing economy, and anyone willing to work can find occupation. I'm not certain that anyone would hire you to command starships at present, nor to work on them in an engineering capacity, but I could be wrong. What would you do?"

More blinks. More emotional overload. It had been long enough that the shock of surrender, capture, and exile appeared to have worn off, leaving only the long decades of emptiness ahead of him.

They stared at each other for a pregnant minute, her unwilling to speak first and him seemingly trapped in some hole he had to extricate himself from.

Finally, something in him broke loose. The tiniest shiver. Only because she was a Seeker under Suka Kuri did Anari detect it, but it was there. A nexus. A decision point.

A fork in the road.

"What is the Corsac Fox intending to build?" he asked, voice hardly above a whisper.

It was as though he considered his own words treason. And they might be, depending on where one was standing to observe.

"A nation where anyone is welcome, regardless of birth, history, or species," Anari informed him, having thought long and hard on the exact words, knowing that she would need to record them for Suka Kuri and posterity. "Citizenship extended to all, equally. Protections under an egalitarian law. Elevating those many species in this region who had previously fallen, and bringing them back up to their own share of galactic civilization."

"He has declared war on the *Auga Empire*," Székely growled, still not quite there in his own head.

"Uly has declared that he will stop the Auga from conquering and suppressing all the other species that are their neighbors," Anari corrected the man, perhaps a bit more sharply than absolutely necessary. "If they can learn to behave, the war would end tomorrow."

That rocked the man back on his metaphorical heels. His head snapped back and his shoulders touched the back of his chair, from where they had both been leaned in like conspirators.

More blinks. More shocks. More history to transcribe.

She waited as he navigated his own emotional turmoil, unwilling to help.

Lead, not push.

"There can be a place for me?" he asked so quietly that she was practically reading his lips.

She nodded, unwilling to break the delicate surface tension of his moment.

"Where?"

"I will let the Governor know that you have an interest, sir," Anari said quietly. "And we shall see what folks might wish to contact you."

Because most of them would need to be much more closely scrutinized, either as potential spies working for the Auga, or folks wishing to do him ill for the simple fact of his birth.

But he was a smart man. Competent and capable. If he could be brought around, there was so much they could learn.

And build.

NINE

Maks had grown rather fond of the little courier *Yosyp Kyrylenko*. Fast. Clean. Comfortable. Reasonably well-armed for a vessel this size. His office was cozy.

Helped that he only needed gun crews and not marines to board someone. And could outrun most trouble.

Doubtful that he'd face any here, but he was making it a point to come into Bastion from a wider angle than necessary anyway. Mostly being careful.

Checking the time, he nodded as the intercom beeped.

"What have you got?" Maks asked, clicking the line.

"We're close enough," Faisal replied from the bridge. "Figured you could haul your ass up here and talk to them instead of making me do it."

Maks laughed. Faisal had come with the ship as the conductor, and was exceptional at what he did, but didn't like people all that much.

"Be right there," Maks said, cutting the line.

One more jaunt, then he'd be back to Rayzian for a time and could possibly relax. Or not. At least he'd get to update Anna on all things he'd done.

He rose and opened the side hatch to the sleeping quarters. Chervonya opened one eye and studied him, then threw off the blanket and sat up, nodding.

"We're there?" she asked, sliding out and smoothing down her tunic from her nap.

"Faisal doesn't want to deal with my mother," he grinned.

"Can't say I blame him," she grinned back. "You Bondarenko folks are too dangerous to be left alone."

"Good thing I brought adult supervision," he said, taking her hand and pulling her up into a kiss. "I can blame you for everything."

"You'd do that anyway," she laughed.

"True."

Maks kept her hand and exited their quarters, headed forward to the bridge. He'd promised to build her a fast cruiser, letting them sail with speed and protection, but circumstances had intruded. Uly was like that. And the Samuur who were repairing that Heavy Striker were obviously going to work slower than a comparable Ononguli yard, because they had to learn so much about more-advanced technology than they had known, in order to get it done.

And it also created an entirely new shipyard in Sector Fourteen. One he owned outright. Capable eventually of turning out the big warships, in addition to the smaller stuff the Samuur had been able to build previously.

Uly would need goliaths in his fleet eventually. Best to start with *Serene Naddoddur* and teach the big cats how to do it.

Faisal sat in the command chair and glanced back as Maks entered the bridge, nodding.

"We'll drop in about a minute," Faisal announced. "Outer marker at Bastion. At least what was the outer marker last time we were here."

"They won't have changed it in the last three months," Chervonya teased.

"It's Maks's Mom," Faisal countered. "Who knows what those people do?"

Maks grinned when she looked over at him. He'd known that his mom had been in the sailing and warfare business when she'd been young. Hadn't understood that she'd been shipmates with Anna

Shevchenko at the time. Or that she'd maintained quiet ties later when the woman became the Lord of the Endless Plains.

Those connections had made him a lot of money. And put him in a position to really help Uly save the galaxy. Those silly Khet would just have to learn to deal with more competition. Wasn't like the Ononguli had ever had their own Trade Factor before him.

"You're live," Faisal drawled as they dropped back into real space. "Four seconds lag."

Good enough. Maks opened a line to the station.

"Bastion Station, this is Maks Sobol, aboard *Yosyp Kyrylenko*," he said simply. "Arriving to meet with the Governor."

He left it at that. The folks who needed to know, did. The rest could draw their own conclusions, assuming they knew the connection.

He supposed that most people did if they were going to spend any time around here. Faisal was all set to go junkyard dog on anyone wanting to cause trouble.

"*Batyr* low and port, sends regards and welcomes," Faisal offered.

Also useful having Sterling Huff handy, already set to pounce on troublemakers.

"Hello, Maks." Mom appeared. "You're right on time. I've let the kitchen know to expect a semi-formal dinner."

Nothing more. The lightspeed lag was still a bit high, but not bad. Not if they needed to talk, but most of what he had could wait.

Maks certainly didn't need to be sharing it with everyone in the damned system, that was for sure.

"Looking forward to it," he replied. "We'll be sailing in now."

He cut the line and turned to Faisal's overall grumpiness.

"All the usual," Maks said. "I'm pretty sure I can score you an invite to dinner."

"I have a book and a frozen casserole I've been saving for today," Faisal replied darkly. "Once we dock, I plan to lock to station life support and flush the atmosphere."

Maks laughed as he rose and pulled Chervonya along with him. There was time to relax before they got there, since Mom hadn't suggested any emergencies he needed to address.

Always a possibility around Uly. Even when he was off pirate hunting.

TEN

Lyra Sobol had kind of inherited the job of Governor as a Bondarenko. Blackmail from Anna. And her sister. And her niece who was one of Uly's wives. Plus, Maks had been here before her.

It ran in the family, so maybe she'd blackmail Zoryana next. Or force Voldomir or Anton to step up. Uly had a lot of allies here, and had drawn in Sobol and Shevchenko as well.

Bastion wasn't an Ononguli system. At present, Ononguli and Khet ran about equal in overall numbers, each about forty percent, with the rest a mind-bogglingly wide selection. The Isann were probably going to be third in another few years, once enough of them had been bitten by the bug to travel much farther from home than most of them had ever imagined. Right before the Samuur did.

Still, she met Maks and Chervonya at the docking lock without dragging everyone else along. Family business before Clan before Nations. That had always been her approach to doing things, and Lyra didn't see any reason to change that now.

She got hugs that were probably a breach of diplomatic protocol in some manual, and didn't care one fig. Ononguli weren't always that tactile, but Khet tended to be. Uly and Dan had impressed it on folks. Probably, the Horde would pick it up at some point.

No, probably the Horde would split into exactly two parts on the topic. Those embracing Uly's vision of the future and the old farts with their wagons still stuck in the mud.

"Welcome, welcome," she smiled, holding hands with both of them. "We have a few minutes of privacy, then the mob. Come, bring me up to speed."

She led them to a side chamber nearby, configured for small meetings, and got them sat down with some tea and coffee.

"Maks, you're looking good," she said, mostly to watch him blush.

What else were mothers good for?

"Business agrees with him," Chervonya offered, slyly grinning as his blush got worse.

"Everything good?" Lyra asked.

These two weren't officially formal, but that was a matter of making the correct announcements in-Clan. Everybody important already knew the truth. One only had to look at who a Human Warlord had picked as his temporary Governor of Bastion while he was gone, to see the new clan alliances shifting.

"Excellent," Maks said. "Eventually, going to build another shipyard here, but that's after I can import a full team of Samuur designers and builders to challenge all the Horde folks living at Bastion who think they know what good ship architecture is."

Lyra laughed. That might be a soft spot in their otherwise tough exteriors, but she understood that her kin would happily rise to the challenge the Samuur presented. Good people. Honest and a little blunt, but a refreshing change from most of the Khet who came to trade.

Those folks tended to talk out of both gill slits at the same time.

"So what brings you, then?" she asked, glancing at both.

"Partly, the need to check on my investments here," Maks replied. "Partly to see if you wanted to send an official representative to Saari when I head that direction next. Uly's new ship should be done shortly. He will be returning from his mission. A lot of things suddenly adjust and take on new courses at that point."

"Anything we haven't discussed already?" Lyra turned serious.

They kept up a regular correspondence, the three of them. Both official and personal, since Chervonya was close enough to being her daughter-in-law at this point, lacking only the wedding and the ceremonial hunt afterwards.

"Nothing new," Maks shrugged. "It's more that I expect our operational tempo to step up a notch when all that happens. Uly will have *Nubia* and *Vauquelin* as heavy units. *Batyr* and a few lighter ships that he had captured or upgraded. The beginnings of a proper fleet, at the time when the Auga might finally be getting their shit together to attack the Horde again."

"Anna's spies think that they are still reeling from the second raid on Zhoralong," Lyra replied, letting him know that the *Vatazhko* was also paying attention.

And sending regular state-level communications.

"That's my expectation as well," Chervonya nodded. "Uly has hammered them several times, in different places all along a wide front. Based on my studies, the *Auga Empire* is likely in the process of a fairly significant amount of soul-searching to figure out what went wrong and if they have to rethink all of their previous plans."

Lyra watched the woman closer. Anna's niece, so someone she knew almost as well as Halyna. At least as smart and sharp. And had been Anna's left hand for years.

If not for Maks, she might have made a great wife for Uly.

"Is there something more we can be doing to help them?" Lyra asked the pair.

"How so?" Maks asked back.

"The Auga are nothing if not deliberate and bureaucratic," she offered. "Uly is a wildcard that upsets everything, over and above all the craziness that the Horde brings whenever the Empire finally decides to attack again. It was like that when I was Chervonya's age. They probably have the basic Horde level of chaos baked into their planning, but only that much. What can we do to disrupt them over and above?"

The Maks who had been a teenager under her roof had been a little hotheaded. Normal for a teenage boy. And had run off and become a pirate, staying with it long after most of his schoolmates had given up the lifestyle and returned to more mundane careers.

That was Lukyan's doing. And Anna was keeping that man close. Wise move.

Maks turned pensive. Eyes unfocused. Head tilted back a little. Breathing shallow.

He looked down and locked eyes with her, and Lyra came to understand that her son had become an entirely new person over the last few years. Calm and deliberate, but also a good match for Chervonya.

And Uly.

"I need Human-level crazy," he announced simply.

"Human?" Chervonya asked, but she understood Humans better than Lyra did.

Had spent far more time around them. Lyra still understood that Ononguli tended to a chaos of individualism, while the Humans were pack hunters.

Lyra watched Maks process his thoughts carefully.

"The Auga are planners," he finally said, nodding at some internal conversation she was only privy to half of. "Ononguli tend to get up in your face and headbutt you. Humans are a next-level unexpected event."

"Meaning?" Chervonya asked.

"Meaning? I think I need to plan something that makes both Zhora-long raids and Nyri look like teenagers joyriding in a stolen speeder," Maks said simply.

"What?" Lyra asked him carefully, both as a mom and a governor.

"I don't know, yet," Maks shook his head. "I don't have to. Uly and Dan will provide the template. My job is building up the support network they need to make it happen. And make it happen now, instead of in another year when I might be turning out Strikers here at Bastion."

"Strikers won't save Uly," Lyra reminded her son. "The Empire can call up thousands of comparable hulls if they have to."

She was not prepared for his ruthlessly serene smile at her words.

"Sure," he nodded. "How will they feed them?"

What?

She blinked. Made a sound. Or Chervonya did.

Maks's smile got bigger.

"Thousands of warships is an impossible formation to engage," he said. "Slow to move. Slow to do much of anything. And they eat a tremendous amount of food every single day. I had to jump through a nearly impossible set of hoops, just to feed everyone when we hit Zhoralong. That many ships consume fuel, metal stock, replacement parts in gigatons. Hell, even spare bodies as people finish assignments and move on. That is their strength. It is also their weakness."

"How so?" Lyra asked.

"They are extremely bureaucratic," he nodded. "Precise planning. Complicated schedules of events. Feeding that many ships in one place would be a nightmare for even a short term. Stretch it out and I might have found a way to utterly cripple the next *Auga Empire* campaign. I'd say I'm surprised nobody ever thought of it before, but nobody thinks like Humans."

Lyra had had long conversations with both Anna and Chervonya. Had come to understand that Maks and Lukyan had turned into creatures halfway between the old Horde hardhead and these new Humans that Dan and Uly foreshadowed.

But to cripple the *Auga Empire*?

"How?" she managed to ask.

Maks shook his head.

"Don't have the details I need yet," he replied. "And the people I need to talk to will be at Saari soon. I need you to detach Sterling and send him with us, either with *Batyr* or I'll carry him."

"Technically, he's supposed to remain here," Lyra said. "Or *Batyr* is, anyway."

Maks nodded.

"Then now might be the perfect time for Yuriy Kovalchuk to take temporary command," he told them. "Because I'm up to no good, but don't tell anyone."

Lyra nodded. She could see that.

"Anything else you've got that's going to ruin my digestion?" she asked.

He grinned.

"Not yet, but the day is young."

Yes, she was afraid he'd say something like that.

PART THREE
SAARI

ELEVEN

Uly smiled as *Nubia* sailed close to the new stardock that Maks had installed.

Old and worn by Horde standards, Maks had bought it used, then had it dismantled and shipped to Saari and reassembled, bringing along a small team of experts who had known from day one that their job had been to train Samuur mechanics and teams to maintain the dock. Knowing that, it was easier for them to learn to repair the captured Heavy Striker Uly had named *Vauquelin*, in order to eventually build new ships from scratch.

Right now, both Maks and the Horde were selling the Samuur a lot of parts, but the man was also in the process of financing local factories to start producing them instead. To turn Saari into a regional trade and manufacturing hub that far outsized this one world and three small colonies they had been a year ago.

Making the Spinward Reaches a place.

"Haydar, what is the status of our new vessel?" Uly asked, looking down and over at the mass of writhing tentacles indicating his Data Officer.

"Current punch list looks like about a week until they are ready to sail out for the first time to see what breaks," Haydar replied. "Certainly there will be things that fail under stress. I'd guess your over/under is about four to six weeks."

Uly nodded. Fifty-percent chance that *Vauquelin* was ready to join the fleet as a front-line warship in a month. Good enough. He would need to make some significant changes at that point, but a good part of the mission to Sector Thirty-Two had been to train up crew members to how he wanted things done.

Once *Kulakhaov* had been ended, they'd managed to repair eleven captured hulls. Uly had put his people on them, then promoted a wide mix of newcomers, heavy on Isann and Samuur, to run things here aboard *Nubia*.

Crash course in on-the-job training, but everyone here had had years of previous experience as interstellar sailors. They had mostly needed to work on a more advanced technology, and with people used to Uly's methods, themselves largely inherited from *Batyr* and Mazhin, based on his first crew.

He turned to Dan, sitting with Suka Kuri and Halyna while the rest were off doing other things. Probably training. No, probably getting cleaned up and dressed so they could provide him an Honor Guard onto the station shortly. The Paramount would appreciate the effort.

"Politics time," he said.

She nodded, drawing the other two women with her.

"Haydar, you have command," Uly said simply.

Not that the Mazhin generally ever wanted it, but it meant that he didn't have to go deal with the Samuur in person all that much. Instead, he would probably sit at his station and write code for some project while scanning every ship in orbit to see what had changed.

As long as *Nubia* was secure.

They exited the bridge aft and fell into two pairs, with Dan beside him and Suka Kuri and Halyna a pace behind.

"Are we meeting with Maks privately before or after the Paramount?" Halyna asked.

Her cousin. Someone Lyra had mentioned she would have liked to set up on a blind date with Maks, but timing had never worked, for which Uly was grateful, because Halyna had turned out to be utterly amazing as a person, once they had relaxed enough to talk.

Almost as impressive as Dan, just in different directions, like all of his wives.

"Paramount first," Dan said simply. "Possibly a full war council at that point, since we got Maks's note that he brought Chervonya and Sterling with him, though *Batyr* remains at home. I'm guessing that the Legal Department will need to brief us, since it looks like Maks brought them as well."

"Everyone in one place," Uly noted. "Good thing I'll have you all armed and protecting me."

"Oh?" Suka Kuri asked.

"At some point, we'll have pissed the Auga off enough that they try to kill us," he noted as they walked. "Personally. I can do what I do because I have the most interesting collection of dangerous women protecting me at all times. It won't be enough."

"What would you propose?" the Elder asked, falling into her favorite Socratic method.

"I have no idea," Uly said. "That's the war council part of this. *Vauquelin* means that I can do more things. Possibly set them up as a commerce raider and turn them loose to materially damage the Auga frontier."

"And psyche," Dan added. "If the Corsac Fox is deliberately raiding them, that will be like inserting needles under their skin."

Uly nodded. She had a vast expertise at those sorts of things, dating back to her time on *Marshall Castillon*, when they had been attacking *Danumash* shipping.

Nobody else did that sort of thing. The Ononguli were generally pirates in peacetime, but that was a different mindset. The Khet traditionally paid pirates under the table to attack other corporate entities.

Only the Humans did war as a formal vocation. Even the Auga were more about patient conquest.

The group entered the aft lock space and Uly noted that the rest of his Wives—the Congress itself—were present. Lieutenant Solomon Wyndham was supervising as Emil Beranger and Gennady Travers handed out weapons and got the ladies sorted. Five of his fifteen total Humans. And not all of them here with him on *Nubia*, as he'd kept stretching things.

But nobody wanted to go home. Not even Emil, whose new cybernetic leg would have qualified him for a full medical pension retirement.

At the same time, what was home?

Uly should have sailed back to Gralbo any number of times, save that he would have had to abandon so many of his friends, because they would not be welcome in *Batyr*. And his former *Danumash* people would have immediately become prisoners of war.

So he didn't go home. Might never.

Looking around the room, he noted four other Humans make that same determination, like they were all Mazhin communicating by scent. Perhaps they were.

He turned abruptly and pulled Halyna into a surprised kiss. Then Dan. Suka Kuri harrumphed at him, so she got one as well. His other Wives grinned and stepped up.

"Another turning point," he told them simply when he was done.

Nods, like every one of them had felt it as well. A charge of lightning building in the ground and trees before erupting.

Uly turned to Solomon. Twenty years old now and probably to a point where he might have finally been testing for a Lieutenancy, back in *Danumash* service. Here, he was Chief of Security, answering only to Dan.

Big. The young man had finally grown into himself. One hundred and ninety-three centimeters tall. One hundred and ten kilos of muscle and toughness. Only the Emro were bigger and heavier in this crew, but Dan had turned him into something of a Sabre School Adept with Suka Kuri's help, though he still had amazingly soft hands when training.

Deadly and quiet. And exceptional.

Solomon met his gaze solidly. No challenge. No emotion. Calm and collected.

Uly nodded with a wry smile, and turned to Dan, then brought Suka Kuri into the conversation as well.

"Starfare School is warships, operating in squadrons and fleets," he said, referencing the new Emro School he was helping create and waiting for them to both nod. "I need a secondary curriculum. Ground combat."

Suka Kuri seemed confused. Dan got pensive.

"You're moving beyond pirates and boarding parties?" she asked, suggesting all the folks she had trained in exactly that.

"Yes," Uly acknowledged. He turned back to Solomon. "How much did you get trained on those sorts of things?"

Once, Solomon might have fidgeted. Hemmed and hawed.

This new gentleman leaned his head back a bit and studied a far wall, eyes unfocused.

"Not much, but I was young when my training for those things was interrupted, sir," he smiled. Even his voice had settled, a resounding baritone. "I do have books I can consult. Those have survived our many transitions, but those tend to be heavy on tactics and theory. I'm not certain how much practicality they bring."

Uly was impressed that someone this young could make that leap, but they were all smart. Most of them had been trapped by circumstances that would have prevented them from fully expressing themselves.

Solomon, for instance, was the fourth son of a duke, and never going to inherit much, save wherever he might have married into, so he'd joined the fleet young to improve his odds.

And been aboard *King Hewitt II* on that fateful day.

Uly looked up at Suka Kuri.

"Can I ask you to review those books and see how we might supplement them?" he pressed. "Or what other experts we might consult?"

Like Solomon, she turned pensive.

Uly smiled that he'd been able to surprise everyone in the room. That usually meant that he had a head start on trouble.

"An Exemplar of Sabre might be your best starting point, but they tend not to travel as much," she replied. "That school falls into two groups, where one believes in digging the widest possible hole to learn from as many people as possible, while the other digs a narrow one as deep as possible. You'll want the former."

"I don't need answers today," Uly told her. Them. Everyone. "I need you thinking about how to do it. I don't intend to invade planets with armies, but I'm not aware of anyone dropping raiding forces onto a surface. Usually, like us, they hit stations and ships. The Corsac Fox will need to do bigger and bolder things to damage the

Auga Empire. That might—MIGHT—be one of them. You'll tell me."

Solomon nodded. Suka Kuri did as well.

Uly smiled at everyone and waved for Dan to get them ready to step through and meet with the Paramount of the Samuur.

He wasn't entirely certain what had just happened, but something had.

Whatever it was, the future had begun.

TWELVE

Dan led the group into a large auditorium, which made sense if they had really assembled that many of the key players in one place. Only Anna and Lukyan were really missing, but Maks and Chervonya could be said to be deputized to speak for the Ononguli Sphere.

What was the most fun for her, though, were the number of Samuur in the room. Not just Paramount Aarne Kallio and Eskil Haldur, but also Kalev Karjalainen, Ursula Nyman, and Matti Lehtinen who'd been the first to visit Bastion. And a few dozen others she didn't know on sight, but an even mix of male and female Samuur, all in those bright orange uniforms they favored.

Dan walked up to the Paramount and gave him a semi-formal bow. The elder bowed back and grinned, so she hugged him as well, then Eskil. Uly joined her, then the entire thing more or less dissolved as the two groups merged and the conversation came up.

The Samuur weren't generally ones for formal meetings around conference tables. They had done that initially because they had been concerned at a mass of aliens that had come to visit, but it was obvious that they had become friends.

Uly was like that in his ability to charm almost anyone quickly.

Eskil stayed close, so she turned to read his ears and whiskers. Not as complicated a language as Mazhin tentacles, but still a thing.

"I have volunteered to meet with you privately later," was all he would say, but the grin was telling.

And if he meant just her and not Uly, Dan supposed that the Paramount might have located a few candidates to join the Congress of Wives. Dan would determine that, but she also knew that Suka Kuri had spoken extensively with the man on the subject, so presumably he had conveyed the correct set of requirements to the Paramount.

Today, it meant more to even qualify for her Combat Team. And Dan had put together a pretty solid list of requirements necessary to justify any candidate getting into the room to talk. Eskil's grin promised that he might have succeeded.

She'd see. For now, she nodded and wandered, even as he stayed somewhat close. Sterling was here, standing next to Maks instead of on his own bridge, so he must have been ordered here by Lyra, who wouldn't have taken such a step lightly.

Uly was close, so Dan slid in off Nasrin's flank, instead of the other way around.

Nasrin's tentacles did a double take at her, so Dan grinned. They were all Uly's Wives. His companions. *His* protectors as well as **her** hands to get things done.

Dan found herself next to Chervonya as a small circle of space developed, even as the Legal Department and the Combat Team broke into groups that were talking around them, however ready everybody was for trouble, whatever form it might take.

"I brought him," Maks was saying. "My mom trusted my judgment on the topic."

"Maks, I trust your judgment," Uly said with a laugh. "I'm more interested in what trouble you might have thought up. Thanks to you and Lukyan, I even made it a point to sail in here on a Wednesday, after all."

Dan laughed with the others, but sailors all had their personal idiosyncrasies. Their superstitions.

Lukyan had infected everyone with *Tuesdays*.

"This is not the place to go deep into details, Uly," Maks replied, sobering and looking so much more mature and adult than the kid she'd first met. "But I think I have some ideas on a future campaign plan that will radically impact your war for the better."

Dan perked up and nodded. Trade Factor Maks was even more dangerous an opponent than Governor Maks had been. Truly turning into the Ononguli he was meant to be.

And a good ally.

She caught Uly's nod as well. This was a public event, with a lot of Samuur folks that the Paramount had to have approved, but not people Dan knew.

Yet.

She turned back to Eskil and gestured for them to move off to a nearby wall, where there was at least an impression of privacy.

"How's the new ship coming?" she asked, ignoring the noise of conversations around them.

"Almost repaired," he confirmed. "I'd have liked it to occur faster—"

"But you had to invent the tools to build the machines to do the work," she nodded. "Back home, most of our gear was hardly more advanced than what you had to work with here, being third- or fifth-hand before we got it."

He nodded as well. That was one of the things that had crossed cultural and species boundaries. The Ononguli tended to build the best small warships, slightly edging out the Khet there, while the Auga were masters of larger hulls.

At least until she had rescued a lost and forgotten Yarikh ship from oblivion.

"Exactly," Eskil said. "Now, we have taken a radical leap forward in our tech. One that will get better as we start building new ships from scratch."

"From scratch?" Dan perked up.

"We have our own designs," he grinned. "Maks and the *Vatazhko* have supplied various blueprints, both theirs and ones for the Auga cruiser Uly stole, so that we could figure out how to repair it. In the lag, the Paramount put together a team of artists to dream as crazy as they could, then added some engineers and others later to help refine their ideas and make them workable."

"And you were one of those, weren't you?" Dan guessed.

Eskil turned serious.

"I have firsthand experience with *Nubia*," he replied. "And with massed battles against Auga squadrons, unique among my people. Art only gets you so far. And most of my comrades really don't understand the deadly nature of what Uly intends."

Dan agreed. Suka Kuri had spoken of how the Samuur were more athletes than warriors. Competition with rules and scoring systems. Still military in nature, but that had been them expecting to have to fend off major incursions by some unknown, dangerous neighbor.

They'd gotten Uly instead.

Only Eskil and Ursula had seen what a real battle might be like.

"Where did your artists take you?" she asked, wondering if Suka Kuri might need to look for more students among the Samuur.

It was one thing to simply draw or sculpt. Hiko was exceptional at almost all physical media, but couldn't sing worth a damn and generally had three left feet on the dance floor.

But an artist *who designed starships...*

"Our comfort zone had been ships like *Virta* or *Niemi*," he said. "What the rest of the galaxy might call light Interceptors. Even our heavy flagship *Tiikeri* only counts as a medium Interceptor as you would measure it, and it is the grand overlord of our fleet. We needed to build something bigger. Fortunately, they had *Vauquelin* as a template, to see what could be done. From there, they broke it down into a series of cubes that could be assembled, rather than welding long struts together and framing out from there. The end result is a bit less durable, but much more flexible in design, because standardization of components lets smaller yards stay involved and the final vessel can be assembled."

"You'll need to talk to Sadeq," she replied. "He's the expert here, along with Marlowe and Kolya."

"We intend to," Eskil said. "If they agree, we can proceed rather quickly."

"Does Maks know?" she pressed.

"Not yet, but we wished to get yours and Uly's approval on our concepts and intentions before asking Maks to throw out his original plans," Eskil replied. "It is his yard, even if it will be our contracts. And his background could find problems we don't know enough to identify."

Dan nodded.

"Send the plans to Uly as well," she decided. "He has a solid engineering background and might see things. How quickly will you be able to replicate your processes and logic at Isann and Bastion, if everybody approves?"

Eskil paused, eyeing her.

"We could send the plans tomorrow," he finally admitted. "Bastion could build it, though they don't have the full yard that Maks intends. Isann and Chief Usupov would need to build a few things first."

"You'll be sending your people to Isann to help them," Dan said simply. "That's a trade network and a cultural connection that doesn't have to go through Bastion. Run it direct, because the two of you are about at the same level today, and both rising. This gets you both there faster, which helps everybody."

He seemed a bit surprised, then nodded sharply.

"Yes," he said. "I had not framed it in those terms, but it makes perfect sense. Pardon me, I need to find Aibek and talk to him."

She nodded and he spun, stalking off into the room.

They needed all the friends they could get, to pull off what Uly intended. It was her job to help them all get there.

THIRTEEN

Suka Kuri didn't think that Uly and the others had paid that close attention, but she'd made it a point to bring Galli Fyodon along to meet everyone at Saari.

Dan and her Team had perked up, but remained silent. Galli wasn't a close combat aficionado by any stretch. Nor did she have any interest in learning it.

What she had was a story. Suka Kuri had pursued that story in some detail.

She directed the Ancyn woman to remain close as she stepped up to the Paramount of the Samuur, Aarne Kallio. Tan fur gone gray on the beard and ears. Eyes that didn't miss anything as he studied the two of them, even as others wandered off to talk to Uly or Maks or Dan.

Not the old woman and the stranger.

"I'm given to understand that Uly rescued your clan from servitude when he finally located and destroyed *Kulakhaov*?" Aarne began, perhaps a trifle uncertain as to where various things were headed.

It wasn't like Saari had many aliens present, beyond the folks Maks had brought and a few Ugotha and Zuath merchants who were really more like itinerant tinkers about to be put out of work if they didn't up their games significantly.

"That is correct," Galli replied, bobbing her headcrest politely.

"And what are your plans from here?" he asked, eyes shifting sideways and up to worry about what a dangerous old Emro woman might be up to.

Not that he was wrong about her, but her plans only tangentially impacted Aarne and his people. Unless he chose to get more directly involved.

Galli noticed and also gave her side-eye. Suka Kuri just smiled at these youngsters.

"They have not really had a chance to come to terms with their freedom," Suka Kuri offered. "Having previously been prisoners of the Auga before her and her group escaped, only to change jailers effectively."

She liked the way Aarne's hair ruffled a little at that. Man was almost as defined by his honor as Eskil. Not that she would take much advantage of him. She like them both.

"Changed jailers?" he confirmed in a dry, hard voice.

Galli nodded.

Aarne looked up at her now.

"What do they need, Exemplar?" he asked simply, but his tone was sharp. Loaded with all sorts of anger directed at people not in this room. "Perhaps another mission like *Kulakhaov*?"

"That will be both unnecessary, and probably impossible," Suka Kuri replied. "The pirates and other middlemen have long since likely vanished, possibly without leaving any trail we might follow. Galli and her folks are anticipated to travel to Bastion with us. Saari was merely the first step back from Uly's mission."

She did like how Aarne turned back to Galli.

"You and your people are welcome here," he said simply. However, it was a promise one might carve into a stone plinth and erect in any major square on the planet.

"Thank you," Galli managed, deeply surprised.

They made a bit of small talk, then Aarne moved on.

Galli touched her arm.

"Will they all react like that?" she asked quietly, still off-balance.

"Uly collects friends in a manner I have never seen another person manage," Suka Kuri nodded. "It is his amazing charm, but he also brings out the best in people, especially Aarne."

"Or Aibek Sulaymanov," Galli replied.

"Any of the Isann, really," Suka Kuri agreed. "All see you as someone wronged, and Uly's people are the kind who will see you set to rights."

Galli blinked slowly, those big eyes a sight to behold as she did.

"Are we better starting a new life here, or Bastion?" Galli asked, leaping over several immense chasms of intervening logic to get to that point in a way Suka Kuri approved of.

"Bastion, I think," she replied. "It is more central to things, regardless of being isolated."

"It will take us farther from our men," Galli replied grimly. "Have you ever encountered male Ancyn this far from Sector One or Three?"

"Galli, I have never met any of your species before you," she said simply. "You were a most welcome surprise, but I'm not sure how we might find you proper mates, this far from home."

"We are never returning to Auga space," the small woman growled tautly. "All they would do is return us to our cells, probably without even letting us into the common yard again for fear of more conspiracies."

Suka Kuri started to say something, then paused. It was a ludicrous idea, which made it all the more interesting in her mind. Galli suddenly got nervous, but that simply reflected her intelligence at noticing how things might have suddenly gone off the rails.

"We'll need the others," Suka Kuri announced quietly. "Come."

Then she set off, using her greater height to locate Uly, currently talking to Maks.

This couldn't wait.

FOURTEEN

Uly saw the look of determination in Suka Kuri's eyes as she approached. And Fyodon's nervousness. His hackles rose. Maks suddenly looked like a man trying to figure out where he needed to throw a punch. Nasrin pivoted to put her back to both of them.

"No, not like that," Suka Kuri waved as she got close. "At least, I don't think so."

Uly nodded and considered relaxing, but didn't act on it. Suka Kuri had gone serious and even more dangerous than usual.

He watched her come to rest. Felt all of his Wives suddenly glance over, shift, and *awaken*, for lack of a better term to describe it.

She reached a hand back and drew Fyodon to stand next to her with a squawk, instead of letting the woman hide in the crowd.

"Galli just mentioned something that triggered a thought," Suka Kuri said patiently, as if expecting to have to repeat herself several times.

Uly glanced closer at the Ancyn woman. Middle-aged, from what he'd come to understand. A politician and leader among her people, until she and her mate had been imprisoned by the Auga for things Uly hadn't really gone too deep into.

"Mistress?" Uly prompted Fyodon, but she was as lost as he was, so he turned back to the Exemplar.

"Going to Bastion with us takes Galli and her women farther away from their men," Suka Kuri explained. "Because they originally came from Sector Three, which, as we know, is in the first ring out from Sector One itself."

Uly nodded, watching both of them. Dan had stepped up at some point, but he'd missed her arrival. Not that he was surprised, given how silently she normally moved.

"At the same time, you have mentioned the need to keep the Auga on their back feet by pressing attacks and raids on random locations, forcing them to maintain a stronger defensive presence along a wider frontier, which serves to tie down a significant portion of their available resources and limits their options offensively."

Uly blinked at the woman. She smiled.

"Uly, I had to review everything you, Sterling, and Haydar created for establishing Starfare as an Emro school," she teased. "I might have learned a few things along the way."

He nodded. Of course she would have. And was smart enough to pick up that very specific vocabulary and use it with the precision of cutting diamonds.

"I had a most ludicrous and evil thought, which I will put down to spending too much time around people who do not have the Empire's best interests at heart," she continued, still grinning. "Why not launch a raid on Stradosha, the world where Galli and her people were held? Where their mates continue to be prisoners."

He could tell that she hadn't mentioned this idea to Fyodon, given the way that woman's mouth fell open. And several others around them.

Normally, Uly would have dismissed such an idea out of hand. Crossing all of one Imperial sector and parts of at least two more to do anything was asking for trouble.

It would, however, poke the Auga in their Third Eye in ways he didn't think he could replicate easily. That alone made it worth discussing, if nothing else.

Around them, the enormity of that question burst silence on the room like a ruptured water balloon.

Uly turned and locked eyes with Sterling across the room, drawing the young man silently close.

Sterling stepped right up to Suka Kuri towering over him and became that same deadly serious Uly had seen at Nyri. Something unspoken passed between those two, then Sterling turned to Fyodon.

"How long ago did you escape?" he asked simply.

"Four standard years, roughly," the Ancyn woman replied carefully.

Sterling fell silent. As did the rest of the room.

Finally, Sterling turned to him.

"That's long enough for them to have relaxed, sir," he said simply. "Recriminations and punishments would presumably have removed that Governor and their associated allies, to be replaced, likely from off-planet, given what I have learned about Imperial politics."

Translated, it meant that Stradosha should have returned to normal finally, instead of maintaining a heightened level of alert after the fears of a tentative uprising around the Ancyn prisoners.

Could he really launch a raid that deep into Imperial space and assume that he could escape again afterwards?

Looking around, every eye in here was focused on him, waiting for his decision. Suka Kuri seemed to think that it could be done. And had rightly identified the current state of the Auga Fleet, defensive and nervous.

Striking past that, deep into the interior, would ripple a spasm of pure panic through Auga civilization itself.

Assuming he could get away afterwards.

"I have an idea," Uly announced to the room, watching them sigh and deflate with smiles, though he wasn't about to mention anything.

Not that he didn't trust the people in this room. The Paramount wouldn't have invited people he didn't trust.

More to the point, Uly's ideas weren't anything more than whispers in the darkness at the moment, and he would need time and his various experts to knead them into shape.

Nothing that he had to resolve today.

"What do you need, Uly?" Maks asked simply, but his tone suggested a wide-open option.

Anything that came up, Maks Sobol would move heaven, earth, and Horde to get it done.

Looking around, the Samuur were vibrating with a similar energy, as were the Isann.

And everybody else.

"Give me a day to think," Uly commanded everyone. "For today, let us celebrate as friends."

The emotions in the room swelled, then shattered in a dozen different directions as voices started speaking again. He glanced at Dan and Nasrin with a promise to explain later, then they all shifted and conversation turned back to the mundane.

For now.

FIFTEEN

Eskil had quietly drawn Governor Maks off when the party began to subside, moving them to a private room with two chairs, a coffee machine, and a faux-fireplace showing holographic flames and putting out a variable level of heat. Thick rugs underfoot and walls treated to look like planed logs gave the impression of being in a small hunting lodge on the surface. Perhaps the one his granddam had built when she'd been a kit.

They settled with steaming mugs and Maks studied him.

"I've heard rumors," Maks grinned. "Art and engineering teaming up. What are the details?"

Of course one of the Ononguli who had come to train them would have sent along a discreet message. Nothing Eskil had heard represented a threat to anyone in the Sphere.

The *Vatazhko* had, in fact, pulled back a significant portion of her forces along the nearest border once enough Samuur vessels had been able to start patrolling that direction, often in tandem with Ononguli warships.

How quickly everything had changed. And all of it because of Uly.

"We had an alternative concept on starship design," Eskil explained, then proceeded to walk Maks through things from the ground up.

It helped that Maks had spent two decades as a pirate, then Governor, then merchant, now Trade Factor. He understood starships at a visceral level.

"I agree that you lose durability in construction," Maks nodded when Eskil finished, thirty minutes later. "And gain significant flexibility in design, though I'm not certain why you need it."

"One hull can be a warship, a cargo carrier, or a diplomatic courier, Maks," Eskil replied. "I don't think that making sections modular and hot-swappable is wise, but if we only have to design one frame, and all three share something more than sixty percent commonality of parts as currently envisioned, it greatly expands our ability to build sections elsewhere and ship them for assembly, assuming we built some sort of small, mobile repair ship that was specifically dedicated to that task."

"Build them here and ship them to Isann?" Maks asked.

"Or Bastion," Eskil agreed. "It means our factories can be optimized for efficiency at a smaller construction scale. And more factories, since the parts would be closer in size to shuttles."

"Diplomatic courier?" Maks pursued, eyes glittering in ways that Ononguli didn't normally do.

Eskil paused and considered how well he'd come to know the species and Maks to be able to say something like that. But Lukyan had trained Maks. And considered Maks to be his best friend.

"I heard a rumor that you needed something larger than *Yosyp Kyrylenko*," Eskil nodded. "Big, fast, and well-armed, while also comfortable for long voyages and able to host conferences. Some of the people who helped you build Bastion's *Watchtower* were among the senior Ononguli engineers here today. I interviewed them about *Treta Envoy*. Not the ship you needed in the future, but it had many of the same functions."

Maks turned pensive. Eskil waited.

"And a diplomatic courier doesn't require the same hard standards of a warship, because it shouldn't be sailing into battle except under duress," Maks nodded finally. "But armed to see of smaller problems making a pain of themselves. I think I need to see your plans, Eskil."

"Oh?"

"I need such a vessel, as you have noted," Maks grinned. "And

Vauquelin will be done soon and out of the yard, where any dock can handle it for most repairs. I'd assumed that your first Striker-class warship would be the next contract executed, presumably providing one Eskil Haldur a new flagship. But I think we might want to build something else first, so that your people are ready, when it comes time to build that one."

"Then you tentatively approve?" Eskil pressed.

"Pending a variety of questions you will have, no doubt, been prepared to answer, yes," Maks said. "It will provide you a training operation your people will need, while solving another of my problems. And perhaps setting you up to turn out something I might classify as a fast clipper."

"A what?" Eskil asked, feeling his ears and whiskers tangle.

"Uly mentioned a type of cargo vessel back home that sacrifices pure hauling tonnage for speed and firepower," Maks replied. "The big ships he has stolen are all extremely slow. By design, mind you, but still they take two to five times as long to get anywhere. If you had a Cargo Striker, a Clipper, if you will, you could get things from here to Bastion or Isann—or even Rayzian—much faster. That might matter."

"I hadn't really given that design that much thought," Eskil admitted.

"Because we all like designing big, sleek warships," Maks grinned. "But let's sidebar on that for a bit, and see where it takes us."

Eskil leaned back and began to talk, based on the design he'd helped create.

Already, he could see how it might radically change things in the Spinward Reaches.

How much better could they make it?

SIXTEEN

Nasrin had offered to swap schedules around, but Dan had insisted on keeping the current calendar, so she had joined Nasrin and Uly tonight in his salon. And Dan would depart later, meaning that Nasrin would be sleeping with Uly.

It was still weird to think about, but Uly had proved to be just as calm and precise there as in other things. Delicate, when she'd had almost no idea what to expect, save that Omid had warned her ahead of time. And been right about Uly as a person and a lover, even though Omid had never—as far as Nasrin knew—been intimate with the Corsac Fox.

Nasrin was on the couch, one curled-under foot just touching Uly's thigh at the other end. Dan sat in the chair across from them. It was late, so she had a decaffeinated, herbal tea with some honey.

"I wasn't supposed to be here tonight," Dan opened with a grin, winking at Nasrin.

Nasrin blushed anyway.

"Granted," Uly replied. "And normally, it could have waited, but I think this might be one of those situations where time really is important."

"You expect a leak?" Nasrin asked.

"Eventually," Uly nodded. "More importantly, something like this will end up having many moving parts that need to be orchestrated before we can even determine the feasibility of such an operation."

"You're really thinking about such a raid?" Nasrin was surprised.

And not surprised. It was Uly.

"Yes."

It was the no-nonsense way he said it that took her breath away. Firmly convinced that it could be done, that it needed to be done, and that they would do it.

Nasrin fell back into tactical thinking to try to wrap her tentacles around it, knowing that starting at the strategic was too big.

"What are the components?" she asked, glancing between the two.

"Resupply," Uly offered. "That's a tremendously long sail, both in and out. Every body that accompanies us has to be fed over that entire stretch. And we'll need ground forces, so I can't cheat and leave most of Dan's battalion behind. If anything, I'll need the larger force we took to destroy *Kulakhaov*. And maybe then some."

"Can we get them that deep?" Dan asked.

"Trojan Horse," he grinned.

It took Nasrin a moment to process that. Human historical references weren't necessarily her strongest suit. Still, it sparked a memory.

"Take *Vauquelin* in and pretend to be an Auga warship?" she asked.

His calm nod at least scaled the situation for her. Sail right into harbor above an Auga world, pretending to be one of the overseers. Break into a prison on the ground. Break out with all the prisoners. Escape. Get home.

The usual.

She grinned. Uly shared it.

"Yeah, I know," he offered. "At the same time, I can't imagine the Auga ever thinking up that sort of operation, against which they might plan a contingency. Madam Fyodon mentioned that once they got to the starport and lifted off, everyone assumed that they were on official business and didn't ask. Had their ship not broken later, they might have made it to someplace like Z'Gosza."

"Or not, considering that we were just starting to clean things up over there," Dan mentioned. "Likely, they'd have run into trouble anyway."

"But we might have heard about it and done something sooner," Uly countered.

And that, right there, was why she compared every other male she met, of any species—including Mazhin—and found them wanting. Why she'd found herself looking forward to being one of his Wives. Of being part of what he was creating.

Of loving him as a person and not just a concept.

He cared deeply about complete strangers.

"Water under the bridge," Dan said, a Humanism it took Nasrin a moment to grasp.

People. On planetary surfaces. Where water fell from the sky and ran on the ground. You had to architect cities to deal with it.

Weirdos.

"Agreed," Uly nodded. "If we can manage it, the entire Empire ends up hearing about it, even if only the ugliest rumors, which would be even better than the truth for my purposes."

"Because they would discover fear," Nasrin observed calmly.

"Exactly," he said. "I can't defeat them by force of arms. We will never have enough ships for that. But they can defeat themselves for me. I just have to inject chaos into their careful system and let things break. And break down. And break loose."

"So we assume a raid to Stradosha?" Nasrin pressed. "Resupply en route and on the return, while being hunted. What else?"

"Do we return?" Dan asked.

Nasrin and Uly both perked up.

"Oh?"

"Do we hit the place, assume that they will quickly pour all of their fleets into trying to intercept us getting back to Sectors Fifteen, Fourteen, or Twenty-One, and go out the other direction?"

"That's one hell of a long sail around their perimeter later," Uly said.

"Understood, but it also puts you in a position to recruit more people along that periphery as well," Dan said. "Maybe locate some Mazhin players and bring them up to date."

Nasrin felt her tentacles sour at the thought of trying to explain Uly to a bunch of old women Clan leaders who didn't think men should be allowed to be in charge, on account of how emotionally unstable the gender could be.

Not that they were wrong, much of the time, but it was Uly. And she'd be responsible for explaining.

And, eventually, banging tentacled heads together to get them to listen.

"Do we short-circuit everybody and go vertical?" she found herself asking instead.

It was fun, watching the other two suffer twisted tentacles, even if they lacked them.

"Huh?" Uly managed.

"The galactic disk is roughly one thousand light-years thick," she reminded him, holding up one hand. "Most systems tend to be in the middle sixty percent, with things thinning out as you get farther away. Folks look at a map and see things in two dimensions when they scale it that big, in spite of how they actually sail between two points."

Then she watched Uly recalibrate his entire sensory network in front of her eyes, blinking twice and nodding. Just frightening to watch, some days.

"I'll need a map," he told Dan. "Scale me out a conic section centered on Stradosha, maybe thirty degrees either way, including other inhabited systems, bases, and anything else you, your Combat Team, or the Legal Department can think of that might interfere with a sail."

"In the top and out the bottom?" Nasrin asked, intrigued.

"Or vice versa, yes," he nodded. "If I don't have to sail around stars or nebulae, we can move faster. And come at them from a direction they probably won't expect. And escape while they try to set roadblocks because they will be in the wrong places."

"While tying up major forces on their part trying anyway," Dan said with a smile. "I'll stay up late and start laying out questions for everyone else to address first thing in the morning. You two don't stay up all night because I agree that the faster we can get this in motion, the faster we can see if it really will work."

She rose abruptly, then leaned over and kissed a blushing Nasrin on the cheek with a grin. Then Uly. Then Dan left.

He held out a hand for her to take. They shared a grin.

"If she wants us up early, we should probably get to bed shortly," Nasrin offered.

"I thought you'd never ask," he replied, grinning.

They rose and she kissed him because he was everything she'd ever imagined he was supposed to be, even before she'd had a name or a face for her dreams.

And more.

SEVENTEEN

Looking around the Samuur meeting room, Solomon appreciated that he was kind of the expert on the topic, but that did not fill him with joy.

Still, he had been raised to duty from the beginning. And fourth sons were born knowing that they had to go out and carve themselves a spot in the universe.

Nobody had warned him that it would turn out like this, but honestly, he couldn't see how it could have been better. Chief of Security for *Nubia*. Sabre School Adept, sort of. Mostly on account of having so much time to focus entirely on close combat training, when Anari and Yanouk were also Moss School.

And those two ladies were going to be Exemplars, one of these days, while he was pretty sure he'd top out around what Dan called Fifth Belt back home. Someone expected to know everything there was to know about a specific art. Where technical knowledge ended and people became teachers of teachers. Eventually the higher black belts, back home, where you were recognized for personal contributions to growing the art, rather than your dojo work.

On the path to Exemplar.

Of course, he was only twenty years old. There were a lot of decades where he could learn new things. Or invent them, he supposed, since there weren't really other Sabre School folks to learn from beyond Dan and Suka Kuri. He had his books and his videos.

And his imagination.

Solomon focused on Suka Kuri, listening to her explain it again. He'd been on the ship when the topic came up. Then had awakened this morning to a laundry list of things they needed from him, so he'd turned everything over to Gennady and spent the morning digging and thinking.

And, he supposed, he was the expert.

She finished and Solomon nodded as a placeholder. Everything Dan had previously explained, fleshed out in about four times the details, mostly backstory from the Ancyn woman sitting between her and Suka Kuri.

All of the Combat Team that had accompanied them were present. Uly had also brought Maks Sobol and the Legal Department to balance things out, but Solomon knew he was on point today.

Weird, because all of his training had gone the other direction.

Then it clicked.

Solomon blinked. Sat up a little straighter, and everybody else turned and locked in on him.

A nod to Dan, because Commander Chastain was speaking today. Chief of Staff of the Corsac Fox.

An officer with a peculiar need.

"You had a thought, Solomon?" she asked in a leading tone.

"My normal job is defensive, sir," he said. "Hold the base while your teams are out taking some station, so I need to provide the anchor and the bulwark behind you. As well as the reaction force if something goes wrong."

Her nod was crisp. She had trained him more than anybody. Turned him into a junior Adept of the Sabre School. Focused him and honed him down to what he supposed was a killing edge, though most of the non-Humans didn't really understand that concept and any Sabre School folks he did meet later would probably find him a bit aggressive and crazy compared to their own styles.

He was reminded of the ancient samurai, who were expected to be scholars and conversationalists when not killing each other.

Solomon made a mental note to start addressing a side of himself he had probably ignored before now. He'd finally stopped growing physically and settled into himself. Shed most of what he'd been born with in Danumash.

Time to identify and create the adult he wanted to become.

"If I understand, the best way forward would be for me to interview Madam Fyodon extensively and use her knowledge and experience to build a defensive network for the prison she was held in," he continued. "Then adapt that to what likely happened after it failed. Then ramp that up an extra level to cover unseen eventualities that allow your team to train as if already on the ground. Yes?"

"Exactly that, Lieutenant," she replied. "Suka Kuri will be involved, because she's exceptional at asking questions and jogging Galli's memory."

"I'll need access to the other women at some point," he countered. "They will likely also have details that might be missed."

He turned his attention to the Ancyn woman in the middle. Gallimanus Fyodon. A name that meant something like mountain mist, if he'd caught the implications.

She watched him with hard eyes. Solomon got that part. He'd been too young to be a threat to the sorts of prostitutes that the officers and older midshipmen had frequented when he'd been in *Danumash* service. But those Ancyn women had been *indentured* into that sort of service, and he was a large Human. Only the Emro were generally bigger than he was.

He would still be seen as a threat, however incorrect that was.

Solomon met her gaze calmly. She could say no, in which case he suspected there would be gaps later that might prove critical.

He waited. She watched.

"I will speak with Loh-An," she finally said. "She'll reach out to the others to see who may be willing or not."

"Thank you," he said simply, possibly surprising her, if she'd been expecting him to force the issue.

The Corsac Fox had knocked that silly shit out of him early. Dan had only reinforced matters in turning him into who and what he was today.

It helped, having an entire Combat Team of dangerous women in charge. Reminded him and any other guy that while they could have opinions, they did not decide things. Dan did.

"I'll start immediately," he told Dan. "I have a few ideas for how the Auga might handle it, based on personal experience many of us share. From that, I can work with Madam Fyodon to refine things."

"Galli," the woman corrected him.

"Ma'am?"

"Call me Galli," she instructed him.

Solomon nodded. If he had the relative ages and lifespans correct, she was about the same age as his mother, the Duchess. Useful to frame her in those terms.

"Galli," he conceded. "I'm Solomon."

"It is a pleasure to meet you, Solomon," she said.

He blushed, but honestly didn't have a lot of experience with women in general, not counting alien soldiers under his command and the Combat Team who were his bosses at the end of the day.

But he could do this.

Uly required it. And might be creating another new Emro school, of which Solomon's books and experiences would be central.

Best not to fuck it up.

EIGHTEEN

Uly nodded to Solomon when he finished speaking, then turned to Maks next.

"I had a note from you that you wanted to try a few crazy ideas," Uly prompted the man.

Maks's smile was warm and compelling.

"You aren't planning to launch a direct assault, correct?" Maks confirmed as an opening.

"Correct," Uly replied. "There is an expectation of possible combat, both on the ground and in orbit, but if we can sneak in and sneak out again later, it would be better."

"You're going to take a force like you did to Sector Thirty-Two, right?" Maks asked, looking around at everyone. "Extra bodies?"

"Probably fewer excess crew," Dan spoke up. "Just as many combat troopers, if not more."

Maks nodded.

"Resupply was a bitch when we hit Zhoralong," he said. "And I speak as the guy tasked with putting it all together. Similar problem here, but framed differently, because I need to get one—one?—ship in and out again. I presume *Vauquelin*?"

"One ship," Uly confirmed. "*Vauquelin*, unless we come up with a different plan."

"Okay, fewer bodies to feed," Maks continued. "One ship, fresh out of drydock and thus expected to be in good shape, though we'll want to push a bit before sailing."

"We're ahead of schedule," Eskil noted from his corner of the table. "Twelve days to freesailing at present."

"Excellent," Maks said. Then he turned back to Uly. "I want to take a bunch of those ships you brought back from Thirty-Two and use them up."

"How so?" Uly asked, intrigued.

Maks had been raised Ononguli, so he'd gone into piracy like many of them did. Had stayed with it longer as a career, until *That Fateful Tuesday*. Since then, he'd turned into an investor, a banker, a Governor, and now a Trade Factor.

"Normally, you pack the ship full of supplies for a long raid," Maks noted. "But here, you'll be carrying a bunch of extra crew, so there won't be a lot of spare space aboard, am I correct?"

"That is my understanding," Uly replied, thinking to himself that the whole concept of the raid itself was less than a day old. He had good people, and they knew how to move when they had to.

"I'd like to take those ships you brought back and strip them down as bare as we can," Maks said, gesturing to include Eskil, and presumably the whole of the Samuur industrial component. "Then load them up with all the supplies they can hold and stage them at certain spots along your path, both going in and coming out. Each ship will be running with the absolute minimum crew we can trust. At each stop, you will take that crew aboard your ship when you empty the vessel of supplies, then abandon the hull in place rather than trying to coordinate getting them out later. Similarly, any fleet hunting you later stands a good chance of getting lucky, but if the hull is empty and the computers wiped, they won't learn anything."

"Just leave them there?" Uly asked.

"You didn't exactly buy them in the first place," Maks grinned. "So you aren't out anything for destroying them later. And Eskil's people have plans to build new vessels that will probably be better than these anyway. So, at best, they were a stopgap measure that Nubia can fill while we're gone."

"We're gone?" Uly pressed.

Maks grinned.

"I might know a few things about long-range logistics, Uly," he pointed out.

"True, but we might not make it back later, and the Ononguli will need you even more if I don't succeed, Maks," Uly said simply.

Maks blinked.

"All those things we've talked about must keep going over the next few centuries," Uly continued. "I need you building out the infrastructure of Sector Fourteen. That precludes you running off on raids into the Auga interior."

"So you'll be going without me?" Maks asked, grumbling.

"Correct," Uly smiled to take some of the sting out of it.

"I beg to differ, sir," Sterling suddenly spoke up.

Uly's head snapped around to the young man.

"Oh?" he asked in a deceptively mild tone, already preparing to snarl at the man.

"You—very specifically—cannot go on this mission, Vanguard," Sterling nodded as he spoke, tones crisp and not giving a centimeter. "In fact, you need to be seen ordering this raid while remaining behind at Bastion. Or Saari or Isann. But not participating."

"Why do you think so, **Commander**?" Uly growled.

"Because you are not a front-line officer anymore, sir," Sterling growled right back at him. "This is intended to materially damage the psychological components of the Auga and their polity, **Vanguard**. That means that you've simply ordered a team to undertake it, because you are already so powerful and secure that you can send ships off on such missions. You, however, are not allowed to participate in it."

Uly started to lean forward. Dan's hand on his caused him to pause, turning to her instead.

"He's right," she said quietly.

It was like a needle piercing a balloon, looking into her eyes. His anger deflated entirely.

Uly drew a breath and leaned back. Sterling was a little pale, expecting to be yelled at. Dan had stepped into the line of fire.

Why?

He paused and considered.

Because, damn it, she was right. Sterling was right.

And Uly had built a thing where people were comfortable challenging him, at least on technical grounds where they thought he was wrong.

Which meant that he probably was.

Suka Kuri grinned when he glanced at her.

"You have trained them all well, Uly," she reminded him. "They are adults now. And officers you trust to execute your orders. They will do you proud."

"That doesn't make it any better," he grumbled, which just made her smile more.

Looking around, though, he was in the minority.

A thought struck him and he turned back to Dan.

"Should you remain behind as well, or does it reflect better that the all-female Combat Team and Congress of Wives, led by you, does this thing at the behest of a group of Ancyn women in need?" he asked, already accepting that he was staying home and moving on.

Dan was caught off guard, obviously expecting more of a fight from him. She paused as well.

Uly looked at Nasrin and read the feel of her tentacles. If Dan stayed behind, Nasrin would lead the Combat Team instead.

Thus, they were all growing up. If Dan did go, this was probably her last mission commanding troops in the field, just as he was likely to turn into Speaker for the Conclave of Species, over and above everything else.

This was what growing up looked like, damn it.

"I think I need to go," Dan said quietly after a moment. "But yes, I think we'll need to move into the next phase, politically, after this. Get the word out to a wider audience that the Warlord of the Spinward Reaches is doing these things to the Auga."

"Got a whole public relations campaign brewing," Ethir cackled madly from where he leaned against the table. "Just waiting to pull the trigger here."

"I also have some ideas, Ethir," Maks offered. "Eskil and Aibek will also be able to help there."

Uly reset himself and considered everything they had laid out so far. He rose and made his way to the coffee robot while everybody else watched him nervously.

Returning to his chair, Uly smiled at them.

"We're going to be here for a while, working it out," he announced. "I wanted first coffee before you folks caught on."

The others blinked and Maks immediately rose to refill his mug, triggering a small cavalcade in his wake.

Halyna reached out a hand and touched his shoulder. He smiled at her. At all of his Wives who were present.

The Auga would never forget what he was about to do to them.

NINETEEN

Dan hadn't spent much time around Galli, but enough to understand that the woman was a leader among her kind. Had that particular charisma that got people in motion. Had the indomitable will to carry them on when they started to flag.

The larger group had broken up into smaller, working teams, once Uly had given his approval for the task at hand and challenged everyone to contribute. Dan had grabbed Galli and taken her to a nearby office.

"I am still overwhelmed," Galli said breathlessly as they settled. "Suka Kuri suggested a thing yesterday. Today it is seemingly already moving with the energy of an avalanche."

Dan nodded. Smiled at the woman.

"That's part of Uly's charm, as you've seen," she replied. "And his power, because he has laid out an overall strategy for folks, and now has them figuring out how to execute it."

"And the young Human, Solomon, will design an Auga prison based on my recollections?" Galli asked, eyes wide and headcrest elevated.

"Yes," Dan said. "Then make it harder, because we want our folks ready for trouble. We'll train against that, then see if we can slip in quietly, free your people, and get back out again later."

"How can you be so confident in your success?" Galli demanded quietly.

"Because we broke out of an Auga prison at Vynchen ourselves," Dan reminded the woman. "Hijacked our transport shuttle with no weapons. Stole *Iron Wasp*. Hit Zhoralong the first time to steal a freighter full of emergency supplies. Then set out to make the galaxy a better place. We have experience. And I'm hoping that we can leverage you and your people into this mission, because there will be other Ancyn on Stradosha. Most of my people are going to be rather rare ethnotypes in Sector Three."

Galli paused and just blinked at her a few times.

"*Why* are you doing this?" she finally asked.

Dan nodded. On the surface of things, it made no sense at all. Nobody would go to this much effort to help relative strangers. Even the Ononguli or Khet might have only helped Galli and her people get this far, then sent them on to find their way in the galaxy.

"Because Bastion needs to be a symbol of something bigger," Dan told her. "Something better. Where you belong without regard to your species. I was just thinking how the Khet and Ononguli would have treated you and yours. At the same time, as Suka Kuri notes, this will radically impact the Auga. Hit them where they live, as a Human might phrase it, because if Stradosha isn't safe from us, what places can be? Can the Corsac Fox get to you anywhere, all the way up to the capital at Ajorn?"

"Thus Suka Kuri has explained it to me," Galli said, shaking her head. "You and the others as well. I simply did not believe."

"Not many do," Dan commiserated with her. "Uly wants to make the galaxy a better place. Right now, that means hurting the Auga. Disrupting them. Forcing them onto the defensive, at least for a while, so that other worlds and other species have a chance to fortify themselves. To make allies of their neighbors against the day when the Empire decides to take them next."

"Suka Kuri told me that you could not stop them," Galli offered.

"Nobody can but them," Dan confirmed. "So we must make them want to stop. To define a peace that they will hold. To become better people, because right now the Empire, like so many other places, defines one species at the top, with everybody else as second-class citizens. And I have extremely personal experience with such things."

"I have noted that your skin color is so much darker than the others," Galli noted. "The Ancyn can be the same, with brown feathers often seen as somehow lesser than gray."

Dan nodded. Galli had gray feathers, with gold and black highlights. Her most important assistant, and probably best friend, was the young woman Loh-An Huang, brown feathered, but apparently everything from her shoulders up would suddenly turn bright red during the mating season.

"Like with the Auga, my tribe were near the bottom of the social ladder back home," Dan said. "Uly's father is a senior politician in the Party that runs *Batyr*, but he simply points out that it gave him a better education in politics and people. You will never hear him describe himself as someone intrinsically better than someone else."

Galli nodded. Paused.

"We could really get our mates back?" she asked.

"That is the plan," Dan said. "The Humans with us don't really have that option at present, though we have joked more than once about doing something similar, save that half of us each came from enemy names back home. And I am the only woman among all the men."

"So we should look at finding the rest of them Human mates when we finish with Stradosha?" Galli asked with a grin.

It was Dan's turn to be taken a bit aback.

"You'd have even farther to travel," Dan offered.

"So?" Galli pressed. "How far is it from Sector Three to Sector Thirty-Two? How would we go about it?"

"Honestly, I'm not entirely certain," Dan replied, well off from where she'd intended this conversation to go. And watching it wave at her in the distance. "The Yarikh are the most like us physically, because they used to be Human."

"Used to be?" Galli asked nervously. "I thought they still were?"

"They have bio-engineered their species," Dan explained. "Sought a perfection of form and programmed it in. Physically, yes, they are like us. Externally. But, internally, who knows?"

"What about the Isann?" Galli asked. "Aibek Sulaymanov, with makeup and a disguise?"

Dan leaned back. Picked up her forgotten coffee and sipped at the luke warm contents.

Shit.

Smaller eyes, generally. Larger noses. Normal ears that came to a slight point, but nothing terrible. Generally shorter and broader, but Humans filled a wide ecological niche. And she remembered one world —currently escaping her memory—where adults 145 centimeters tall were average. Someone barely coming up to her collarbone.

"I'm not saying that is impossible," Dan temporized.

"If we've gone as far as Sector Three, and intend to escape, should you keep going, and find more Humans to assist you before returning?" Galli asked. Dan started to speak and Galli waved her off. "Yes, I am aware from my rescuers that Humans are considered vastly more dangerous and violent than other species, as a rule. I'm not suggesting you unleash them on the galaxy. But I understand what it means to live among strangers. To never have children. Or never to see yours again, because you had to send them off to be raised by your parents or siblings when you went to prison. Trust me, Dan, I understand loneliness."

And Dan supposed that she did. And might have children who hadn't seen her in years. Nor known what had happened to their mother.

None of the *Danumash* or *Batyr* men with her could expect to have children of their own, save Uly, and they had taken pains to put that discussion off for a time.

Did Bastion need a proper Human colony added? Several hundred Human women and men who could start families? Be happy?

"I had expected that such a mission might still be years in our future," Dan began, but again Galli cut her off.

"No," the woman said simply. "Do not wait. Do not hesitate. We did not, even knowing the probable cost, though the men were unable to break out with us for reasons we never learned. Merely that the time came and they did not join us, so my women took a vote and decided that they would rather be free. Go find more Humans, Dan."

Dan was aghast, but remembered that Galli was a mature, middle-aged woman as the Ancyn counted such things. Perhaps her aunt, all things considered. And had spent much of her time with Suka Kuri since being rescued, so she would have picked up that woman's modes of thought.

Of asking hard questions, then pursuing answers to conclusion.

And Galli wasn't wrong. At least Dan didn't think so.

"I will need to talk to the others," Dan said. "To see what they think. And if they think it can be accomplished. It might delay rescuing your men."

"They have waited years," Galli replied. "A bit longer won't hurt. Not if it opens us up to something even bigger."

Dan contained her sigh.

It might work.

Then what?

TWENTY

Suka Kuri had learned to retain perfect outer calmness when listening to Dan explain things. The youngster Dan had been raised in a world where her sex and skin color often counted against her, compounded by her low military rank at odds with her obviously overlooked intelligence. *Batyr*, for all they had turned out someone like Uly, were still fools, as far as she was concerned.

Dan finally ran down and fell silent. They were alone in the gym where Suka Kuri had redone almost everything to her scale, adding only a few chairs and such for tinier folks. It let her work with Yanouk and Anari as Seekers preparing to become Adepts of their own, combining the best elements of Moss and Sabre into a new thing.

Her life was one of new things. The two schools had been created specifically to seek out the novel and incorporate it, often jettisoning the old when it was no longer useful.

Traditions frequently went stale. Stodgy, even.

Suka Kuri had dedicated her long existence to resisting such silliness.

But Dan's face demanded seriousness.

Suka Kuri took a deep breath and smiled, letting even that little bit help relieve Dan's stress.

"Such a thing does not represent a bad choice," Suka Kuri said.

"Even if it does stretch us tremendously. And, I will point out, you do not ask this thing for yourself, because you have Uly. It is the other men who might benefit, though I suspect that any Human woman that might somehow catch Sterling's eye at this date would have to be at least as exceptional as you, given how close he and Anari have grown."

"Or Kit and Melpomeni," Dan nodded. "Though that is far more fraught with complexities."

"She is entirely alien," Suka Kuri noted. "Kit asked me for advice at one point and I pointed out to him that if he saw her as a large Isann or a tiny Emro, it would make it easier for him. He did. They are not as close as Sterling and Anari, but they have become more comfortable. Within limits."

"And I will challenge that, if we proceed," Dan said. "Disrupt it, even."

"A wise man once said that anything that can be destroyed by the truth deserves it," Suka Kuri smiled. "This is no different. If anything, it might impact the Ononguli the most, since Anna Shevchenko already sees Maks and Lukyan as cast in a semi-Human mold."

"More clans wedded to Humans?" Dan asked.

Suka Kuri liked that hint of wonder that came into Dan's eyes. She didn't claim to have all the right answers, thus pausing to listen and think regularly.

Thinking was the key.

"It further cements his ties with the Horde," Suka Kuri nodded. "Already, many have chosen to move to Bastion. Others will take up service at Saari, helping uplift the Samuur. Or Isann, which I believe is next on Maks's list. All of this represents a great blending of peoples that might be unique in this era, as far as my studies have reached. I like it, and demand more."

"Demand?" Dan asked, yet more confused, which just meant that she was open to new ideas and hadn't processed them yet.

Such were the joys of being a philosopher. As long as she didn't take advantage of the youngsters all that often.

"Demand," Suka Kuri confirmed. "I will talk to Aibek, but I suspect that you and Uly need to immediately trek at least as far as Bastion, if not to Traiffe itself, to recruit a few folks who can pretend to be *Batyr*

Humans for long enough to fool people. You are not enough. Kolya, Gennady, and Emil are not enough. The others are all *Danumash* folks, and you do not want more of that kind, at least at first, much as I love Drew, Sterling, Kit, Marlowe, and Solomon. You want people from *Batyr*, because they will be closer to understanding the universal truth of what Uly is building."

She paused, watching that worm slowly eat its way deeper into Dan's mind with new ideas.

"This just got huge," Dan murmured.

"And thus you see why I spent so much time with Galli," Suka Kuri grinned. "She could be an Exemplar herself, one of these days, though I am not sure what school she might invent to convey it. She is not, however, right for you or Uly. One of the others might be, but I have not gone deep into the rest of the clan, partly to give them time to heal. And partly because I believe many of them left mates behind, though I have not asked."

"Most, yes," Dan offered. "I think they wrote it down, but that wasn't a detail that really mattered at the time."

"Nor does it matter now," Suka Kuri said. "They have a need, and you will address it. Then, I believe, it is appropriate for you to press home some sort of mission to Gralbo, or at least some fringe Human colony where you might invite the adventurous to join you."

"Iethert, Masym, or Gorge," Dan mused. "Places I have visited, back in the before, where we went to dispose of captured goods we took from *Danumash* vessels, trading them for supplies we needed in our formal piracy days."

"Exactly," Suka Kuri nodded. "You and Uly head out immediately. Take Maks and his ship. Leave Sterling and Haydar in charge here to get things organized for when you get back."

"Just like that?" Dan asked.

Suka Kuri focused herself into the seriousness of a granite cliff face.

"Just like that."

TWENTY-ONE

Maks was surprised when the call came in. Late in the local day at Saari. Most folks would be either asleep or counting down to it.

But his private line had beeped in his cabin, so it was someone who needed to talk to him now, instead of leaving a message for him to address in the morning.

He kissed Chervonya and listened to her grumble about business as he slid off the bed. Both had been reading, and probably an hour from actually turning out the light.

Uly's face greeted him. It was a serious, sober face that had Maks already locating the nearby alert button in his mind, in case he needed to mash it and bring his crew into combat in thirty seconds.

"What's up?" Maks asked carefully.

Chervonya heard something in his tone, because she shifted on the bed.

"I need to make a high-speed run to Bastion, possibly as quickly as a ship can be resupplied," Uly said. "Probably on to Isann and Traiffe from there. How soon were you planning on traveling with *Yosyp Kyrylenko*?"

"Like, now, Uly?" Maks asked, already doing an inventory in his head.

"Like now."

"What's up?" he repeated himself, cringing.

"Dan and the others have come up with a most interesting addition to the mission," Uly said. "I need to gather up several more Isann or Yarikh folks to accompany Sterling and Dan."

Maks tried to assemble that into some sort of coherent whole, but it refused to come together. He glanced at Chervonya and got a definitive shrug.

Helpful.

"Why?" he asked, dreading the answer already.

"She thinks we should make a long run to a Human colony on the far side of the *Auga Empire* to recruit," Uly said simply.

Maks wondered if there was something wrong with the gravity on his ship, as he pulled out a chair and settled into it.

Utterly insane. That's what it was. At the same time, it made a perverse sense, if they were already looking for a run that long. He'd dreamed of something crazy to mess with the Auga.

And maybe they'd need to circle around to Z'Gosza, or at least into Sector Fifteen.

Or not, looking at Uly's dangerous eyes.

"I feel like this might completely disrupt everything I had been planning," Maks offered.

"Agreed," Uly nodded. "Except that it really just means that one of your ships needs to be something that can sail into a Human port without standing out. That's not *Vauquelin*, obviously, but we have a few options. Crew won't be a major problem, except where I'll need folks who can pass for Human long enough. And a hull large enough to bring back an additional mob."

Maks did the math. Turned back to Chervonya, hoping she could read his mind.

Her nod was helpful. Maybe.

He turned back to the screen.

"I can send the ship with you in a couple of hours," Maks offered. "But I need to remain here for a variety of reasons, so I will have to meet up with you or it later. Possibly when you get back. I don't know."

"Nor do I," Uly said. "But the faster I can put this portion in motion, the better. *Vauquelin* needs a solid shakedown for this kind of mission anyway, so I have time. You and Sterling can work out a target somewhere on the near edge of Human space, then find them a ship to sail there. One where Dan and Kolya don't need many folks to run it, but can load up colonists. Solomon will be in charge of security, with non-Humans riding herd. Can I impose and steal your ship?"

"Certainly, Uly," Maks replied, getting a nod from Chervonya.

Uly was the reason he was what he was these days. Him and Lukyan, but mostly Uly.

And Dan.

Time to start paying them back for all the help along the way.

Because things were about to get weird.

TWENTY-TWO

Sterling awoke to a note to see Uly or Dan immediately, but it hadn't been critical enough to wake him early, so he showered and put on a nicer uniform before moving to where Solomon told him they were.

When he got to the big conference room, both looked to have been up all night, the opposite of crisp and fresh.

"Good, you're here," Uly said, breaking off from a conversation he was having with Mr. Ramezani on a screen.

Because Haydar preferred being on a quiet bridge somewhere away from people when possible. Introvert, like a lot of them, just moreso.

"Sir?" Sterling asked.

The room was full. Lots of folks moving around, including the Paramount and Commander Haldur.

"There isn't time to do this properly, but that's because time is entirely of the essence, Sterling," Uly said, rising.

Everyone else rose, too. And fell perfectly silent.

Sterling fell into parade rest so automatically that it almost hurt. At least everyone was smiling.

"Commander Huff, it is my privilege to promote you to commanding officer of the Bastion naval vessel *Vauquelin*," Vanguard Fortier announced formally. "You will take command of the final reconstruction process and delivery into service. During that time, you will work with various teams, including Lt. Wyndham, Trade Factor Sobol, and the government of Saari, to plot the necessary components of the expected raid deep into Auga territory, such that it will be as close to ready to execute as possible when I return."

Took a moment to absorb that, then Sterling nodded. He'd been expecting it. Everybody had been expecting it, to be honest, with Uly adding a second major warship into his fleet.

"Where will you be during this time, Vanguard?" Sterling asked, because obviously he had missed something.

"I will be departing in about an hour for Bastion aboard Maks's courier," Uly replied. "Dan and I need to recruit you some extra assistance for the latter portions of your mission, which Suka Kuri will be able to flesh out if you have questions."

"The latter portions, sir?" Sterling asked.

Didn't sound like a run straight in, bounce up and over, then out. Not that such a thing would be expected by Auga military bureaucracies, but at least it was predictable. Unlike Uly.

"After Stradosha, Conductor," Uly added. "You will undertake to continue outwards, in the company of a second vessel—to be determined—and send an additional mission to a Human colony in Imperial Sector Seventeen for recruiting purposes."

Sterling blinked. Blinked several more times. *Danumash* had trained him to be able to stand perfectly motionless and still breathe in the face of the sorts of abject stupidity that certain senior officers, men like Captain Winter on *King Hewitt II*, could get up to.

Insanity like this was close enough. At least he hoped so.

"Our plans for that portion are, obviously, a great deal more flexible at present, Commander," Uly smiled, taking some of the weight off Sterling's shoulders. "You and Maks work out how that goes. Also know that I intend to disguise any Isann and Yarikh that I can recruit to pretend to be Human during that portion of your mission."

The Isann would be all over that sort of thing. It practically defined them as a civilization.

Sailing Into Darkness.

The Yarikh would be far more interesting. And easier to disguise, obviously.

He wondered if he could convince Uly to bring Anari with him when he returned. She was kinda the ambassador to the Yarikh, though technically that was Kit when you got down to it.

Still, duty. He understood his.

Sterling nodded.

"I'll need a command crew as well as a full vessel crew, sir," Sterling said.

"For now, I'm keeping everyone aboard *Batyr* in their new roles," Uly replied. "You have full permission to inquire with anyone else for lateral transfer, excepting my senior folks like Drew and Haydar."

Sterling chuckled. Uly looked confused.

"Sadeq probably already lost that coin toss," Sterling reminded him. "Might need Kolya for his species. Probably need Kit if you can add some Yarikh."

He paused and turned around until he found the face he wanted, sitting next to the other face he might have selected, had circumstances been different. But Sterling already knew that the next big warship coming out of the graving dock would belong to Eskil Haldur. Whether it was the new flagship of the Samuur fleet or one he commanded for Uly didn't matter today. And it might be both anyway.

Sterling locked eyes with a pudgy, middle-aged Isann sailor next to Haldur.

"Aibek, I appreciate that this is short notice, but would Ainura or your kids mind if I offered you the First Officer slot on *Vauquelin*?" he asked.

Uly smiled. Dan smiled. Aibek looked like a man who had swallowed down the wrong pipe.

Sterling liked the man. And appreciated his calmness and competence. And he should have his own ship again, after Uly had nearly destroyed *Moonlight* at Bastion when they'd first met.

Before the *Karaŋgılıkka*.

"Are you certain, Commander Huff?" Aibek asked.

"Utterly," Sterling replied. "You are one of us now, and I look forward to training more Isann sailors, just as we will train Samuur to those same standards."

Commander Haldur nodded and smiled, so he understood. And probably could supply a list of sailors who Sterling could interview, many of whom had gone to Sector Thirty-Two with Uly and flown home captured pirate hulls, so they would know their business.

Sterling turned back to Uly.

"We'll get it done, sir," he said.

"That's why I rely on you, Sterling," Uly replied.

Sterling pasted that smile on his face and turned a pair of chairs around so Aibek could bring him up to speed and then they could dig in on Maks and Haydar.

He might be close to going home. Or at least as close as he thought he ever wanted, short of sailing into harbor with Uly and a full fleet of Heavy Devastators.

Wouldn't that be fun?

PART FOUR
BASTION

TWENTY-THREE

Uly had come to appreciate Maks's courier. He and Dan had moved into the main cabin without even emptying the closet, merely packing enough clothes for two drawers.

Cozy. Comfortable. They'd teased in the past about stealing such a ship, just the two of them, in order to return home and sneak in.

Now he was close to sending Dan. Or at least closer.

They would be arriving at Bastion shortly. Maks had warned him that Faisal would expect him or Dan to be on call to talk to the station when they arrived so that Faisal didn't have to.

In many ways, it was like dealing with Haydar, though Uly hadn't figured out what Faisal the Ononguli did in his off-time. Still that same introversion and intelligence.

"Boss, we're here," Faisal announced on the intercom.

Uly had a screen live in Maks's quarters, watching the countdown. He'd already recorded a message that he transmitted as soon as they emerged, looking at about a four second lag.

"Thank you," Faisal said immediately, so he'd been paying attention.

Uly's message didn't say it was him. Everyone would be expecting Maks, and Uly had simply typed a note that they needed to dock and talk to Lyra as quickly as could be arranged.

It wasn't that he was concerned about broadcasting, but he and Dan had grown a bit more circumspect about things, knowing that he didn't have *Nubia* or the Combat Team protecting him right now.

Any fool pirate could do something stupid right now.

He'd rather they didn't.

"Got docking lane assignment and schedules," Faisal replied ten seconds later. "Anything I need to worry about?"

"Resupply, in case this is the first step sideways," Uly reminded him.

"Already put in my orders." Faisal actually smiled at that, which was good. Fellow was relaxing.

Docking went quickly. And Governor Sobol was utterly flummoxed when the hatch opened and Uly and Dan emerged.

"Uhm...?" she began.

"It's complicated," Uly said. "We might not be here long, but that's because the people I probably need are elsewhere."

Dan stole a hug. Uly followed. They ended up back in Lyra's office, where he brought her up to speed.

"Utterly nuts, Uly," Lyra said when he finished. "I like it."

"Good," he replied. "I'd like to grab Anari, Kit, and Melpomeni at a minimum."

"And I sent all three of them to Traiffe," Lyra grimaced. "Probably just arrived there today, or maybe tomorrow."

"As to be expected," Uly shrugged. "Thank you for handling all the strangeness of diplomacy with my various neighbors while I've been gone."

"Sounds like you might be back here sooner than you expected?" she asked. "At least on a semi-permanent status?"

"Likely," Uly agreed. "Dan will take longer, so I'll need you handling Chief of Staff duties if I can continue to impose, since Dan and the Congress will be busy forward for this."

"I have Voldomir already talking to various architecture firms," Lyra grinned. "At least one of your towns on the surface needs to be the sort of paradise that drags Ononguli down off their ships. And we might have found a bay that will similarly appeal to the Khet, such that both would be happy."

"Even better news," Uly said.

"What do I need to be doing?" Lyra asked.

Dan smiled.

"The Legal Department had some ideas on homesteading," Dan interjected. "All the folks currently in place will have a chance to double their holdings, then we'll need a full land survey based on the new rules, and we can start selling land, either on a cash basis or bank loans, or in kind over a longer horizon, depending. Ethir assures me that the first and third options work best, but that's outside my expertise."

"No, he's right," Lyra replied. "Farmers will provide goods or sell them on a local market as it develops. Ranchers will do the same. The cities will, for now, be run on Ethir's weird mix of Auga, Ononguli, and Khet rules, but they left detailed instructions for how to read various sections. We have a few towns down there, but wanted to hold off on siting a capital city until you had more time to walk the ground."

"And this isn't the time," Uly said. "You send a packet with me that has everything I need and I might start having opinions when I get back."

"Should you take *Batyr* instead of *Yosyp Kyrylenko*?" Lyra asked. "Probably not as fast, but much better armed, which might be important back there."

Uly considered it.

"Yes, and it lets me see Yuriy and his crew work, after they've been promoted and before I start pulling some folks off to rearrange my crews."

"And start a training school," Dan spoke up.

He turned to her, eyes inquisitive.

"Ground school," she said. "Most of the sailors you have now are experienced hands. We'll want a basic training institute. And eventually a place to formally start training new students in Starfare."

It was the calmness as she spoke that really rammed it home. Building an entire nation required planning for those little steps. Sailors knew how to do these things, but he wanted them to do it a particular way. Everybody. Every time. And yes, officers trained in Starfare.

He nodded.

"Add it to your list," he said. "Or delegate it down, since you'll be months on a mission and probably need to start now."

That caught her just as off guard, which was his intent.

She was his Chief of Staff, but that really meant that she was his other half in just about everything. Even the other Wives weren't nearly as good at understanding him. Not yet, anyway. Maybe never.

"Yes, we'll take *Batyr*," Dan decided. "I need to talk to Bello as we sail. He'll have a cousin or relative. The Ononguli don't really do it that way, relying more on on-the-job training, but the Khet have schools. We can hire a few instructors to start forming a curriculum at some point."

Uly nodded.

He could do all these things, because he had her.

It would be the time alone that would be the hardest.

TWENTY-FOUR

Yuriy wanted to pinch himself, but refrained. Uly smiled. Dan, standing just behind Uly on the bridge, also smiled. Everyone on the bridge of *Batyr* smiled, so he must not be dreaming.

Yuriy was still afraid of waking up.

"Lieutenant Commander, sir?" he asked Uly, mostly to confirm.

"That's correct," Uly replied. "It originated in the idea of a Lieutenant commanding a small boat instead of a Commander doing it, then got formalized into a rank between the two. Since we're using a complicated mix of *Batyr*, *Danumash*, and Ononguli ranks for things, I can add one temporarily. Eventually, you will be a full commander, but it's time to get used to command, Yuriy, though I know you have it in you."

"Who'd have imagined, sitting in that cell, listening to the Songbird," he mused.

Dumbass pirate. He'd been one. A lot of folks, looking back on the *Iron Wasp* days with Adrian, used the same vocabulary as a way to underline a future they'd moved into.

And yeah, he'd helped steal this very ship, leading Uly and the others to this bridge because he'd been qualified to sit engineering watch up here back then.

Now, he was officially in command.

At least everyone was smiling. And he didn't think he was dreaming.

"How soon can you depart, Mr. Kovalchuk?" Uly asked.

"We've been generally topped up on supplies, sir," Yuriy replied, turning to Vitali.

Lt. Vitali Havrylyuk had been his Gunner before, and taken on the First Officer job when Yuriy had stepped up. Probably needed to find a new Gunner soon, but it didn't have to happen today.

Or maybe First Officer. Vitali might want to go back to Guns. They hadn't really talked about it before now, assuming that Uly would do things over the next several months, rather than showing up out of the blue, promoting him, and setting sail.

"Can we make it to Traiffe on what we have?" he asked the man. "Or Isann, both directions?"

"If we're adding people, Traiffe is my outer limit on what we have loaded," Vitali nodded. "Assuming we can convince them to resupply us."

"Assume a stop at Isann," Uly said. "We'll want to give them warning to pack. Plus, we can check in with the Chief of Chiefs. Maks sent me a message pack for him, laying out their next two years of building."

"Isann is easy, sir," Vitali said.

"Good," Uly said, turning back to Yuriy. "Our gear came aboard when we did, so as soon as you're ready to go?"

Yuriy kept his grin professional and contained. Sterling had loved the idea of random pop quizzes to get everyone used to shit going suddenly sideways. Like half the bridge crew ordered to go to lunch in the middle of a training alert, representing crew injuries.

He recognized another pop quiz in Uly's eyes.

"Mr. Temitope, do you have a course laid in for Isann?" Yuriy asked.

"Affirmative, sir," Bello replied.

Yuriy nodded.

"Let the station know we are departing," Yuriy ordered. "Then begin acceleration and transition to warp as soon as you clear the outer markers. You have my permission to exceed standard speed limits in harbor, as long as nobody is a threat to our line of passage and we can convince the warlord to wave traffic fines later."

Uly's smile suggested that he was doing okay. Yuriy settled back into his seat and brought up his screens as Uly and Dan moved to side stations to watch.

Lieutenant Commander Kovalchuk, Conductor of *Batyr*.

And no, he really wasn't dreaming.

TWENTY-FIVE

Kit wasn't about to say that he was used to Traiffe. Or comfortable being here. In fact, it weirded him out even more to be in a place where the only so-called *alien* face he saw was Anari and everybody else looked Human.

Weren't, but he still thanked Suka Kuri for that concept. Small, dark brown Emro. Good enough.

It was Melpomeni that kept him on his toes. She was one hundred percent woman. And zero percent, but one hundred in the right ways.

He just generally skipped over the part where she'd mentioned off-hand that her last lover had left more or less about the time he'd been born.

He looked up as the hatch—no, door, planetary surface and unpowered—opened and she entered the little workshop he'd been permitted to play in. After having almost all of the powered tools removed and replaced with stuff he'd brought with him. Easier to understand, less likely to bleed, and stuff the Samuur and Isann would have access to.

None of this Tools of the Gods bullshit, thank you.

Still, she was smiling. It was a pretty smile. Distracting. He put the tools down before he started bleeding again and smiled back.

"You haven't moved in three hours," she said simply.

He stopped and realized that she was correct. She was usually correct.

Melpomeni held out a hand and pulled him to his feet when he took it. Stuff got put down. Tools got put back where they belonged before he went anywhere, so he could find stuff later.

Ya gotta stay organized on a starship, and ground was no reason to break those habits. Especially not if you could bleed when you weren't careful.

He leaned in and got a kiss; careful, though, 'cause he really didn't understand women and even then he was pretty damned sure that she wasn't going to be like any he might meet on some future date.

Rather than speak, she kept his hand and started walking. He got pulled along, caught up, and they wound up outside pretty fast, except that the building wasn't really a building. More like a series of rooms and hallways, only half of which had walls or roofs.

Helped, when the city was located in a paradise.

Kit walked. Kept up with her, and she was in better shape than him, but she cheated. Had been designed better. Or upgraded from baseline.

They got to a place where someone was serving a picnic. Sort of. Table with several troughs of food and one of those ultrasonic doohickeys that kept bugs away. Melpomeni more or less shoved him into line, so he got stuff.

Butter that was yellow was still weird after so many years of eating Khet cooking, but he was adjusting. Bread was great. Noodles. Sauce the softest pink. Protein of a critter he couldn't identify by shape, color, or texture. Might have come out of a vat. Didn't ask.

Glass of water with ice. Basic stuff, though he'd noticed that they had started adding spices and flavors to the stuff since he'd been here.

Melpomeni blamed him for busting them out of a rut. Kit appreciated how bland their food must have been before. He was still bringing more spices next time and making them ramp it up another notch.

"What have you been working on this morning?" she asked as she settled across from him.

"Got an idea for improvements on a standard Isann life support generator," he replied. "Picked apart the ones the Samuur use and I've taken it as far as I can. The Isann still have spots where theirs can be made better."

"Why not use standard tech?" she asked. "It's more advanced."

"Sure, but I keep circling back to how we might take their stuff and eke out more improvements with what they can build now, rather than retooling their entire economy," he shrugged.

"You haven't asked me what the Yarikh might offer," she noted carefully.

Kit put down his spoon and fixed her.

"You told Uly that you would help, but not how," he reminded this woman. "Or when. Figured you needed to talk with the Scholar to see what she would approve in terms of tech transfer. I assume you folks have access to all sorts of fantastically interesting gear, but none of it helps the Isann or Samuur in the short term. They'd have to be retrained on it. Then tear out everything they are doing now and build new whole factories to build new parts to build new systems to even consider building new ships. That's out a ways, any way you cut it. Better life support now means they can have larger crews, or sail greater distances with what they have, especially if the fix is something small that can be done in place."

Her face got serious, then she grinned and looked so much younger. She generally looked an incredibly well-preserved and hot fifty-something, but suddenly she looked his age. It was the smile.

"And weapons?" she pressed, still grinning.

"*Nubia* mounts 15s," he nodded. "Already stupidly powerful and a step beyond most of the rest of the galaxy, at least until the Auga decide to build some. I have no doubt that they have plans for something similar somewhere, just didn't need them before now because a 12 is a solid standard. Explorers need more range to wander. Maybe improved Variable Pulse Spatial Generators so they can get places faster. Weapons and shields are pretty well balanced right now. Uly's always going to be hurting for trained crew, so I gotta figure out how to make him better ships."

"And automation systems?" she asked, turning more serious, but not super serious.

"That's Haydar and Roshan," he shook his head ruefully. "They are always writing tighter code and designing cleaner control systems. At some point, I figure Uly or Maks challenge them to clean-sheet design a new starship. That's when it gets fun."

"Oh?"

"Mazhin live on ships," he said. "Don't go down to planets all that often, so things have to work. Have to work without a handy repair yard if it breaks. Have to be durable measured in decades or centuries. My contribution is life support. Good at that."

She paused, studying him. Kit grabbed his spoon and shoveled, wondering where she was going with all this. Wasn't like he was the deepest guy. Or anywhere close to the smartest, ESPECIALLY on this planet. He just tinkered.

And occasionally got to ogle hot babes like her.

She opened her mouth, closed it again, and apparently started over in her head. Eyes gave it away.

He shoveled, wondering when it would get more weirder. It would. It always did.

And technically, Anari was the Ambassador to the Yarikh, but that was the official stuff. Melpomeni and him had gotten...

Something.

Kit still didn't have a vocabulary to describe it, and probably needed a woman like Dan or maybe Suka Kuri to help him understand what he'd gotten himself into. Anari, for all she was smart, was way less experienced at some of these things than he was.

"The Scholar suggested sending some new designs for improved systems," she finally said. "And you've already utterly punctured that logic without even thinking about it, because, as you noted, the Isann or Samuur would have to retool their entire economies to support such things."

"Build your factories at Bastion," he nodded. "Central, and can export to the others, plus drawing them in to face Uly."

She blinked. Kinda like he'd surprised the shit out of her.

It happened occasionally. Blind squirrels still stumble across acorns.

"We would probably need to send our people to train everyone," she said carefully.

"Assumed that," Kit said. "Only way to make it work, since you don't want them coming here in the numbers that you'd need."

More surprise. Wasn't like he didn't let backbrain think through these things constantly while the hands tinkered. Only so many ways to scale that fish, as the Khet would say.

"Would Uly approve?" she asked.

"Utterly," Kit smiled. "Kinda the whole point of this thing, when you look at it. Bring everyone together as one big crew. Yarikh are just one more flavor in the gumbo."

He didn't mention the part where they looked Human. Would be taken for Human, because they'd started off that way. Blair had been pretty certain that they were a fully different species now, as such things were technically classified. But the Yarikh women that came might be compatible with folks like Cleve and Leon.

At least physically.

"Then I have a different question, Kit," she turned way serious now. "How far do we take it?"

There was an ambiguity in her eyes that spoke of more than just tech. At least he thought so. Personal stuff. Cleve and Leon and some of the other guys involved.

Kit took one of those big steps backwards in his head and focused on the little things instead.

Call it cowardice if you want. Still not going there.

"As far as you think is safe," he countered, letting her decide what he was talking about.

Pop had warned him about how dangerous older women could be. The need to treat them respectfully. Listen to them. Appreciate them. Maybe get them to cook you breakfast if you did your job right.

Kit wasn't sure he'd ever meet a more dangerous woman. At least in those terms. Dan didn't count.

"We'd be disrupting things," she offered. "Changing everything."

He shrugged.

"Hopefully, making it better," he challenged. "Happier for everyone."

He really hoped that they were still talking about life support systems, but felt like he'd fallen into a river and could hear those rapids approaching.

"What would make Kit Simonson happier?" she asked, kinda blunt.

He paused to frame the words.

"I am not the deepest guy," he admitted. "Never set out to be a hero. Not like Uly. Not like Dan. Just a dude down in engineering, learning how to fix shit from Marlowe. An apprentice at the time, though I suppose I've moved up since then. Uly wants to stop the Auga. Needs a lot of friends. A lot of help. That's you. That's the Isann and the Samuur. The Horde and the Corporations. I've kinda wondered if the Yarikh really could move everyone far enough ahead that they could poke the Auga in their Third Eye and make them stop, but you've never said anything. How far do you want to take things?"

Kinda rude, tacking that on the end there. He went bland as his words caught up with her. Hadn't ever actually seen the woman blush before. Kinda hadn't thought it was possible. Especially as dark as that skin normally was.

Just added to the cuteness he found so distracting.

All that, **and** brains.

She suddenly shook her head ruefully, grinning at him.

"You're bad for me," she chuckled. "And good. You keep me from sliding back into stodgy."

He grinned back at her. She'd mentioned them inverting their whole culture overnight when a lost tribe of Humans suddenly showed up to say hi. Most of them had started to fall back into the old ways, he'd been given to understand, but some still had what Mel called the fire of adventure.

She chuckled some more, then turned and waved at someone.

Kit looked over as that someone approached, then nearly dropped his spoon when it turned out to be the Scholar herself. He started to stand automatically, caught his legs on the table edge, nearly fell on his ass, then she waved him back down.

How much trouble was he in this time?

'Cept that she was smiling. Both women were smiling.

And damn, someone had designed Yarikh woman to be hot, even with curly, gray hair.

He smiled, too. The Scholar slid in next to The Engineer and both watched him.

His water needed some juice. They didn't do those sorts of things, but if he was spending a lot more time on this rock, their cuisine was going to need the Spatula's touch. Or one of his trainees.

Something.

"What have you told him?" Scholar Marinos asked.

"Nothing," Mel smirked. "He keeps turning the conversation around on me, but I think we have come to certain understandings."

He wanted to ask about what, since most of that had been teasing, but supposed that that counted.

Scholar locked hard on him, but had friendly eyes.

"Uly asked for help," she reminded him. "We have decided to provide some technical assistance. What do you need?"

"People willing to come to Bastion," Kit replied automatically, feeling shit get eyeballs-deep serious enough that he wished Anari was handy. "To teach everyone there how to build better systems. And to improve the ones they have now, because we're still talking years to get things where Uly needs them, and he might not have that time. Not if the Auga get pissed enough to send a fleet to Bastion after him."

Woman nodded. Sage. Brains. Babe, but brains. And brains.

"We have discussed founding a second Yarikh colony at Bastion," she said simply, but his jaw dropped so hard that it hurt. She nodded. Smiled even. "That many of us will necessitate sending a squadron of our defense vessels to protect them, which will also protect Uly. Or at least his home because we have surmised that he will continue to travel far too much for a leader."

"Founder," Mel broke it. "Warlord. He's actually within parameters there."

Kit turned to the woman and remembered just how smart she was. Not like he forgot, but things occasionally jumped out at him.

"You have *parameters*?" he asked.

Mel nodded, then grinned. He felt a little safer.

"Historians have cataloged such things," she told him. "And we've had reason to review their findings recently. Uly fits a number of paradigms as a national founding hero."

Wow. Just kinda wow. And he *really* needed Anari. Or Suka Kuri. Shit had just gotten real, like she'd pulled back a curtain and let him peek into the next room.

Kit nodded. Not much to say there.

"What will Bastion need?" the Scholar asked, echoing Mel without all the subtext.

At least he really hoped so.

"I got a list," Kit managed. "Or I can write it down in two columns. Was just talking to Mel on the topic."

"Good," the Scholar nodded. "You do that, while we start our preparations here."

Then she rose, smiled again, and walked away. He turned to Mel and caught her grin.

"Uhm?" he asked.

Her smile expanded.

"Logic, Kit," she replied. "You bring it to the table, along with a variety of other gifts. The only way to stop the Auga, according to experts who have studied such problems, involves helping Uly. Now. Today, because every year we delay allows the Auga that much more time to grow in strength."

"Conversely, it also improves the odds of an eventual imperial collapse," he said, blessing Suka Kuri for taking him aside and giving him a crash course on certain things she knew he would need here.

And she'd been right. Like Mel, Suka Kuri usually was.

Mel blinked at him, then the smile came back, even warmer.

"Not a chance we wish to risk," she nodded. "We've worked too hard around here to let them screw it up later."

"What do you need from me?" he asked, seeing her face suddenly take on a different look.

He hadn't meant it that way, but her smile offered certain suggestions. Brains as aphrodisiac? He supposed it could go both ways.

"You're taking the afternoon off," she informed him. "Tomorrow, we'll start formalizing that list."

He finished his food quickly, then let her take his hand and draw him in the direction of the personal quarters. Whatever he was doing, he was apparently doing it right.

TWENTY-SIX

Dan was impressed by the speed with which they'd made it to Traiffe. Then how quickly the Yarikh had reacted to welcome *Batyr* then get her and Uly to the ground to meet with the Scholar and her people.

Instead of the usual conference rooms where Dan seemed to live when she wasn't in her dojo, this was a park. Of sorts. On a perfectly gorgeous day.

Anari sat close to translate, but Uly was generally conversational these days, the result of all Dan's work reading and listening to those logs and teaching him. Kit and the Engineer sat close to one another to one side, touching more than was probably necessary.

Good.

Scholar Nomiki Marinos looked so much like several of her aunts that it almost hurt to sit close to the woman. All of them reminded her of home. Of the family she'd largely given up on ever seeing again.

And this next mission would just make it worse, as tantalizingly close as they would get.

Not close enough. Probably.

It was a shame that Aurtan wasn't closer to any border she might slip across, or she would be tempted. Nobody would look twice at a crew of Yarikh arriving there, if they didn't say anything.

Uly finished his portion of the explanation, covering the Ancyn they had rescued and the mission to go free more or them. He turned to her with a warm and helpful smile.

"Then you take command," he said simply.

Dan nodded. Scanned left to right to see everyone watching her with an air of expectation. Kit was Human. They had recognized that immediately. He was still pale and washed out compared to the dark brown Yarikh. Anglo, with light-colored skin and straight brown hair instead of her kind.

Dan looked like the dark faces looking back. Her people.

Something stirred deep inside and gave her a power she could hardly remember ever feeling.

"From there, I would like to recruit a handful or more Yarikh," Dan said. "Folks willing to travel to the far side of the *Auga Empire* and assist me by pretending to be fully Human."

The Scholar started to speak and Dan waved her off.

"I know," she said. "I also know that you and I only appear to be the same species. This will go beyond that, because you'll be impersonating folks from *Batyr* in dress, manners, and language. In culture. I know you can pick such things up quickly, so it won't be a problem."

"Why?" Engineer Michelakos asked.

Blunt, but not hostile.

"Because our intent is to sail to a Human colony along the outer edge of *Danumash* space," Dan replied. "Most of those worlds are largely independent of *Danumash* and *Batyr*, and will trade with any ship that comes in. They will know a bit about aliens, because I learned such things when my old ship called on those worlds. As to the why, I intend to recruit up to several hundred Human colonists to join us at Bastion."

She watched the shock ripple hard across the entire group.

"Several hundred?" Michelakos asked in a voice hardly above a whisper.

"We'll need sufficient diversity of blood lines to retain viability over the long haul," Dan nodded, knowing that Michelakos would understand that language.

Engineer, but in the context of scientific advisor to the woman in the middle.

The Scholar.

Dan watched Michelakos share a knowing glance with Kit. One that suggested those two had sorted out as many of their issues as they probably could, given all the other things involved.

And folks who might be willing to help their distant and primitive cousins, if medical science needed it.

She'd ask Blair to step in and charm everyone at some point. He was still the most species-cross-trained medic in the galaxy right now, even if he refused to act like a proper doctor most of the time, but that was his personality, and not his knowledge.

Marinos turned to Michelakos. Some unspoken conversation occurred, but that was two old friends and not any sort of telepathy. Dan had spent too many years around Mazhin—and now Samuur—learning to read alien body language.

The Scholar turned to Anari, who had been largely silent up until now. The only alien face in the crowd, of a sorts, but only when you measured skin tone and physical size.

Her intellect guaranteed her place here.

"Anari, why don't you explain the discussions we've been having?" the woman in charge suggested.

Anari nodded. Like Suka Kuri, she tended to kneel, even though her hosts had apparently manufactured a few chairs and benches to her size and mass.

It made her look like one of the ancient samurai of legend. Poised equally for battlefields and salons. And she was.

So utterly was.

"Without knowing of your impending arrival, we have been negotiating details of a small Yarikh colony that would come into being at Bastion," Anari said.

Dan was touching Uly, thigh to thigh, so she felt his shock, even though he made no other move.

"Such a thing, as Kit reminds us, would help them to train various folks to manufacture and maintain technology upgrades from what everyone currently has, ranging up from Isann and Samuur to Auga and the warship *Nubia*," she continued. "It would require time, though, so there have also been discussions about immediate improvements that could be shared."

"A full colony?" Uly asked, voice carefully neutral.

The Scholar nodded.

"We presume a decade of work, at a minimum," she replied. "While that is a much smaller fraction of our lifetimes than yours, it still represents a significant investment."

"Are there that many Yarikh willing to travel away from Traiffe for an extended period?" Dan asked, drawing the woman's eyes to her again.

"We expect somewhere between six hundred and one thousand," Marinos replied.

"That many?" Dan pressed.

"They will need to protect the teachers and the mechanics," Anari spoke up. "To do so, they have proposed a squadron of Yarikh warships permanently assigned to protect the system and the colony from outside threat."

Dan could only think of one true threat at that point. She caught the Scholar's nod.

The Auga would not be allowed to take Bastion. Possibly ever, if her cousins had decided to stop the Empire from subsequently threatening Traiffe.

Better to let the barbarians fight it out, way over there. Not that Dan was offended. She and Uly would fight. Yarikh assistance meant that they could do a better job of it today, rather than spending the rest of her lifetime building up the infrastructure and hoping that folks four hundred years from now maintained it.

And didn't turn out to be just as bad as the Auga.

This generation of Yarikh wouldn't be alive to see it. At least she didn't think so without asking pointedly rude questions. However, not that many Yarikh generations would pass between now and then. They would remember.

"Of those thousand," Dan said. "Might there be a few dozen willing to depart shortly? To visit their distant cousins? The Lost Tribe?"

Another ripple of surprise, but Dan understood that part. She'd read and listened to all of Selene's logs, both official and personal.

The Yarikh didn't come from Traiffe. They had chosen to settle here when they'd withdrawn from the galaxy. Back when they'd still been Human.

Some of Sterling's newer calculations had suggested that Humans might have originated somewhere on the far side of Imperial Sector Forty-One, out well beyond Z'Gosza and across a deep stellar rift.

Not anyplace Dan figured she'd visit in her lifetime, but Sterling might be able to suggest a vector and send others that way.

Were there yet more lost tribes to be found?

"I will," Elias Ioannidis spoke up from opposite Kit and the Engineer.

Every head turned toward him.

Middle-aged Yarikh male. Hair gray verging over to white, kept short enough to barely have any ringlets in his curls. Tall and thin. Overdressed for the situation. Or simply bad at fashion.

Historian to the Court. Anari had found him to be a strange mix of pompous and personable, depending on the topic. As smart as all of them. A little too full of himself at times, but much less so in others.

"Elias?" the Scholar asked.

"There is literally nobody better educated or suited to such a mission, Nomiki," he replied evenly. "And I'm not certain I would trust the reports of any who did go, excepting Melpomeni."

That drew smiles.

The man turned to look at Dan. She studied him. Imposed her will on him silently, because his body language shifted.

"If you would have me," he amended.

Dan nodded. Didn't do her any good if someone wanted to challenge her authority at every turn because he thought he came from a more advanced civilization.

All they had were better toys.

She turned to the Engineer next.

"At least to Bastion," the woman answered. "Probably, I will need to travel to Isann and Saari to help them from there. Possibly Rayzian, but that's less certain. But I will begin locating the adventurous ones immediately for you, assuming Nomiki approves."

They were back to the Scholar.

"Ten years suddenly feels like it will run much longer," the Scholar said.

"All of you would be welcome to remain past that," Uly replied. "Or found new colonies in the Spinward Reaches."

"Got a list of worlds we surveyed," Kit added cheerfully. "And a few we skipped. All of them are habitable and abandoned, near as we could tell."

"There you go," Uly said. "Many places you might claim. Or surrender your claim and have new neighbors, possibly including long-lost kin."

Dan watched all of them digest that tidbit.

A year ago, they had thought themselves the last Humans left in the galaxy. Today, they were discovering how wrong they were.

And Anari had mentioned how a few of the younger ones had suddenly woke up one morning chafing at the limitations that had been acceptable to their elders.

Not like she had any experience with that.

Dan watched the Scholar. The woman nodded.

"We will do this thing," Nomiki said somberly.

"You will come to appreciate the wider galaxy," Dan promised.

"I hope you are correct."

TWENTY-SEVEN

Uly had a good vantage from the bridge of *Batyr*, having settled after a week on Traiffe that had been more of another whirlwind romance with an entire culture than a series of planning meetings.

Or both.

What frightened him—concerned him, perhaps—was the ship currently docked with the main station across the way and how it dwarfed the others. He had seen scans of the ships Anari had first encountered on arriving. None of them had been as big as *Batyr*, while running power curves comparable to at least Light Strikers.

Dangerously powerful defensive ships, designed to protect Traiffe from any fool demanding access. Luckily, he had asked politely.

And sent Kit.

Sometime in the last year, they had started building a larger ship. *Batyr*'s equivalent for displacement. *Nubia*'s for power. At least.

He could only imagine what they had for weapons, with that many years to think about such things, even if they hadn't built them.

Until possibly today.

They called the class Blackbird, just as *Nubia* had once been of the Skyhawk-class. And named it *Searcher*.

What they were searching for was left to the imagination for now, but it would carry the first several hundred colonists and their immediate gear. Along with other things that Uly felt were almost gifts from the gods. Or the fey.

Things the Scholar felt would help him, both immediately as well as over the short and long term. Help him build out the Spinward Reaches into something bigger. Something better.

And it hadn't taken them long to load *Searcher*. He'd loaded up on supplies at Isann, so he could run home. Chief of Chiefs Usupov was already sending people directly to Bastion to meet Dan. She would fly aboard *Searcher*, her and Anari and Kit and the others, where they would have already started working things out by the time they met again on the far side.

Uly drew a breath, aware that Yuriy and Vitali were watching. Waiting.

He turned away from the screen and nodded.

"What is their status?" he asked simply.

"Awaiting our readiness, Vanguard," Yuriy replied. "We're loaded and set, awaiting the order."

He would see her again briefly at Bastion. Then not again for however long it took to succeed, but he already missed her.

"Take us home, Mr. Kovalchuk," he ordered.

TWENTY-EIGHT

Dan had immediately felt at home, the first time she had walked the corridors of *Nubia* that had once been the Yarikh Skyhawk *Invincible*. Khet corridors tended to run wider, with lower ceilings. The Ononguli were the exact opposite, accounting for horns and skinnier builds.

Searcher was also like coming home. A Human-engineered vessel. Anari was as cramped as ever, but giddy at the prospect of seeing Sterling again. Of him coming with them on the long mission, where those two would have the sorts of together time she had had with Uly since leaving Saari.

Elias Ioannidis had taken on something of the role of a tour guide, though she knew ships better than he did. But he'd been planetbound for most of his life, and she'd already spent a decade and a half in space.

He did, however, understand how hungry she was for his professional expertise. They sat in a lounge, not *surrounded* by many of the volunteers, but more crowded than due to mere chance. He spoke, she listened. Anari absorbed it nearby, but that was Moss School and the need to relay every iota on later. To Suka Kuri if nothing else, but the Lost Tribes were going to meet, and would need to know things.

"At that point, we closed off the sky," Elias concluded. "Built the defensive forces adequate to annihilate any bothersome pirates as we cultivated an image of a terrible dragon to be left alone. At least until Kit and Anari arrived."

At least they understood that Kit had been symbolic, and Anari the Ambassador, though both had shifted their roles around somewhat, like good teammates did.

Elias really was a good storyteller. Fortunately, he also knew to poke fun at that same pomposity. Anari had said that such a change was his adaptation to the new future.

"What about Sector Seventeen?" he asked as the room turned to her.

Dan knew that they would need to know many things, even as she was planning to hold the role of ship's captain when they got where they were going.

Or should she take on First Officer, allowing her to visit the ground while someone like Elias remained in orbit? Not that he would. The man practically demanded to be at her side, studying everyone, and she would honor that.

And she didn't need to decide anything until much, much later.

She drew a breath and leaned back, focusing not on anyone in the room, most of whom felt like a family reunion, but on a spot she could see in some incredible distance.

Her dreams, maybe.

"There are two Human realms over there," she began. "The *Seven Kingdoms*, also known as the *Combined Crowns of Danumash*, are where Kit and several of the others were born. Beyond that, closer to the galactic rim, is *Batyr*. That's where Uly and I come from, but we currently aren't planning to visit either."

"Because you would not be welcomed home?" one of the younger women asked from a corner.

Most of the ones that had joined them were young. Teenage rebellion, and all that. That one might pass for her actual cousin by looks. Dionysia Stavrou. A young adult, which meant about Dan's actual age, in spite of her looking more like a precocious seventeen-year-old.

"Either place we went, there would be questions we would rather not answer," Dan corrected her. "The Humans live in their own bubble of space, well removed from any other inhabited stars. Almost a desert that way, rather than a rich river plain like Auga Sector One or some of the other lands. It has kept them bottled up for the longest time, when they might have turned into a threat to the rest of the galaxy otherwise."

"Did they choose that intentionally, if they are Yarikh who chose to ignore the recall?" Dionysia asked.

Dan shrugged and turned to Elias.

"That's your culture more than mine," she pointed out.

"And I would tend to agree," he nodded. "We presume that they ran a tremendous distance, then settled where nobody would ever find them. That would have been some seven or eight thousand years ago."

"And I'm not a Human Historian to tell you much," Dan replied. "Nor Uly, though he has much more formal education. But we're going to one of the outer colonies. There are several of them on the far side of that wide gap that few other species have crossed. We knew about the existence of some aliens, but even then they were rare. And *Danumash* obviously had encountered Mazhin, because our original group of ten came from several different ships that they had taken."

"And yet they never expanded?" Elias pursued.

"I think geography helped," Dan answered. "*Batyr* would have, but *Danumash* is essentially defensive. They hate other Humans based on skin tone alone. Aliens would have been a whole other level of people to oppress below that, save that those Mazhin were all sophisticated and trained. Slaves, being transported from one facility to another when our ship intercepted their convoy and rescued them."

"Which is why you needed Yarikh to infiltrate Human spaces," Dionysia noted.

"And Isann, who can be disguised adequately," Dan replied. "There will be others who remain out of sight. Ononguli and Khet combat troopers who will protect us from pirates."

"Do you really need Isann for this mission?" the young woman asked, perhaps a touch pointedly.

Dan laughed.

"They would never forgive me if I left them out," she said with a smile to take the sting out of her words. "*Karaŋgılıkka* literally means *Sailing Into Darkness*, and is their primary cultural touchstone. Once Uly understood that, he had the keys to turn the entire species into some of his best friends and most loyal supporters. They will be more excited to travel with us than anybody, and happy to wear makeup later. It lets them go someplace none of their ancestors ever even dreamed of."

She let them chew on that concept for a bit. They might be physically older, most of them, but Dan had seen far more of the galaxy. It made her feel a bit old and jaded.

The Yarikh were confused, but they were willing to step out. To leaving their homeworld, when their parents had never imagined such a thing. It made them more Isann that way. She smiled at the thought.

"And Humans on one of these worlds will just pack up and sail halfway across the galaxy with you?" Dionysia asked.

Elias turned around to look at the woman.

"You just did," he pointed out quietly.

Dionysia looked crestfallen. The others laughed.

Dan nodded.

"That is something we all share," she reminded her. Reminded them all.

"And all the others?" Dionysia asked. "These strange aliens we never knew?"

"All friends of Uly's," Dan told her. "And they are just people, same as you. It is going to be a grand adventure, but first, we must sneak into the *Auga Empire*, where all of us will have to hide out of sight to rescue a group of Ancyn."

"How will you do that, if so many of these species are unknown there?" she asked.

"Because I also have many friends," Dan smiled.

PART FIVE
VAUQUELIN

TWENTY-NINE

Sterling was still adjusting to the weird way that the Auga built their command spaces, but supposed that he could eventually rip this whole space out and redo it. When they got home.

Nubia was arranged on levels, with the Conductor able to look over the shoulders of the four in front of them without standing. *Batyr* had been set with his chair somewhat aft in the room and the others all facing forward in front of him.

Trust the Auga to have everyone but the Conductor around an oval-shaped bridge, facing a blank bulkhead for a station. Sure, he had space to pace and wander around, but he had to imagine that everyone else was cramped, at least psychologically.

He had started a list of suggestions and questions for Mr. Ramezani and Mr. Anyari to make all this better. And maybe Suka Kuri and Omid for the aesthetics.

Efficiency of form occasionally had to give way to art. He'd learned that from them. Should he locate Hiko Seiichai and ask him to travel with them for his sculptural abilities? Hmmmm.

"You appear to be about ten thousand light-years away," Aibek Sulaymanov noted as he stepped close.

Sterling rose from his...call it a command throne. Wasn't far off.

"Thinking how we can rip everything out in here and make it...prettier," Sterling replied. "What do you have for me?"

"Your reminder that we need to meet Maks and Eskil at the station," Aibek said.

Sterling checked the time and realized that he had been daydreaming. Possible when the ship was ready to go, but still docked and waiting portentous events. Like the thing that might be the biggest and most dangerous raid the Auga had ever suffered.

Certainly the most audacious.

So far...

He turned to locate his Sensors Officer. *Danumash* didn't do things that way, nor *Batyr*, but Uly did. And it helped that Mr. Ramezani filled both roles, so it had been natural for Sterling to adjust *Vauquelin* onto a similar path.

That, and he'd found a diamond in the rough with Maikki Hudaibirdi. A Samuur woman, she'd taken a transfer from *Ahonen*, where she'd been First Officer, so she knew the job here.

"Ms. Hudaibirdi, you have command until we get back," he told her, watching the tall woman immediately nod, rise, and begin pacing, like she would.

Not as tall as Anari, but still tall. Solomon-sized, if anything, with shoulders, but not a lot of hips. Muscles. Woman was as jock as they got when you got her talking about herself. As competitive as any Samuur he'd met in every athletic field you suggested.

Sterling grinned to himself as he drew Aibek with him.

"What's so funny?" the much-smaller, middle-aged Isann asked as the hatch closed and they headed toward the docking airlock.

"Remembering the day I first met Uly," he said. "Well, Dan came through the lock first. Uly stepped up and broke Eldridge's jaw for the racist bullshit he threw at Dan, then looked at me like I was an overcooked steak on a plate."

"And?"

"Comparing that dumbass Astronomer's Mate I was then to where we are today, where my First Officer is Isann and I just turned over command to a Samuur woman without a thought until now," Sterling laughed. "I kinda like who I turned into, but that young *Danumash* gentleman I might have been would have been utterly aghast. He was also a racist shit. Specist, too. Thank all the gods that I met Uly, Dan, and everybody else."

Aibek nodded at that. The Isann were in their first generation of leaving their home system, and that man's galactic horizons had also grown enormous from when he'd been a dumbass kid. They'd bonded over that, in spite of Aibek being about the same age as Sterling's dad.

"And now we're off to rescue the Ancyn," Aibek said with a smile. And a bit of a jaunt in his step that Sterling felt, too.

Quickly, they passed through to the station and in to where Maks and Chervonya were. He had to remember to think of them that way, instead of Mr. Sobol and Madam Borisov. They had both put their feet down on the topic.

Weird, but it was Uly, and Sterling could appreciate that.

They settled around a conference table.

"I have a note that suggests Uly will be here the day after tomorrow," Maks opened.

"Of course," Aibek replied dryly. "Wednesday."

That got a laugh from everybody. Even absent, they all understood Lukyan's issues with *Tuesdays*.

"What I wanted to talk about today was *Polat*," Maks said. "The ship itself is generally ready to go, having undergone a significant overhaul. Thank you, Sterling, for your suggestions, by the way."

Sterling couldn't help but blush. Maks was important people. But, he supposed, Sterling was, too. At least he had ideas about turning an old passenger transport into something with enough guns to be a threat to any pirate thinking to try to capture it.

That would be a lot of fun, once Dan had several hundred of her troopers aboard, but there would be a stretch where the ship had almost no crew and a lot of supplies aboard, setting up for the mission to Imperial Sector Seventeen.

Sterling was just sad that he wasn't going with them.

"Do you have an initial crew identified?" Sterling asked.

Maks nodded.

"I put out the word and found a few Ononguli folks that have experience with some of the regions in between," Maks replied. "When Uly gets here with *Batyr*, there will be any number of folks that were with Adrian when Uly and Dan were captured, so they might also know some of the closer portions of Seventeen. They will also know both Nine and Fifteen, because that was where *Iron Wasp* normally operated when Adrian was in command. Depending, I've also lined up a few Samuur and Isann adventurers."

"No Khet?" Sterling asked. "Rabiu Khadijan might actually be a good candidate for command, in spite of him being part of the Legal Department these days."

"You think so?" Chervonya leaned in.

Sterling nodded.

"We should ask," he replied. "I think he could handle an independent operation, if he had quality sailors doing the actual work. Plus, Fifteen is more Khet territory than anybody else, so if they have to cut diagonal, his connections might come into play."

Inside, he grinned because of all the aliens he knew. Liked. Trusted. Him.

"I'll talk to Rabiu," Maks said. "It will be a weird job."

"Not really," Sterling interrupted. "If anything, a long survey mission, since we'll want to know what those edges of Seventeen and Fifteen are like, when we decide to go back and recruit more Humans later. And we'll want to make sure that we can do it in such a way that the Auga don't decide to go conquer Human space."

"Could they?" Chervonya asked.

"The Auga could conquer anyone, if they set their Third Eye to it," Sterling replied. "I've tried to cultivate Conductor Székely, whose ship we stole. Nothing military, mind you, but me asking him about the *Auga Empire* from the standpoint of a complete stranger, letting him talk about his homeland. They have literally tens of thousands of big warships, if the Emperor decided to assemble a fleet and send it off. Granted, Maks here is already planning how to lame and cripple such a formation, but it wouldn't take that many Devastators to simply annihilate the *Danumash* fleet, before moving on to do the same to *Batyr* itself. Then you give them the choice of surrendering or having their worlds bombarded. Even Humans will smile and take the easy way out. At least initially."

"Initially?" Aibek was suddenly concerned.

"About a generation later, twenty to thirty years, I would expect a whole bunch of rebels waking up one morning and deciding to do something about the Auga," Sterling nodded. "Something well out of proportion to their numbers. It would be worse if they were Imperial recruits, like I would expect. Imagine Anari. Now multiply that by a few million angry, Human troublemakers."

Their shudders meant that they understood.

He knew enough non-Humans to appreciate how crazy his people would get. Best if it never came to that.

From there, the conversation wended around on any number of technical details. Both he and Maks had been Governor at Bastion, so they could work out a lot of things that Uly would need, probably better than anybody.

"Before we go," Maks said at the end. "Sterling, can you talk to Rabiu and see what he thinks?"

"I'd love to," Sterling nodded. "We have some time to identify a replacement if he doesn't want it, but I think he will."

After all, that crazy Khet had run away with the pirates and found himself, to hear him explain it.

What was this, but the next phase?

THIRTY

Rabiu was working on commercial statutes dealing with importing and exporting live fish at Bastion when the hatch opened and young Sterling Huff slipped into his office.

Anything for a break, so he hit save and leaned back.

"Welcome, young man," he said. "How can I ruin your afternoon?"

"Might be the other way around, Rabiu," Sterling grinned as he took the seat across the desk.

At least he didn't have that crazy serious look on his face. Rabiu had been in battle with the guy when he and Drew went places nobody else could in their minds and attitudes.

"Should I already be looking to steal a ship and run like hell?" Rabiu asked, unable to help the way his gills flared a little.

Even in jest.

"Your name came up in conversation," Sterling replied. "Maks asked me to inquire."

"About?"

"Taking a long working vacation from Bastion," Sterling nodded. "Assuming command of *Polat* for the purposes of sailing it over to where you'll meet Dan and me when we're done at Stradosha, then transporting Dan and her people on to their next target before bringing them back here."

And there went the gill slits. And the headcrest. Even the eyes bulged a little.

All this time knowing the guy, and Sterling could still surprise the shit out of him.

"You're serious?" he asked. Demanded. Something.

"Yes, sir," Sterling said. "Maks was planning a largely Ononguli crew, drawing on folks that sailed with Adrian in the old days and knew the border zones between Imperial Sectors Nine and Fifteen. I suggested that you had better political and social connections in Fifteen, if the ship needed to loop wider to escape pursuit. Plus, he hadn't thought to include many Khet, and I found that a little rude."

Rabiu recalibrated his opinions of the kid. Yet again.

He remembered the youngster. A little uncertain. Maybe a bit full of himself, but what teen wasn't? Raised by folks looking down their snouts at aliens like him or the Ononguli.

And now stepping up and demanding that Maks remember the rest of his allies. Uly's allies, but the Horde's, too.

"I don't know how to command a ship," Rabiu offered, looking for a way out.

"We'll make sure you have a sharp crew," Sterling countered. "Experts, because you will be a long ways from help, in a big ship that pirates would love to steal. I want you to take the time remapping things out there while you wait for us to catch up. I have stars and vectors, but names, species, and economies are the sorts of things Uly will need when he extends his Silk Road from Z'Gosza eventually to the *Institutional Republic of Batyr* itself. That's several links, so we need to know where to anchor things as we draw a firewall around the Auga."

Who the hell was this guy? Except that Uly had mentioned that he considered Sterling Huff to be the best Astrogation expert **he'd** ever met. And Sterling had picked up Uly's logic of lateral trade, cutting off those spokes running into Auga today, and turning them into a barrier, however much it only existed on a map.

And in Auga minds.

"That's it?" Rabiu asked.

"I can send along the full training course for Starfare, for you to audit or take," Sterling replied. "Not that I expect you to become a war fighter, but all the introductory stuff really focuses on becoming a better naval officer."

Rabiu nodded. Probably useful, since Sterling, Uly, and Haydar were the principle teachers.

"What about on the far side?" he asked.

Sterling shrugged.

"We need to get you to a place, but I haven't narrowed down the options yet until I know who is coming with us," he said. "The ship is ready. The crew, as well. I thought you should represent the Khet Corporations on this mission as a reminder that we're all in this together."

Which made sense, considering. A great many species had all signed up to help Uly. And more would come.

They stared at each other for a moment.

"You in?" Sterling asked with a grin.

"Yeah," Rabiu replied. "Though I'm not sure what trouble Ethir and Piruz will get up to without adult supervision."

"They've run out of time for that," Sterling reminded him with a laugh. "From here on in, they'll be working directly with Uly and Lyra."

Rabiu matched the grin. Those two were in for a surprise.

And yeah, if Maks was turning fully into a Trade Factor, maybe Rabiu needed to consider going the other direction and becoming a warfighter pirate?

There was probably a lot more money on the table, if they were about to find ways to trade with the Human worlds soon.

THIRTY-ONE

Eskil had gone to see the Paramount. Kallio had an enormous office with a wide picture window porthole showing the dock where *Vauquelin* had been for the longest time, filled with only emptiness today.

The Paramount watched him for a long moment as Eskil envisioned the things that would take shape there soon.

Not tomorrow, as *Vauquelin* might come back for repairs after Huff gave the ship the sort of hard shakedown cruise required, but maybe the day after that.

"A Marke for your thoughts," Kallio commented, drawing Eskil back to the present tense.

"What we build after Maks gets his new ship," Eskil replied.

"You have questions?" the Paramount asked. "Concerns?"

"Governor Maks gets an upgraded courier, as quickly as we can bring it all together," Eskil turned back to his boss. "Probably not the best version he could get, especially if he commissioned something from an Ononguli yard instead of us. I appreciate why he's doing it here. And what it will mean to us, being able to keel-up something bigger than anything we've ever imagined possible. Still torn with the entire design aesthetic we should be pursuing as a navy."

The man leaned back, whiskers and ears focused intently, so Eskil continued.

"Uly has a great many small ships at his disposal," Eskil noted. "Mostly taken away from pirates, but a few he bought or got as gifts from the Ononguli and the Khet."

"Piracy in both regions relied on such things," Kallio reminded him. Eskil nodded.

"And *Batyr* used to be one of the heaviest such vessels at that scale," he said. "We've studied it and come to understand what it can do."

"You think we should turn out more like it before building something large?" Kallio asked.

Eskil shrugged. Paused. Wrapped his ears around…

Yes. That was it.

"It frames us as a people, going forward," he admitted. "If we build big ones, we might stop building smaller. Vice versa as well."

"Is that a problem?"

"We need a lot of small ships to train crews," Eskil said. "To train up the officers and commanders that Uly will need later. But those small ships can't necessarily stand in the line of battle with big warships. That much was painfully obvious at Zhoralong, where I would have been destroyed, save that Lukyan threw himself into the path of death instead. And it was still a close-cut thing, where we might have still been lost with all hands, had the battle gone on much longer."

"You aren't normally this morose, Eskil," Kallio said.

Eskil nodded.

"We stand on a cusp, Paramount," he offered. "From knowing almost nothing two years ago, to stepping into the battle line against the largest and most dangerous empire in the known galaxy. It stopped being a game, I think. Do we lose too much of ourselves in becoming more like Uly and Dan? In growing deadly serious and forgetting that we used to be defined by our sports?"

"I think I shall blame Suka Kuri for turning you into this new person," Kallio said with a grin that went all the way to tips of his ears.

Eskil grinned back. The man was not wrong. The Exemplar had expanded his mind tremendously by stretching his horizons, then filling in some of that new space with many exotic ideas. And he knew she did it to allow him to translate those things and transmit them to the Samuur in terms they would understand.

In that way, she was probably more dangerous than Uly.

"What about the mission to the Human worlds?" Kallio asked.

"Perhaps that weighs on me as well, Paramount," Eskil admitted. "The Isann and Yarikh go. A few Samuur as well, but not as many."

"Your distant cousin Maikki Hudaibirdi is third-ranking officer aboard *Vauquelin*," the man reminded him. "Your doing, if I have to remind you."

"And a wise choice," Eskil nodded. "And your distant cousin, too. Sterling will come to appreciate her. Maikki or her sister would also both be candidates for Dan to meet and possibly recruit to the Combat Team as their Samuur representative. I have less concerns there. It is the shape of the *Illuminated Solidarity* over the next generation that concerns me."

"I intend to build us a new flagship," Kallio stated in a stark tone. "Something that can stand with *Nubia* and *Vauquelin* when it comes time to attack Auga systems."

"It is when the Auga come here that I am concerned about," Eskil replied. "One warship can be easily overwhelmed. At the same time, we fought against a cluster of tiny vessels at Zhoralong. They were annoying, but not a particularly terrible opponent, because they were too small. There must be some medium we can attain."

"If we build something entirely defensive, it does not need to be configured for long voyages," Kallio offered. "Patrol boats that stay generally local, or make short runs directly to other places. Heavily over-armed for their tonnage."

Eskil blinked and smiled.

"Yes. Just as we suggested to Maks," he said sharply. "A combat version, a diplomatic version, and a cargo version. Start with a foundational design, then have three different middle sections that can be inserted during construction. We can turn out explorers that are decently armed. Or cargo vessels to trade with more distant neighbors. Or swarms of smaller ships that can force the Auga to behave."

"You think so?" Kallio asked.

"*Vauquelin* represents a standard design for their Heavy Striker," Eskil replied. "Three triple turrets of 12dm. Six 1dm defensive mounts, plus four 2dm mounts that can be offensive or defensive as needed. Six neutron Omnipulsars. And that's their heaviest hull short of the Devastator. If we could launch a veritable barrage of 1 and 2dm bolts, across a full hemispheric front, they have to go entirely defensive, possibly using 12s to stop us. That or flee."

He paused, blinking rapidly.

"I'll need to reassemble as much of that design team as I can, understanding that both Maikki and Taija won't be available," he said quickly. "We'll take the same logic, and scale it down to a small Interceptor. Something comparable to *Virta*, *Niemi*, or *Koski*, but modern and specifically inverted to provide a porcupine defense locally, while the next generation of those ships is the exploration hull, with more supplies, fewer weapons, and better comfort for sailing."

"And the cargo ship will do away with most of that?" Kallio asked.

"I think so," Eskil agreed. "Commonality of parts to make manufacturing them easy, while letting us protect Saari orbit and start significant trade, both back towards Uly and up and over into Ononguli space via Daicia. We can adapt our existing yards that way, and leave Maks's platform to turn out those bigger ships that we'll need when we go on the offensive as part of Uly's fleets later."

"I will expect a preliminary report with estimates on my desk in three days," Paramount Kallio ordered. "You have my clearance to gather that team back up, minus the sisters, and turn them loose, if we're still building the next two big hulls currently on order."

"I don't see a reason to change that," Eskil replied, rising with excitement to get started. "It's the secondary yards that will need to prepare. That, and I think I need to send a message to Isann, asking the Chief of Chiefs to send some of his people, because both of us will be able to build these newer, smaller designs, while Maks works on getting a new yard built at Bastion. Isann will be a number of years before they can turn out Strikers locally, so we might need to work with them for their own new flagship."

"Three days, Haldur," Kallio grinned.

"Three days," Eskil agreed.

He headed towards the hatch, almost bounding with excitement. There was so much to do.

THIRTY-TWO

Maikki scowled at Eskil Haldur on the screen. She had retired to her private quarters at his request, and turned on the cryptographic protections that the Mazhin Ramezani had insisted on before having this conversation.

She was not pleased.

"Of course," she growled. "You had to wait until I was just about to sail away for six months to pull a stunt like this, Eskil."

His grin was irrepressible.

"Honestly, Maikki, it came up this afternoon, talking to the Paramount," he replied. "Or I'd have found a way to split your time to help."

"Taija will be furious at you," she reminded him.

"Noted," he nodded. "Not a lot I can do there, except have you relay a message to her to start a new design notebook and fill it with crazy ideas that we can review when you two get back."

"I'm half tempted to make you tell her," Maikki said.

"Fair," he agreed. "Let her be angry with me."

"Good, you call her directly after this," Maikki said. "And you better not be delaying another Striker. I ought to be up for promotion when we get back. Especially after a graduate level course in command from Sterling Huff. I appreciate that you said he combined youth with

165

incredible skill, but I really didn't understand the implications at the time."

"Oh?" her cousin asked.

"He might have taken that whole War Patrol, back when they first went to Bastion, if Kalev had forced his hand," she said. "I've reviewed his notes and reports as part of my training. Plus what he did at the Auga port of Nyri."

"Uly is an exceptional commander," Eskil nodded. "And he speaks of Sterling and Drew both ascending to a higher plain of consciousness when battle comes. And yes, your name is tentatively penciled in for the next warship hull."

"Tentatively?" she scowled, growling individual syllables at him.

Flagship Commander and First among Equals he might be, she'd still tear a strip of fur off his ass if he gave her a reason.

"You are about to undertake a war patrol deep into Auga space with Sterling Huff and Dan Chastain," Eskil remarked soberly. "I make it about fifty/fifty that you end up stealing another warship along the way and needing to sail it out underhanded. Uly has the most amazing fortune that way, when you count all his ships. Including the one you are currently sitting on."

Maikki paused and considered relenting. Her cousin wasn't wrong. Had, in fact, touched on one of those things that occasionally kept her up at night. Suddenly taking command of some new vessel and dragging along enough crew to somehow get it home.

It helped that *Vauquelin* had a significant Samuur crew aboard, with Khet and Ononguli filling most of the senior spots. And most of Dan's ground army.

Maikki nodded.

"Any other rude surprises?" she asked finally.

"No," he said. "And I will contact Taija as soon as we're done and draw down all her fire on me."

At least he was grinning as Maikki cut the line and left him to her sister. She liked her cousin, but this was one where her and her sister would be left out.

However, honestly, would she? While he was designing new classes of ships to build, she'd be Third-in-Command of *Vauquelin*, with her sister serving as an Engineering and Damage Control officer, something she understood had been Uly's specific job before he went rogue.

No, this felt like she'd stepped entirely past anything Samuur, and was part of Uly's new nation. That filled her with as much joy as it did trepidation.

Now, they just had to undertake the most impossible war patrol in Samuur history.

And make it home again.

THIRTY-THREE

Suka Kuri listened to Sterling's explanation and laughed with joy, possibly surprising the young man.

"Would it be better if you took Hiko with you on this mission?" she replied when he was done. "That would allow him that much more head start to begin designing things, understanding that he can't actually tear out any systems until much later."

"I didn't wish to impose, Exemplar," Sterling replied. "He is an Adept of Moss School, and teaches many students."

"He is also an adventurer, though not in the ways of the rest of you, Sterling," she nodded. "He sees the galaxy through different eyes, but I think that he would enjoy such a thing."

"As long as I'm not disturbing him, ma'am."

"Sterling, Moss School—like Sabre—is all about going out and learning new things," she told him, turning serious. "Thinking new thoughts about old ideas and improving how everyone does it. He paints and sculpts, yes, but interior design is just as much art as science. He might not have the technical inclination to handle wiring and such, but creating better *feng shui* with your command spaces is something I think he would see as a permanent, outdoor art exhibit. And he probably could be taught the wiring portions of things easily enough, if you needed it, but I suspect that the rest of your crew is better suited."

"Thank you, Elder," Sterling replied. "I'll reach out to Hiko shortly and ask. I still think of him as the Seeker he was when we met, and I don't think I had truly internalized what it meant that he was Adept now."

"Many young people have begun to grow up, Sterling," she said, mostly to delight in the way his face turned bright red for a moment.

"Thank you," and he was gone.

Suka Kuri poured herself some tea and smiled at the galaxy. At history. At everything. She found herself yet more excited at the prospect of a Moss School Adept called upon to assist with starship design. It wasn't a thing they did, but she couldn't think of any reason why not, save that such tasks were generally viewed more as Sabre in inclination.

Save that Sabre would tend toward brutal efficiency rather than art. And that pretty much described the Auga approach here. She had never liked that space, and hadn't identified why until now.

Nobody could make eye contact with anybody except their immediate neighbors on each side.

Sterling and Hiko would fix that.

Yanouk entered her dojo after a time. Paused at the look on her face, then moved nearby and knelt in silence, waiting patiently like a Seeker should.

Even one destined for her own greatness in several more decades.

At least Suka Kuri's grin was infectious.

"I feel like I'm coming into some practical joke in the middle," Yanouk finally offered.

"You are not entirely wrong," Suka Kuri nodded. "I have been giving thought to the mission."

"You are NOT allowed to assault an Auga stronghold," Yanouk replied bluntly.

Suka Kuri laughed some more.

"It may become necessary," she informed her Seeker.

"How?"

"Not counting the Ancyn who accompany us—and may be recognized in spite of the time gap—I likely have the most experience with those sectors of the Auga social structure of anyone Dan might call on," Suka Kuri told her. "While assaulting an enemy fortress might be a bit much for these old bones, I suspect that it might be necessary for me to lead."

Yanouk fell silent and watched her. Like Nasrin, she was young, though she had grown tremendously as a person and student over the last several years, shaped as much by Dan as by herself.

A young woman now. A Wife, as well as Scholar and Warrior combining Moss and Sabre with her sister Anari.

"Scout?" Yanouk asked after a long pause.

"Something to that effect, yes," Suka Kuri nodded. "An invisible, old woman who will be ignored by almost everyone because too many men think that no woman can be sexy after thirty. Or dangerous. And too many women will not wish to be reminded that they too will grow old someday. It will allow me to do things that others would be challenged over."

"Such as?"

"Walk right up to some guard somewhere, pretending to be utterly lost, both physically as well as emotionally, and demand assistance," Suka Kuri offered. "Letting me get far too close to them to stop me doing things if I find it necessary."

"You are NOT allowed to assault a fortress," Yanouk repeated sternly.

"No, but I may need to disable a guardian," Suka Kuri countered, sobering. "While I might be old and weak compared to you or your sister, people do forget that being Emro means I start from a much different position, when it comes to physical capabilities."

Yanouk fell silent. Suka Kuri watched her eyes, seeing the Adept she would grow into, one of these days. Both her and Anari might have already reached that stage, save that both had chosen to pursue Moss and Sabre equally, making them doubly dangerous. And doubly interesting.

"Would an old woman walk with a cane?" Yanouk asked quietly.

Suka Kuri was momentarily taken aback at the question. Sabre taught physical fitness at a scale where folks tended to live much longer than normal. Assuming that they didn't fall in battle.

But then she saw it. Saw the character she would portray on the surface of Stradosha. Elderly, which she was. A bit frail, which was only technically true compared to the dancer she'd been at Yanouk's age.

But a cane... Any sort of close-combat weapon. Oh, that did open all manner of interesting possibilities.

Suka Kuri felt her face light up with excitement. Yanouk nodded and rose, walking to the hatch and punching in a number on the intercom.

"Security. Wyndham."

"Solomon, it's Yanouk. Could you join Suka Kuri and me in her studio? Oh, and bring a one-point-five-meter staff or piece of tubing."

"Uhm. Sure. Give me five minutes. Do I need to change?"

"That will not be necessary, Solomon," Yanouk replied. "This is merely educational."

"Be right there."

Suka Kuri watched her student—her eventual candidate to become an Exemplar herself—nod and return, standing close.

"Oh?" Suka Kuri asked, noting the seriousness on Yanouk's composed face.

"Dan has a form," Yanouk replied. "It evolved from short-staff combat, but is equally functional with an umbrella or walking stick. I know it to a certain degree as part of Dan's curriculum, but Solomon has taken it to mastery as part of teaching boarding party actions to her troops. Dan's Icemace is lovely, but obvious, as is Uly's Shadowwhip sword. But I agree with you that a cane of some sort is probably an even more effective disguise."

Suka Kuri chuckled. After a few years, you really did learn how to read someone's mind by their face, and she had made no attempt to hide her thoughts from Yanouk.

"So you approve?" she asked impertinently.

"Absolutely not," Yanouk grinned back. "Is there any chance at all you'd listen to me?"

"None," Suka Kuri laughed. "None whatsoever."

She could hardly wait.

THIRTY-FOUR

Dan was on the bridge when *Searcher* came out of warp at Saari's outer markers. Elias and Dionysia had joined her, along with Melpomeni and few others.

Kit was busy tinkering somewhere. Anari was vibrating with excitement, but she'd been separated from Sterling for too long and ached to see the man.

Dan understood that. Her own trial was coming.

"So many ships," Elias noted with a touch of quiet wonder in his voice that was unusual.

"Bastion will have even more," Dan replied. "And a wider spectrum, as there are few Zuath or Ugotha here as of yet. Mostly, Ononguli and Khet, plus Isann and a few others."

"There's *Batyr*," Dionysia pointed. "And that's *Vauquelin*?"

"It is," Dan nodded. "Since Nomiki is serious about sending ships to protect Bastion, *Batyr* will probably stay here on guard. The Samuur build excellent ships, but simply weren't up to the technical achievements of everyone else until recently. That will change."

"It will be interesting, meeting so many new species," Dionysia replied. "We knew they were out there, but none were welcome."

She turned and Melpomeni nodded. But then, Kit had charmed all of them in his nerdy, enthusiastic way. Melpomeni had merely taken it several steps further. Or perhaps gotten her claim in first, though Dan didn't mention that.

Uly had more than one Wife, after all, even if she was First.

Quickly, they retired to the shuttle bay and rode across to the station. Behind them, *Searcher*'s crew and passengers would start assembling a small station they had carried to serve as living quarters while things got sorted out. Dan knew that the Paramount would welcome them, but the Yarikh would need to occasionally retire from being around people as they got used to new species.

Their entire culture had been one of introversion and introspection for the longest time.

Uly was there when the airlock hatch opened, surrounded by a sea of friendly faces. He grabbed her and welcomed her home with almost as much enthusiasm, despite the short separation.

The long one was coming.

She stopped kissing him long enough to note that Sterling had brought a small platform to stand on and was kissing Anari with equal energy.

Melpomeni stood to one side with a grin that made Dan blush furiously.

She moved into the mob, still holding Uly's hand.

"Paramount Kallio, this is Elias Ioannidis, Historian to the Yarikh government," she began introducing people. "And Dionysia Stavrou."

"Be welcome," Aarne grinned with whiskers and ears. "Come."

They all cycled through to a larger conference room. It had a small table to one side, but was dominated by chairs and couches. Comfortable. Cozy, in spite of the volume.

Dan spent the next twenty minutes bringing everyone up to speed, because Uly had specifically not told them much, other than that his mission had been successful and a ship would be arriving with more friends.

Always more friends. It had taken her time to understand how he did it, but he'd also worked his charm on her.

"Where does that leave us?" Eskil asked as she fell silent and took a long drink of fresh juice.

"Most of the Yarikh who accompanied us will remain here," Elias said, turning to include Maks in the conversation. "They will work with the Ononguli and Isann engineers to both improve current systems, based on work Kit has done, and lay the groundwork for incorporating new system designs into the process. Subsequently, they will travel on to Bastion and perhaps Isann after that."

"And that vessel?" Aarne Kallio asked.

"*Searcher* will remain here," Dan said. "It is not as well armed as the squadron that they have sent to Bastion, but it is a capable warship. Once it gets unloaded, it can also provide a base, or travel to other systems as needed. You will exercise command authority for the most part."

Aarne nodded. Saari had grown exceptionally busy lately, but most of it was trade traveling in and out, rather than things they were manufacturing for export. Maks had mentioned that he intended to change that, and would be able to make more progress with more hands.

Dan caught the nods and turned to Sterling. Commander Huff, just as she was technically Commander Chastain. Uly's principal combat commander meeting his Chief of Staff.

"How soon will you be ready?" she asked.

"I'm ready now," Sterling replied. "We've been working out everything at this end, but I needed to check in with you before sending out your resupply ships. Especially Rabiu and Phase II."

"You have it mapped and plotted?" she asked.

"I do," he replied. "In over the top to Stradosha via a series of cargo ships like lily pads, then out the bottom and lateral to where the *Free Trader Polat* will be hiding, waiting for you. Nine additional ships are queued up to depart later, establishing a chain of resupply to get you home on the return leg."

"And you?" Dan pressed.

"Once we're successful and have rescued the various Ancyn prisoners, you'll transfer your team to *Polat* and I will slip back home to either Bastion or Saari, depending, with Krilic as a backup if necessary," Sterling described. "We've sent the *Vatazhko* notes mentioning things in vague and somewhat coded terms that probably only Lukyan will understand, from what Maks tells me."

Dan nodded. She understood now what Uly said about simply aiming his team, then getting the hell out of the way. It was her team, too. Perhaps more so. And she would be taking all of them with her on this one, leaving Uly a little bereft until she got back.

Then it would be her turn to hand everything over to the rest of them. Uly's Ambassadors, just as Sterling, Eskil, and Aibek would be his combat commanders.

She needed to recruit some female commanders, obviously, to remind the rest of them from time to time.

She turned to Nasrin next.

"What do you need?" she asked her friend and Second-in-Command.

"A launch date," Nasrin grinned back. "We've got a campaign plan in place. All it needs is when we're sailing *Vauquelin*, in order for everyone else to be in place along the way."

Dan shook her head in wonder.

"How soon could we leave?" she asked, nervous at the answer.

"Two hours," Nasrin replied. "I'd prefer a couple of days to make sure we didn't miss anything that you or Uly would spot immediately, but everyone at this end has poured over it with everything they had."

"Two days sounds like a minimum," Dan said, turning to Uly. "We have folks to introduce here and get settled."

"That's my job," he said simply. "You go rescue Galli's people."

Hell of an inversion from how things normally worked, but she supposed that it was the obvious outcome of training people to be independent and operate on vague orders. Even her and Uly.

"Three days, then," she decided.

Then she would be taking her war directly to the heart of the *Auga Empire*.

PART SIX
RAIDERS

THIRTY-FIVE

Sterling had brought up all three screens around his station, watching internal systems as well as one showing warp space outside. Technically, Aibek could handle most of this, with Sterling off doing paperwork and meeting people, but Uly had made it a point that a commanding officer stood watches on his own bridge.

You needed to know the people around you. Especially when many of them were relative strangers. Sure, the Ononguli folks knew their business. The Samuur and Isann as well. Still, folks who hadn't been with him all that long.

Ms. Hudaibirdi entered and caught his eye. She stepped close as if she wanted to discuss something, but didn't look like she wanted it public. At least that was the way he read her whiskers.

Knowing Mazhin folks for so long had sure helped.

"My day office?" he asked, watching her body language.

"If that would be possible, Commander," she replied.

Sterling turned to his Khet Pilot.

"Mr. Kaita, you have the bridge," Sterling called. "I'll be nearby if something happens."

The man nodded, but his shoulders seemed brittle. Sterling understood. All of them were new, and Sterling accepted that he had a reputation these days. Generally good, but they all knew that he wouldn't hesitate to plunge them into battle.

As long as he could see a way to win. There would be circumstances coming up where running like hell might be the wisest course of action. He'd reminded Aibek a few times to remind him if and when they got there.

Aibek understood what it meant to be looking at overwhelming force coming down on you like a hammer.

He and Uly had been a bit brutal that day.

Sterling rose and gestured for her to precede him. Out the bridge hatch, down the hall a short distance, to a hatch with alcoves on either side. He'd learned from Conductor Székely that armed guards were usually stationed there in Auga service to protect the commander.

Sterling thought that said more than most people really understood about the Imperial mindset. And not in a good way.

He moved behind the desk and gestured her to sit, watching the tall woman. Samuur had a similar sexual dimorphism to Humans, just in the other direction, with the men usually around his size and the women bigger. She had perhaps half a head on him. And similar shoulders. Solomon-sized.

At the same time, she had exchanged the orange uniform of the *Illuminated Solidarity* for the medium blue of Bastion, trimmed in scarlet and red. It looked good on her. Professional. Sharp.

"What can I help you with, Lieutenant?" he asked.

Other than Aibek as a Lieutenant Commander, all of his officers were lieutenants these days. Eventually, he and Uly would change that, once they knew who was staying put and who might be returning to their national fleets. And once they built out a full naval rank structure that incorporated everything they had learned.

Hudaibirdi looked like she was staying.

"I encountered questions from the Emro Moss School Adept Seiichai, sir," she said, pausing.

Sterling nodded.

"I asked Hiko to redesign the bridge," he said. "And a few other spaces. Suka Kuri mentioned that they were perfectly efficient. Brutally so, she called it."

"You disagree, sir?" she asked, more curious than anything from her tone, but they were still getting to know one another.

"Oh, I agree with his assessment," Sterling said. "I find it unnecessary. Other ships I have been on tended to line people up, all facing forward like *Nubia*, or face everyone inward, so they could see their commanding officer's body language when things got loud or focused."

She sat back, watching him.

"That would improve efficiency?" she asked finally, confused.

"Social efficiency," he corrected her. "Team building, when everyone needs to be able to react to everyone else, without having to maintain a whole series of small images along the edges of your screen to see what anyone is doing."

"And Seiichai?"

"Moss School is art, Lieutenant," Sterling noted. "I'd like the bridge to be a friendlier space, considering the amount of time I expect to spend there. I'll have him redo this room, once he has a design aesthetic in mind."

That surprised her as well. From what he'd seen of Samuur ships, they tended towards the brutalist school, at least internally. Necessary, given their low starting point. It would still improve things to have them much more artistic and warm.

"Crew morale, Hudaibirdi," he continued, nodding.

"He asked me to consult, sir," she said quietly. Confused.

"I sent him," Sterling confirmed. "Eskil told me that you and your sister were on the team that is designing new vessels for the Paramount. I would love to bring that expertise to bear here, as well. Hiko will be excellent at the frosting on the cake, if you will, but not necessarily at baking the cake underneath. Nor will he care much, other than understanding that all the stations need a certain standardization of form and function so everyone can be trained once."

"So he won't handle wiring and communications?" she asked.

"I doubt that he even understands how any of that works," Sterling replied. "This will be an art installation when he is done. And it will be gorgeous. I want you and Taija to make sure it's functional, with durability and redundancy built in from the start. This is still a warship. I'd like to be able to hand the yard updated plans as soon as we get back and ask a team of mechanics to rip everything out and make it better."

"But not until we return to Saari, sir?" she asked, maybe surprised. Maybe hopeful.

"That's right," he replied. "If we go into battle between now and then, I want this ship as brutally efficient and durable as possible. We'll retrain folks later as needed."

"Unexpected, sir," she finally managed after three false starts.

"I'm not always about warfare, Hudaibirdi," he grinned. "Sure, when Kalev, Ursula, and Matti showed up that first time, it was extremely tense. And I've been called upon a few other times. Depending, I'll either remain in command of *Vauquelin* for a significant period of time, or perhaps be promoted to *Nubia*. In both cases, I want a bridge that's nice to look at, as well as functional. That's why I have also asked Nasrin Monfared and a few other Mazhin to be involved in Hiko's work."

"Sir?"

"What do you know of Mazhin tentacles, Hudaibirdi?" he asked.

"Less than I thought apparently, sir."

He nodded. Most people underestimated them. He'd known better from early on, watching them have conversations by semaphore and scent.

"Their tentacles also have something like taste buds," he explained. "They can taste the air. And any surface they lean into. Omid was extremely strict about how any ship she was on did laundry, which is why ours smells so nice. She trained those people to her standards, which mirror Dan's or Uly's in many ways."

"I see," she said, probably not seeing it, but at least aimed in the right direction.

She was a great officer and sailor. At the same time, a little lost about the wider galaxy she and her people had stepped into, so he supposed that his job today needed to lean more into the educational. It would make her a better officer later to know these things today.

"The paint we eventually use will have to leave a pleasant aftertaste to them," Sterling continued. "I doubt that anybody else could tell, though Samuur noses might be sensitive enough. If we have time, I'll have the whole ship redone, though we might just sell it on later, once Saari is turning out new designs that I presume will be better."

"Better, sir?" she asked.

"*Vauquelin* is brutally efficient there, too," Sterling reminded her. "But the design is conservative and a bit outdated. The Auga move slowly. Design a ship. Build a few thousand copies of it. Update the design to incorporate new ideas after a generation. Build more. Slow and certain. Because Uly brought together experts and handed them a blank piece of paper, they can strive for something better."

"Eskil's team?" she asked, eyes blinking with surprise.

"Uly's idea, working with Maks, from what they told me," he said. "Inventing the future not just of the Samuur, but all of Bastion, too."

"But Uly trusts us to do it right, sir?"

"You're here," Sterling agreed. "I had a long list of candidates to pick from to fill my senior officer slots. All of them were good. You brought a whole list of secondary skills to the table that I felt I needed. Your sister is the same way."

"That's a lot to think about, sir," she said, seeing some of the scope he'd tried to lay out for her.

"You're doing exceptional work, Maikki," he nodded. "Keep it up. That's all I can say at this point."

She nodded back and rose, leaving him to smile.

He didn't mention Eskil's hints that both sisters were available to Dan, if they met her standards for inclusion in the Combat Team after a long try-out period. Dan would make those decisions.

Putting the Hudaibirdi sisters where Dan could see them operate meant that they could soar or crash as they would.

Halyna Bondarenko might have started as a political thing, but she'd worked out well enough. All the Congress had impressed Dan with their ability to think. To act.

And to dance. Or at least learn how, once Dan made her decision to include them.

THIRTY-SIX

Dan exulted in having her entire team—the *Congress Itself Assembled*—present. To train. To talk. Simply to be. It had been a while, given various missions, such as sending Anari to Traiffe.

Even Suka Kuri was here, though Dan understood Yanouk's concerns that the Exemplar was likely to cause a great deal of mischief. People still forgot that even an elderly Emro outweighed any other species. And Suka Kuri's training meant that she was as least as strong as many others half her size.

They had been diving deeper into the cane form for fighting. Solomon had taught a few classes, mostly to polish everyone since they had the basic form. Until recently, it had been one of many they knew. No better nor worse as a tool.

Extremely useful for an old woman pretending a limp.

Among the younger ones, Yeong-Suk as a Guezal could walk Imperial streets without notice. Three Emro women might excite comment, but if one was the grandmother of the other two, less so. Nasrin might be a bit exotic, but the Mazhin were known to trade inside the Empire just as much as outside. Perhaps not as much in the inner ring of Sectors, but Human, Khet, Isann, and a pair of Ononguli would instantly raise alarms.

That was the last thing they needed.

Galli and Solomon had joined them, mostly to watch Dan and her Combat Team train. To better understand what they could accomplish, rather than merely hearing stories about it.

Completed, they had gathered around a small projector Solomon had brought. At this scale, it allowed one a god's-eye view of the prison Galli had escaped from. Scaled up, one could walk those hallways, though there was a risk of assuming the map was the territory in training.

It was only a good approximation, and left large areas of the facility blank, simply because none of the Ancyn women had ever visited more than one third of the volume.

"A goodly chunk of this region was dedicated to male prisoners," Galli explained, pointing a laser at one side. "We think that they took up about half of the space, while the women took up roughly one third, leaving the other sixth for administrative offices. Kitchens, laundry, and maintenance were contained within each gender-split zone. Even the exercise quad was split with a cyclone fence."

"Is that fence electrified?" Ciah asked.

"It can be, but normally wasn't when we were there," Galli replied. "That allowed us to see our mates and talk to them. It also let us plot our escape. As Solomon notes, I have no idea what changes they might have added, but leaving the fence active most of the time is likely."

Dan agreed. At least assuming the warden figured out how the breakout had occurred. As they had at Vynchen and Zhoralong, sometimes folks did crazy things that the Auga and their pets weren't prepared to understand. And might not be able to adjust their defenses appropriately without significant time and recriminations cast about.

It had probably been long enough in this case.

"I assume the towers on the corners are equipped to prevent someone from landing in the quad?" Anari asked.

"I've built that into the scenario," Solomon nodded. "Presumably something capable of shooting down an air taxi or stolen delivery truck. Additionally, the guards are known to have weapons to punish or kill prisoners who get out of hand below in the quad."

"We won't liberate them there," Dan said. "If anything, trying it means we have to fight our way through too much of the facility to get out again. Not that we couldn't, but time will be our greatest enemy. Once an alarm goes off, we have to presume more and more police and military forces will be dispatched to stop us from escaping."

"Helps that those idiots built it right in the middle of a city," Halyna offered. "What could they have been thinking?"

"From what I heard while I was there, it was originally somewhat remote," Galli replied. "The city grew up around it later, providing personnel and support services. Nobody really considered that anyone would be crazy enough to attack a place like this, so they didn't enforce any sort of setback on the walls."

"Can we bore our way in?" Yeong-Suk asked. "Literally. Physically. Explosives would make too much noise, but maybe some sort of auger that we could set up and drill?"

"Anything is possible, but those walls are thick and I expect that it would take considerable time to do it quietly," Galli replied.

"We won't have that luxury," Dan stated. "We'll be arriving aboard a stolen and renamed Auga Heavy Striker on official business. I plan to walk right up to the front door with orders to transfer some subset of male prisoners to a different facility. Possibly to Ajorn itself. The troops we'll be hauling are to look good, but they are also available if we have to shoot our way out."

"As with other assumptions about Auga behavior, I presumed that orbital defenses would generally be smaller vessels," Solomon nodded. "Search and Rescue. Anti-smuggling gendarme patrols. That sort of thing, mostly limited to hulls in the Seeker or even Sloop rating if we get lucky and there are not major naval units handy, though I can't predict that with any accuracy. Not a significant threat to *Vauquelin*, except perhaps in massed numbers that would surprise me to see."

"Correct," Dan said. "The problem will be later, when they figure out that they've been had, and send fleets after us."

"And all of this will be handled on the fly?" Galli asked, still a little shaken at the concept.

Dan smiled.

"We don't have any choice," Dan replied. "Not if we want to do this."

"And you will," Galli nodded. "What part can I play?"

"You've already done most of it," Suka Kuri spoke up. "Prepared the battleground, so to speak. The rest of us will step up at this point and handle it."

Dan had her doubts, but she also understood that the Exemplar expected to lead on this mission.

Certainly, the Auga would never see it coming.

THIRTY-SEVEN

Maikki had come on duty half an hour ago, Commander Huff having specifically reset the watch schedule so that his current bridge crew were all the senior people. Him. Lieutenant Commander Sulaymanov who was Isann. Her. Gunner Andrii Dovzhenko the Ononguli. Pilot Jatau Kaita who was Khet.

A mixed bag by species, but she had begun to appreciate that Huff hadn't just picked one of each species as a representative. The others were as good as she strove to be on a daily basis.

"Mr. Kaita, what is the countdown?" Huff asked in a normal voice.

Not bored. Not angry. No particular emotions at all. Professional.

"Two minutes to first rendezvous, sir," Jatau replied.

"Mr. Dovzhenko, bring the ship to alert," Huff continued. "Ms. Hudaibirdi, I'll want a hard, short-ranged ping when we drop, followed by an ongoing passive review in case someone is parked out at some distance preparing to drop on us suddenly. No reason to expect it, but now is a good time to train how we'll fight."

She nodded and focused on her boards. The Mazhin, Haydar Ramezani, had laid out his expectations for how things like this should be handled, as well as how he had seen Huff do things in the past, when he'd been Uly's Gunnery Officer.

They came out of warp a little distant from the coordinates, just in case someone had prepared an ambush. Maikki hit the button to trigger everything short range, while leaving on the passives set to a level where there would be any number of false positives over the next several minutes.

As Ramezani had said, better to spook at shadows than to miss a shark.

One signal noted. The cargo vessel that Maks Sobol had dispatched ahead of them, packed to the rafters with food and equipment resupply that let *Vauquelin* travel with a larger crew than normal on a grand voyage.

"Conductor, I confirm *Flame of Neeri*," she said over her shoulder, already better appreciating how this bridge might be more socially efficient if she could see the man working. "Nothing else close on scanners."

"Excellent work, Hudaibirdi," Huff replied. "Mr. Kaita, take us in. Mr. Dovzhenko, lock one forward turret on *Flame of Neeri* and keep the other ready to react. Rear turret set neutral aft in case someone comes up behind us."

Maikki nodded and watched her boards. By the same book Huff himself had written, with the help of Fortier and Ramezani. Precise and careful, always with the note about jumping immediately to any of several chapters on starship combat if trouble approached.

The Samuur didn't work that way. Then she corrected herself to the past tense.

Hadn't worked that way.

That was probably going to change in the future. They had gone from a small stellar nation largely surrounded by darkness to the middle of a large playing field with several other teams competing around them. Half friendly. Plus the Auga, who would have simply rolled over everything the Samuur had, if they had arrived first.

Maikki understood how primitive their old ships were, and looked forward to what Eskil and the others came up with while she was gone.

"*Flame of Neeri* hailing," she said as those folks woke up.

Not perfectly sharp, but not a bad delay, given the range of arrival times calculated before *Vauquelin* had departed.

She brought up the image of the Ononguli man currently acting as conductor. He and his people would unload the ship, then join them on *Vauquelin* for the next stage.

"I'm already cutting local gravity to ten percent," he said as soon as he recognized her. "That will save us about an hour in crossloading after you dock."

"Stand by," Maikki replied. "Jatau, did you catch that?"

"Affirmative," Jatau said. "Maneuvering now. Have them rotate about forty degrees to port and bring their stern up ten degrees."

She relayed that, then sat back and kept watch. Chastain and her people would board first and secure everything, then a mob of troopers and small powered trucks would start moving boxes, before *Flame of Neeri* ended up abandoned.

Maikki understood that the chain of transports had been selected from the hulls in the worst shape. The least valuable.

Still, she wondered if someone intended to come back later with more crew and recover them. At least those outside of Auga territory. Perhaps inside, given that the Ononguli tended to engage in piracy as a hobby as much as a vocation, strange as that was.

Samuur probably looked just as exotic to them.

What other things was she going to learn on this voyage?

THIRTY-EIGHT

Aibek had joined Dan and her team aft, understanding that he was just support, there to stand around and watch without doing anything else until she told him so. And she was bigger and stronger, so she could just pick him up and carry him somewhere if he pissed her off enough.

That put a grin on his face as the hatch opened, then she and Nasrin went through, along with twenty killers known as Scout One and Team One.

Aibek had another mob of killers surrounding him, then a second mob of strong backs behind that with carts and trucks. He watched the first group vanish and felt someone come up beside him.

Taija Hudaibirdi, younger sister of Maikki. Almost as big. Basically a full head taller than him. Sharp on the technical stuff. Maybe a little sheltered on the rest. Or just extremely introverted, compared to the Isann he knew. And Eskil, who was kind of an extrovert.

"Everything ready aft?" he asked, mostly to break up the oppressive silence.

"So far, sir," she nodded. "I have my people ready to flood the zone on the all-secure call and swarm the goalie."

Took him a moment. Isann weren't nearly the sports nuts that Samuur were, so their idioms were confusing. And Taija was far worse than Eskil. Maybe worse than her jock sister, though that would be measured in millimeters.

Nasrin emerged quickly and waved him into motion.

"Go get your people," he turned to Taija, then started forward.

As First Officer, he wasn't likely to get his hands dirty today. Not too much, anyway. Maybe.

Mostly stand around and answer questions, because he had the most starship experience of the officers present, since Suka Kuri had stayed forward.

Flame of Neeri was a pretty standard design. Everything flat on a single level, with control spaces and living quarters forward then engines and generators aft. Three-quarters of the ship in the middle as a series of cargo bays that could be isolated as needed.

Boxes. Lots and lots of boxes. Most of it was food, assuming that mechanical parts would hold this long and *Vauquelin* had enough on hand already.

Vauquelin was still nearly filled with bodies. Space for another fifty to be crammed in, a bit uncomfortable until Dan and the secondary team rendezvoused with Rabiu and offloaded, at which point *Vauquelin* would pivot away and start playing a game with the Auga to get home.

Aibek didn't think those fools were up to it, but he also understood Taija's concept of flooding the zone with bodies. Or ships in that case.

Only took one to get lucky and call down everyone else if they got away from Sterling.

If they could get away from Sterling.

He smiled again and found a spot near the main airlock hatch to plant his butt. Out of the way but handy. Aibek didn't even have to handle a clipboard today. Merely look good and remember not to move suddenly when gravity was only ten percent of normal and he could jump over these piles if he wasn't paying attention.

Taija led her team through quickly, pausing exactly long enough to scan the room, then point at the stack she wanted removed first. Since she'd packed it in the first place, she had the choreography.

Aibek watched her move and nodded.

Sharp. Crisp. Expert. All the things he wanted in a damage control officer.

The new body next to him turned out to be Ciah Dambe.

The *Troublesome Warrior Child* as she had renamed herself. She wasn't especially troublesome anymore, but it made a great story to fool people.

"Everything good?" he asked.

"Sure," she nodded, looking up.

One of the few folks around shorter than him, as Ononguli, Humans, and especially Samuur tended to all be bigger.

"We just unload and go?" Ciah asked.

"Unless someone bothers us, yes," Aibek replied. "Sterling's on the bridge for that reason. I'm here in case we need to back away suddenly and decide if crews are left or evacuated. It would have to be serious trouble for that, though."

"Someone selling information to the Auga," Ciah said. "Like we figure happened at Zhoralong the second time."

He paused to consider that, aware of the general consensus on the topic.

"And we never have figured out who might have done it?" he asked.

"Someone Ononguli," she said, turning cold, even for Khet standards. "And screwed up in underestimating Uly and Maks, so the Auga didn't have overwhelming firepower on hand."

"They had three Striker-class hulls," Aibek pointed out.

"And we stole this one when we were done beating the shit out of it," she chuckled. "And put Sterling in command. They better bring six next time. And if I ever find out who it was..."

Aibek nodded and swallowed. He was originally a civilian conductor. A raider, he supposed. Not military in the way Sterling and Uly did it. And he'd gone through Starfare, but again, vocation and not art form or life goal.

Still, someone attacking Sterling probably did need three times the mass, just to make it even. Even the Samuur reviewing his previous battles had privately rated that first meeting at Bastion as a probable draw, their three to his one, had Sterling come out and they'd tried to jump him.

"Are we hunting whoever it was?" Aibek asked, intrigued.

He had only recently moved into an Inner Ring type of position of authority, having previously been merely one of Uly's many advisors, most of whom were smarter than him.

He'd brought luck to the table. It had kept him alive this long.

"Not actively, from what I understand," Ciah shook her head. "But I know Lukyan was pissed enough to grind somebody's horns off over it."

Aibek had seen that. Hadn't put two and two together, thinking how protective the man had been for Eskil and Ursula.

But yeah, if you pissed Lukyan off, you'd best defect to the Auga and hope the Empire could protect you.

Boxes were moving now. Out the port-side three-quarters of the hatch, with the starboard side for bodies returning.

Fast. But then, Taija had set it all up in the first place and then trained her teams to do it a certain way.

It was always acceptable to be early to a meeting. Late had other connotations.

And this mission involved nearly thirty ships, strung out like pearls on a rope.

Lots of chances to screw things up, but Aibek understood how good these players were.

And how lucky.

THIRTY-NINE

Sterling nodded contentedly.

"Mr. Kaita, detach us and back away slowly," he ordered. Dan had joined him on the bridge, looking exhilarated, but that was emptying the holds of *Flame of Neeri* without any significant fuss.

Now they knew how it would go the next time. After number four, they would be crossing into Auga-claimed territory. At least on a map. A two-dimensional map that didn't take into account how thick the galactic disk really was, when viewed edge on.

A thought twisted his mind around, so Sterling turned to Aibek.

"Mr. Sulaymanov, you take charge of this operation," Sterling ordered, noting that heads around them nodded like this was yet another pop quiz.

At least they'd all grown a little jaded at the unexpected instead of seizing up.

Aibek popped out of his station and strode to the center of the bridge. Dan turned a questioning eye, so Sterling waved her to join him and headed aft to his office.

Except that he put her behind the desk and took the outer chair.

"What's up?" she asked as they settled.

"Been thinking about what we're doing," he replied, still looking for the right word or concept. "How we're sliding in over the top and down to hit Stradosha from a blind side, then going out the bottom and away."

"Okay?"

"What's to stop them from doing the same thing to us at Bastion?" Sterling asked. "Or Rayzian or any other place where ships located on a flat patrol boundary might be skipped over?"

She paused, possibly also seeking words.

"There's generally not a lot out there in open space worth taking," she offered.

"Understand that, Dan," he nodded. "I'd presume some sort of hard strike to blow things up, rather than an invasion force, if only because of all the added logistics troubles inherent in maintaining that baggage train. Us, if we intended to drop out on top of whatever base Stradosha had in orbit so we could pound it into scrap metal, before going after orbital factories and warehouses."

"Armaments, for one," she replied. "More importantly, we're aliens here, Sterling. The Auga have their bureaucratic checklists for things, and I think that what we did at Ixtin will further convince them to stay on list rather than suddenly striking out sideways off schedule."

"The Ononguli are pirates..." he began, then stopped himself. "And they drydock the big ships in peacetime and prey specifically on shipping, because they want to steal things, rather than blow them up. Does anybody ever intentionally destroy things? Salt-the-earth kinds of aftermaths?"

It was her turn to fall silent, eyes flickering back and forth.

"Even *Batyr* really didn't do that," she said. "Or *Danumash*, at least from what I saw. We'd damage a ship or force them to surrender, so we could materially impact their operational capacity, but I can't remember any mission where we intentionally set out to target civilian industrial facilities. The costs were always too high."

"Agreed, but we have 15s on *Nubia*," Sterling countered. "That means standing outside of defensive range and salvoing, especially if we had a team of sharp escorts close to us where a station's big wavebolts were less dangerous at the end of a long run."

"Where are you taking this?" she asked.

Sterling started to shrug. Stopped it. Listened to that voice whispering in the back of his head.

"Maks," he said simply.

"Maks?"

"His plan to send a swarm of small pirates after the cargo ships that Auga might send to resupply a forward fleet, if they ever got around to assembling something so big that nothing could resist it," Sterling said. "I was reading studies on the Auga conquest of Semeonis, during the last war, when they showed up with a small armada of Devastators, a mob of Strikers, and a horde of smaller things, driving the Ononguli completely out of the system before dropping troops on key cities and threatening mayhem if the locals didn't surrender. By then, the Ononguli had already suffered hugely, so they accepted another one-sided peace treaty, surrendered the planet, and evacuated their population elsewhere."

"Not one I'm familiar with," she replied, but he got that.

Nobody else really put their nose to the grindstone on tactics and strategy and history like he did, either. Him and Solomon, opposite sides of the same coin, maybe.

"Because nobody fights a real war," he muttered, voice suddenly filled with wonder as it suddenly became clear.

"Repeat that?"

"They are always fighting like thalassocracies, Dan" Sterling said. "Maritime trade empires generally focused on cargo moving around, instead of planet-based nations focused on farming and ranching in the old days, or industrial facilities more recently. Auga is generally defined by trade, like everybody else is, where only a few major industrial worlds produce the vast majority of heavy stuff, while light manufacturing happens almost everywhere for regional consumption. Specialist economies. Crap, I need the Legal Department, but left them all home. This exactly the kind of question they'd have an answer to."

"Talk to me," she ordered. "We have smart people here on the ship."

Of course. The Congress. The Wives. All tremendously smart and dangerous. Just look at Anari.

"What if we started going after their big cargo ships?" he asked. "The ones like *Wren* or *Workshop*, that can haul amazing amounts of material around, which is exactly what they need to invade anyone. Doubly so if they want to build a station like at Ixtin."

"Ignoring smaller ships?" she pressed.

"The Auga would need to redirect a significant proportion of all their shipping to make up for that loss if we were successful," he said. "Which further materially damages their economic capacity, if I have my vernacular right."

"You do," she nodded.

"They can't have both," Sterling said. "Either they can haul goods between worlds, or they can invade, if we ignore warships and go after megafreighters routinely. And not to capture. Blow them up, or at least damage them so badly that they end up being scrapped, or worse, they take up an entire drydock bay for a year. That's a year not building anything new, like more warships."

"How long until they figured out what we were up to?" she pressed.

Sterling paused to consider it.

"I need your experts," he decided. "Anari, Suka Kuri, Yeong-Suk. Folks who have lived inside the Empire as adults. I mean, I can guess, but as you said, we're aliens. Way more aggressive that way, because we're willing to embrace total war rather than slap fights in a sandbox."

"Any of this impact our current mission?" she asked. "Or my subsequent one?"

"Negative, sir," he replied automatically. "This is a long-term thing I'll go deeper into when I get back home. Grand strategic operations, because it starts to impact the kinds of warships Uly might want to build, if he decides to go down that path. I'll need to refine a significant number of details first. It might be enough to hurt the Auga in a way that they understand, though. Force them back, which is what Uly needs."

"What everyone needs," Dan replied. "That all you required from me?"

"Think so, sir," he said. "Lots to think about before I even write something up and ask the Combat Team for how to make it better."

She nodded and left him alone.

Sterling could see the shape of it in his head. And how the Auga might respond by building something large enough to make an epic voyage to Bastion to attack it, one of these days.

It also gave him a couple of ideas on how to handle both the offense and defense in that situation.

Because those Auga were going to be pissed at him when he got back from Stradosha.

FORTY

Yeong-Suk still occasionally paused to marvel at how utterly beyond bizarre her life had gotten, since waking up to Dan and Nasrin preparing to steal the ship at Nyri. All of the men who had been prisoners with her—all older, too—had gone on to other jobs and careers with Uly, mostly at Bastion.

Only she had moved into a position of authority.

Hell of an outcome for a pickpocket and con artist. And where the hell would she go next?

Today, she was in the wardroom with Loh-An Huang, talking about the prison itself. Back on Stradosha. And ahead.

"And that's really about all I can recall," Loh-An concluded. "Solomon thinks that the men's side is likely built like the women's side, with the extra space being dedicated to more cells for the men, instead of the warden's office and such."

Yeong-Suk nodded. They'd all gone over it any number of times, to the point that most of her sisters knew how many paces it was from any given pair of doors, based on the Ancyn having to walk those hallways so many times.

"I'm more interested in the social geography," Yeong-Suk replied. "The warden and his people."

"You don't think they replaced him after so many of us escaped?" Loh-An asked.

"Oh, that was probably the first thing they did," Yeong-Suk smiled, feeling her fur crease. "But honestly, the person they brought in to replace him probably wasn't all that different. At least psychologically."

"You think so?"

"Willing to bet my life on it," Yeong-Suk nodded, still grinning. "I expect another Auga in charge, simply because this was a political prison, rather than the sorts of places I knew when I was Imperial."

"That matters?" Loh-An asked.

"Pickpocket," Yeong-Suk said. "Petty thief. Anarchist only in the sense that I grew up in extreme poverty and there weren't jobs for us. You hustled or you starved, and the Auga really didn't give two shits about us, except as they had to sweep the *favelas* occasionally and throw us in jails. The troublemakers like me got shipped to another Imperial Sector entirely to serve our sentence, then dropped on the nearest planet instead of getting sent home. Great way to break up families. Lousy way to prevent recidivism."

"I don't think I understood that before," Loh-An nodded. "We were all political prisoners. But I talked to Ethir Ewin, and he had a similar story, come to think of it."

"Lots of us like that," Yeong-Suk said. "Born in the Empire, but not really part of it emotionally. That's why I wanted to get your impressions of the old warden. Already drained Galli of everything she knew. She suggested you next."

"I was probably the second worst problem child of the group," Loh-An laughed. "At least among the women. Some of the men were worse, but they tended to be locked in isolation chambers pretty quickly, while the women got dinged on benefits, like money that families would provide to buy little things would be penalized. Or extra hours working in various support shops."

"Women less of a physical threat to the guards, and all that?" Yeong-Suk asked.

"Yes, maybe," Loh-An nodded. "A quieter revolution, at least until Galli suddenly led us to freedom. Except that the men were supposed to join us and never did. Still, nobody talked, because we got away. Mostly away."

Yeong-Suk nodded. Sometimes, you had to make hard choices—accept bad conditions—if you wanted to survive. She'd never been in anything nearly as bad as Galli and Loh-An, but she could see it shaping them as people.

"So the warden," she said. "Likely a bureaucrat's bureaucrat?"

"If the new one is like the old one, yes," Loh-An said. "Patterns and processes that don't adapt well to changing circumstances because nothing is ever supposed to change in a prison except the people running the place and the folks trapped inside."

"Excellent," Yeong-Suk replied. "Let's talk about how the average manager went about his day, based on times you had to deal with him or his immediate lackeys. When was that?"

"We had to wait, in order to get yelled at personally," Loh-An smiled. "Berated for unsocial behavior that was jeopardizing our opportunities to reintegrate properly into society when our sentence was done. Our old warden often had a religious overtone to such diatribes, but I'd heard from older prisoners that they were all like that. Plus, he saw prisoners every day immediately after lunch, regardless of when they dinged you. Maybe you sat in the hole all night. Maybe you were cuffed to a chair in his outer office and didn't get to eat. He was always on a timeline."

"Yes," Yeong-Suk grinned. "Let's talk about those sorts of timelines. I want to add them to my list for Dan."

She sat back and listened to the woman ramble. Little of it was new, but it formed an image in her head.

Bureaucrats could be turned into their own worst enemies, if you knew how to attack their foundations.

FORTY-ONE

Suka Kuri had taken to hosting meetings made up exclusively of the Combat Team in her gymnasium. Partly, she had the space for three Emro to be comfortable. Partly, because people tended to give her a wide berth they thought was respectful.

Usually, that meant she had to go right up and step on their toes to get their attention.

Yeong-Suk finished her briefing last, having spent time with Galli and Loh-An on the social engineering aspect of things. Of this group, Yeong-Suk was the best qualified to talk about the Auga as a people and a political entity.

Suka Kuri had spent the most time inside the empire, but mostly wandering from Emro community to Emro community as a Moss Adept, teaching and creating. Granted, the Auga had hardly changed in her lifetime, but Yeong-Suk had a radically different mindset.

"From there, I think we can walk right in and take hostages," Yeong-Suk concluded. "If it all works, we might be able to simply own the place until we're ready to leave, with all our imperial prisoners left tied up for someone else to find after we go."

Suka Kuri turned to Dan. They all did. Dan was in charge. Entirely, with Uly left behind.

"Audacious," Dan offered tentatively, but that was more a note of how wide their margin for error would be when they arrived, than concern that they couldn't pull it off.

Suka Kuri smiled.

"You had a thought?" Dan asked.

"My mother used to call it her flustered housewife routine," Suka Kuri described. "Pretend like you have completely missed the joke and force someone to explain it in excruciating detail. Pretend like you've gotten some key detail wrong in the situation and harrumph extravagantly until someone comes along to fix it. She got far too much mileage out of it. However, I suspect that she was having too much fun, though she'd never have admitted that out loud."

"Obviously, you were adopted," Katya Zehlennko offered in such a dry, underhanded tone that Suka Kuri nearly fell out of her chair, howling with laughter that the others shared.

It took her nearly a minute to regain her composure. Katya's knowing grin set her off twice more.

She sighed and contained the last bit of giggles, but they kept trying to escape.

"As it may be," she continued finally, "I believe that such audacity as Yeong-Suk lays out utterly works in our favor here, because it is so far outside the normal behavioral zone of the Auga and their minions that it might get utterly garbled in the communication, further confusing any attempt to explain what happened afterwards."

Dan nodded.

"Back home, we used to call it The Chain," Dan said. "One person whispers a secret to a second, who tells a third, slowly working its way around the circle until it comes back and you compare the original to the final. Yes, this will confuse them. Better, if we can keep casualties to a minimum, we have the opportunity to make them look like a clown show instead of a government. Bullies can tolerate being insulted. Being laughed at undermines everything that upholds them."

"It is certainly a twist on our original plan," Anari offered. "Will it work?"

"More so, I think," Suka Kuri nodded. "Organizing ourselves this way actually compounds the overall confusion, when someone attempts to go back later and sort out what happened. Dan, I'll still be thankful if I don't call on you, but you will be there to rescue an old woman, yes?"

"Yes," Dan grinned. "And I'll have overwhelming force handy if we resort to the hammer. As with this, I'd like to watch you pull it off, if only because then you can all go home and school Ethir on pulling a bigger con game than he and his cousins have ever managed."

"Dan, I'm not sure how many people have ever managed something like this." Suka Kuri turned serious. "If anything, the previous events that might come close are all things that many of us were directly involved in."

"At what point will the Auga finally catch on?" Yanouk asked.

Suka Kuri turned to say something, but Halyna leaned in and touched her arm.

"Never, if we can confuse them enough," the Ononguli woman noted. "Haydar's little surprise ought to confuse things in orbit for far longer than necessary, such that it requires years of review of logs and outside analysis to even fathom the outcome."

"Can we?" Yanouk asked. "Confuse them that badly?"

"That is the central tenet of our enterprise," Halyna stated. "Audacity. Deception. Confusion."

Suka Kuri nodded. That really did cover it.

"What will be interesting," she said, drawing everyone back to her, "is if we can manage it so thoroughly that we can do it again at a later date. Much later, after they have had the chance to learn all the wrong lessons from this operation."

Dan's smile was promising, as were the looks from the other women.

On the one hand, it was a pity that Uly had needed to keep many of his male advisors home, as he moved into the next phase of his Warlord-hood. On the other, the Auga and several others tended to lean a bit far into their male chauvinism, to the point that she found herself looking forward to the trouble that she and a group of women might cause them.

It was going to be wicked fun.

PART SEVEN
WARLORD

FORTY-TWO

Uly was home. Lyra was still acting as governor, while he commanded from *Nubia*'s decks. Today, that involved her coming aboard from the station via shuttle. And bringing the Legal Department with her. Or at least Ethir and Piruz, with Rabiu off playing pirate.

They settled around a table. Lyra was the one most concerned, while Voldomir had an irrepressible grin. Uly addressed him first.

"What have you found in terms of a proper capital city?" Uly asked.

"Khet like water," Voldomir reminded everyone. "Yarikh do as well, from what I'm given to understand. Isann, given a perfectly blank slate, will go sideways into a mountain and terrace it with patios facing the sun, depending on the latitude. The Ononguli, of course, long for the Endless Plains, so I've spent extensive time with satellite imagery, then high-level flights, then low-level explorations. And a lot of walking on the ground. At this point, I'm probably in better shape than I was when I married Lyra, but I think I have a place to start. Assuming you want a great big pretty city for trade and cultural events. Auditoriums, universities, that sort of stuff."

"I'll still need to visit," Uly reminded him.

"Understood," Voldomir said. "Number three on the original list I sent you, because if we build a couple of flood control dams upriver, and maybe turn one of the channels of the delta into a big drainage ditch, the rest of the city won't have any serious water problems. And you get a lot of river to use for recreation and even trade, when you go mining up in the mountains with the Isann."

Uly nodded. Not the sort of thing he ever imagined needing, but the Sobol and Bondarenko clans had both gone horns-in on helping him be successful. That meant finding all his knowledge gaps and working to fill them before he even understood he had them.

It helped that a small tax on trade had generated a tremendous amount of cash, over and above what he had cleared in his anti-piracy operations.

People really did appreciate not having to fear being jumped by pirates. Maybe being killed, but certainly having their entire livelihood stolen out from under them.

He turned to Lyra next.

"You got my note about the Yarikh?" he asked, having sent it directly from Isann before he'd gone to Saari.

"I did," she said, horns bobbing. "An entire squadron of small warships dedicated to protecting Bastion from outsiders?"

"Indeed," Uly replied. "And available for short-range patrols, out to the closest ring of nearby systems when those start filling up with population, but primarily here. *Searcher* went to Saari, where it will also anchor things, but the Scholar presumed that the Samuur would maintain their own naval forces, so they didn't need as much there. At least yet."

"Bastion's going to be on the bullseye," Piruz inserted. "Specifically you, Uly."

"I'm aware of that," he replied. "At some point, I will have to turn over command of *Nubia* to the next conductor. I'm also aware that I don't have enough blackmail on hand to make Haydar do it."

Piruz put his hand back down and nodded with a grin. There was only so much Uly could get Haydar to do for him. And once he was on the ground semi-permanently, he probably needed Dan on one side and Haydar on the other, plus the Legal Department and the Combat Team, with many of those folks taking their turns as Ambassadors on a regular basis.

"As I said, *Nubia* with a new conductor," Uly continued. "Maybe Sterling. I don't know yet. The Isann and Samuur will contribute significant forces, possibly equal to the Khet and Ononguli, so I will have a rich pool of potential conductors I can promote."

"How do we turn you into the government?" Ethir asked. "Lyra's been great, same as Sterling and Maks before her, but you're here. What's next?"

"I think we build the Conclave," Uly said, looking at his friends. "Send out a message to every world we're friendly with and invite them to send ambassadors here for now, and then figure out who wants to actually pay taxes and belong, as they send both permanent representatives and members of the Conclave of the Many Species. From there, we can start executing a legislative function that is more than just me or Dan deciding how things will go. Or you as Governor, Lyra."

"We have laws," Ethir noted dryly.

"Largely inherited from Khet business practices," Piruz offered sideways. "With some Ononguli thrown in, a heaping of Mazhin, and some weird stuff that *Danumash* and *Batyr* contributed. Kinda a mess, when you get down to it."

"Necessary at the time," Ethir growled at the larger man.

"Agreed, but hey, let's throw a bunch of technocrats at it and have them start massaging it into something a little less messy?" Piruz grinned.

"Send out an invitation under my name," Uly said. "All of the Legal Department, my senior advisors, the Combat Team, and a few others will be on that list, but many of the important players won't be here, so whoever gathers won't be doing anything critical. I expect them to meet for maybe three or four months out of every year, then approve a budget and go home to update their people. The Presidium as a council will handle the important tasks and direct the growing bureaucracy. Right now, that's those same people, making decisions in council as a representative body."

"Just the Spinward Reaches, right?" Ethir asked, head turned a little sideways like he got when he had a con going.

"Not even all of it," Uly replied carefully. "Those worlds we wish to protect from Auga incursion tomorrow, if it happened. And we are not claiming any world as far from here as the Silk Road between Rayzian and Z'Gosza, but they are welcome to send people as representatives of foreign powers."

"Gotcha," Ethir nodded. "You do realize that they'll come, right?"

"That's my intention," Uly said. "The more people who look to us to protect them from the Auga, the stronger we'll be. Get them to trading away from the Empire instead of into it. Lateral, too. Strengthen the rest of us at the Empire's expense. Remember, I intend this thing we're building to outlive me and Dan by a long time. All of us. Laws help, but social patterns are more important. Schools that raise kids to an equality of form, so they are all part of one nation."

"It'll be different, that's for sure," Ethir whistled.

"I'm aware of that," Uly said. "We've had success changing minds about piracy in Sector Fifteen. And even in Sector Twenty-One. This is the logical next step."

"In that case, let's talk budgets," Ethir nodded. "Rabiu isn't here, but he left us a stack of ideas…"

Uly leaned back and found his coffee mug. Dreary, technical stuff, but it was the foundation of any nation that was going to survive longer than a single dictator. Or even a series of them.

Empires like Auga were built on the strength of their immense and capable bureaucracies. Temper the ambitious and resist the dullard.

Build something bigger than any one sentient person.

If he could.

FORTY-THREE

Lukyan had put his foot down, then discovered that Anna wasn't about to budge a centimeter.

Stubborn woman, like he liked them. Sometimes a pain in his ass. As a result, she'd put him on *Storm Crow*, with Dmytro taking command of *Fire Diamond* for now.

He hoped it was for now. Anna could play rough when she wanted.

They arrived at Bastion on a Saturday, because he already had enough on his plate to add a *Tuesday* on top of it. Klyment Gavrilyuk was still conductor, a man in firm control of his bridge and his ship. Technically, flag commander of the Horde, if they ever got that silly, but framing it that way let Lukyan see him in a light similar to Eskil Haldur, and that made things way easier.

"We're being hailed by the station and *Nubia*," the comms officer nearby announced in a matter-of-fact tone.

Gavrilyuk turned a superior grin at Lukyan. They'd had some long and fulfilling conversations on the way out here, but Lukyan was never playing poker with the man again.

He keyed the switch live.

"Greetings, Bastion Station, this is Lukyan Chayka, aboard *Storm Crow*. Maks said I could find Uly here."

He left it at that. The lime green uniform already made him itch, but that was entirely psychosomatic. Note, the green was fine. It was the Rayed Sun of Rayzian in gold on his collar that felt like it weighed as much as this ship.

He'd lost that argument, too. Good thing he didn't mind it when she was right all the time.

Uly appeared on the screen. Studied him for a long moment. Nodded.

"Ambassador looks good on you," Uly said with exactly the same sly grin Gavrilyuk had going.

He glanced over and Klyment seemed to be laughing to himself.

Lukyan drew a breath and pretended to be immune to it all.

"Your fault, Uly," he said.

"You could have sailed away at high speed, never to look back," Uly teased.

Klyment snorted. Lukyan scowled at both of them.

"No longer an option," Lukyan said.

Reminded him. Reminded all of them.

Uly got deadly serious in an eyeblink. Human serious.

"Trouble?"

"I'm not certain," Lukyan replied, aware that there were limits to signals encryption, even involving what Haydar could do when challenged. "Need to chat directly."

"*Nubia* or the station?" Uly asked.

"I think *Nubia*," Lukyan said, aware that he'd been in flight for a while and Maks had kind of scared everybody back home with the little he'd been willing to share. "But Lyra should join us."

Might impact the Bondarenko and the Sobol, at the end of the day.

Certainly, Anna had been concerned enough to pull him out of *Fire Diamond* and send him to Bastion on *Storm Crow*. As her formal Ambassador.

From there, they'd see where things went.

FORTY-FOUR

Haydar liked the Ononguli, but found that even Lukyan could be a bit of a drama queen at times. Listening to Lukyan's update from the *Vatazhko* and from Maks, Haydar thought they were all overreacting a bit.

Something must have shown in his tentacles, because Uly paused mid-breath and turned a question his way instead of speaking. Then a nod for Haydar to proceed instead. Lyra was equally intrigued.

That was the problem with having someone like Uly around. He could read minds. Tentacles, at least.

"The reason we didn't include that many details was because Krilic was a fourth fallback," Haydar explained.

Lukyan didn't appear convinced.

"You're raiding a planet in Imperial Sector Three," he noted.

"And Sterling got input from a lot of people on how to handle it," Haydar replied, keeping the profanity out of his tentacles. For now.

"What's that likely to do to the Auga?" Lukyan asked.

"How many raids have you suffered over the last few years?" Uly asked.

"Fewer than predicted," Lukyan acknowledged. "Far fewer."

"Like they were all set to start the next war, and somebody caused

219

them to panic and recoil?" Uly asked. "Maybe reset everything and dig in while they sorted out how much threat they were under? That sort of thing?"

Lukyan didn't have tentacles. He was almost as easy to read as a Mazhin. Haydar only grinned a little.

"Maybe," the man admitted grudgingly.

"And what do you think the Auga will do if somebody hits a target in Three?" Haydar pressed mercilessly. "Better, gets away afterwards, because honestly, we spent more time planning the approach and escape than we did the in-system parts of the mission. That's Dan's part, with Sterling available if he has to get mean with a newly refurbished Heavy Striker."

Lukyan turned to scowl directly at him. Haydar nodded, tentacles loose and calm.

"Anna's afraid that they will lose their shit and lash out," the man finally admitted.

"That sounds like an Ononguli response, not an Auga one," Lyra noted from her quiet corner of the table.

Watching Lukyan, Haydar wondered if turning that dark crimson with blush actually hurt. Certainly, jolting your tentacles into a knot did, but he hadn't asked an Ononguli what the equivalent was. Hadn't thought about it before now.

"The natives are getting restless," Lukyan offered, tone much quieter.

"Afraid that I got them into a war, then left them holding the bag?" Uly asked.

"I didn't say it made any sense, Uly," Lukyan responded. "But there was enough grumbling that she appointed me Ambassador to the Barbarians and sent me out here in the fastest warship she had to get an update. Maks refused to provide any details."

"He wanted you to talk to us," Uly said. "Man has his hands full there, building up the Samuur into dangerous allies who can hold our middle flank later."

"Middle flank?"

"The Isann are defined by the *Karaŋgılıkka*," Uly said as Haydar nodded, having heard this speech maybe too many times. "The Samuur are defined by honor to a degree I haven't really encountered outside of story books. One of these days, the Auga will catch a clue and try to build a new fortress right in the middle of our new trade road, separating the Horde in Sector Twenty-One from the Spinward Reaches in Fourteen. That runs into the Samuur as soon as the Auga push to any depth past it. Maks wants Eskil to be able to push back."

"And that Yarikh ship I saw?" Lukyan asked.

"Nomiki has promised a small squadron to protect Bastion as well," Uly said. "I expect them at almost any time. They'll give me flexibility to do things like spend more time at Rayzian. Obviously, I've been gone long enough that some of the old hotheads have had a chance to talk themselves into delinquency again."

Haydar like that term. It really summed up a couple of the Lords of the Endless Plains. Especially Teke and Pasternak.

"Uly visiting would be good, but there's a problem," Lyra interrupted. "The Combat Team is all with Dan on her mission."

Not how Haydar would have phrased it, but he supposed that Lukyan wasn't one to take offense. Not around here.

"Not following," Lukyan replied.

"Somebody on Rayzian told the Auga that Uly was going to hit Zhoralong," she continued in the sort of blunt tone that you got with people who had evolved to bash horns together at high speed. Mazhin didn't like bruising their tentacles that way. "They failed to prepare adequately, but they were still there. Have you located your leak in the palace and executed them?"

Haydar kept his tentacles flowing, even as Uly winced and Lukyan hunched like she'd just punched him in the belly.

"We have not," the man replied after a beat.

"Then I can't imagine that Uly is safe," Lyra ground on. "Anna's not a threat. You aren't. What about *everyone else* in the building?"

Haydar wondered at what point she might just knock the man down and start kicking him. Might be less painful, especially as Uly wasn't stepping in to stop her.

Nor was he, come to think of it.

"Suggestions?" Lukyan asked when he realized that he was outnumbered three to one in here.

"I need to go," Uly said firmly. "I presume that Anna is asking me to visit to consult?"

"Roughly, yes," Lukyan agreed. "A show of strength, because they thought that the Auga must be up to something when they pulled back."

"As opposed to freaking out and reinforcing their entire Ononguli frontier, in case we went even deeper into Sector Fifteen and hit places like Vynchen and the like?" Haydar asked.

Nicer tone than Lyra's. Still a low bar to clear.

Lukyan had the intelligence to look abashed. Haydar understood. The Ononguli had been alone against the Auga for centuries, but that had been their own damned stubborn intransigence that hardly even allowed Mazhin traders to do more than stop at the frontier, then withdraw.

Until Uly. Haydar could see them backsliding a bit without the Corsac Fox immediately in sight.

Haydar didn't want to suggest that the Ononguli were afraid they'd been abandoned, but he also wasn't going to ask.

"Lukyan, we can send a message on to Rayzian, or you can carry it," Uly offered simply. "That gives Anna some time to prepare, but I don't think that we want to raid the Auga in the near future."

"Why not?"

"They will be pulling back forces from that same border to hunt for Sterling and Dan," Uly said. "Given the methods we've plotted for them to sail out, I don't think they will find *Vauquelin*, but every day they spend searching randomly is a day they are not threatening the Horde. Let them be looking back over their shoulders instead of at you. It gets them focused on the internal sectors. We like that, especially if we intend to drive them back and make them surrender former Ononguli worlds."

"Would they?" Lukyan asked, astonishment obvious on his face.

"That has always been my goal," Uly said. "As to the current circumstances, I'll make a stop on the way to Rayzian and gather up a new bodyguard that ought to impress even the Ononguli."

"Who?"

"I'll ask the Paramount to provide them."

Haydar couldn't help the snort that escaped.

"Oh?" Uly asked.

"Ask Aarne for an all-woman bodyguard," Haydar offered blandly.

Uly laughed and laughed and laughed at that. It took Lyra and Lukyan a few moments to catch up.

Yes, that would be utterly rude, considering how big Samuur women were, especially compared to Ononguli. Almost as much fun as an all-Emro force, if they ever decided to recruit enough of those folks.

Haydar made a mental note to ask Suka Kuri what she could do.

FORTY-FIVE

Eskil felt his ears go back so far that someone could probably pin them together on a mat without a lot of effort right now.

Uly's grin didn't help.

At least Aarne was no better, sitting between Eskil and Haydar with a look of pure shock smeared across his face.

"How many?" Eskil finally managed to gasp out.

Haydar the Mazhin leaned in, grinning with face and tentacles at the same time.

"At least twenty women," he said. "Half of them the deadliest killers you can find, the other half the biggest troopers you have."

Eskil blinked. Blinked again. Turned to Aarne, glad that there was somebody else handy that could maybe make sense of it.

"I understand the why," Aarne finally managed. "What I don't get is the message you are sending."

"My people—Lyra, Haydar, Lukyan—have gotten it into their minds that I'm at personal risk," Uly explained. "Normally, I would have some or all of the Combat Team along as bodyguards, but Dan took them with her on her mission. At the same time, the Ononguli have a leak at an extremely senior level, so folks at Bastion presume assassins as a potential threat."

Eskil couldn't help but bristle. He understood assassins at an intellectual level, but any Samuur who went down that path lost all honor. For all time. Possibly dragged their families and even clans down with them. A few had done it, historically, such that their descendants had to change their names to escape any potential connection with such fools.

"And women?" Aarne asked.

Uly stood up and walked over to one such trooper who happened to be close. Inari Johansson, who suddenly looked like she'd rather be anywhere else in the galaxy at this moment.

But then Eskil saw it. Snorted. Grinned, even, matching Uly.

Inari was an entire head taller than Uly was. And broader in the shoulders. Might weigh half again as much.

The Ononguli tended to be Uly's height. And generally about as skinny, to the point that Dan was bigger than most of them.

Eskil nodded to Inari that she could relax.

"Thank you," Uly turned to her and said before returning to the table.

The rest of the room was slowly coming to understand the joke.

Except that it wasn't a joke. It was a size thing. A species thing, because any Ononguli troublemakers would be looking at women like Inari, who would have been specifically selected for mass, power, and seriousness. Looking **UP** at them.

Then he had a thought so ludicrous that he started laughing before he could contain it.

"Oh?" Haydar asked, tentacles mostly locked on him, though a few were tracking Inari's ongoing discomfort.

"Dan took the entire Combat Team and her battalion with her," Eskil said. "Yes?"

"Yes," Uly replied patiently.

"You have *Nubia*, but none of those men and women that make up the assault battalion," Eskil continued, turning to look at Aarne, because it would be his decision, assuming Uly approved. "Should we recruit a full replacement force to travel with Uly on this mission? ALL female, but some hundred and fifty, give or take, plus the additional bodyguard element over that exercising the same sort of command authority that Dan usually does, and the unit commander subordinate to Solomon?"

"Solomon went with them as well," Haydar pointed out. "He had certain expertise they needed. Abadi Nwachukwu, a Khet, is currently handling things."

"Male?" Eskil asked.

"Luck of the draw," Uly replied. "Abadi's assistant is an Ononguli woman named Jelyzaveta Stasiuk. But yes. A temporary full force adds a level to the message we probably need to convey to certain folks on Rayzian. Aarne, is it possible? Could it be done quickly if you approve?"

Eskil turned to his boss and cousin to attempt whatever mind control he might have to get the man to agree. Uly had come to them looking for folks he could trust sight-unseen.

Was there a better definition of honorable to be had? Anywhere?

"It can be done," Aarne replied. "Eskil, since you understand the situation, I'll charge you with putting it together. Assume my approval ahead of time and get Uly and Haydar to sign off on things."

Eskil smiled.

Ground forces weren't his forte, but he was First Conductor. People would listen to him.

"Since timing is critical, may I make a suggestion?" Haydar asked.

Eskil nodded.

"Find three units that are all reasonably gender-imbalanced," the Mazhin said. "Pull out all the men on paper and see what that leaves you with, since we'll want a force capable of meshing well. Especially since it will be somewhat scratch-built."

Uly nodded. Eskil did the math and nodded as well.

"I'll need a few days here to identify them," he offered. "At the same time, if we have a count of bodies, we can start loading supplies immediately, then get them aboard at the end."

"Sounds like a plan," Uly said. "I need to meet with a few people here, so you and Haydar work it all out."

Eskil grinned.

It wasn't a practical joke to play on the Ononguli. The stakes were simply too high.

It was, however, a novel way to look at things.

Here, then, was the future arriving.

Again.

PART EIGHT
STRADOSHA

FORTY-SIX

Sterling watched carefully as the pearlescence of warp slid away, dropping them back into the real galaxy. On his personal screens, he had split things to show his image as it would be transmitted to the station.

Which was really weird to see, because Mr. Ramezani and Mr. Anyari had come up with an entirely new system. It took Sterling's image and made him look and sound like an Auga when he sent it. Not quite Conductor Székely, but they'd used him as their original model for shape and voice before adjusting things.

And it was eerie, but Anari assured him that it worked. She had the most experience with the Auga fleet, little though it was.

He trusted her judgment.

"Standard Auga hail incoming, sir," Maikki said, voice just a hair off normal with stress.

Because *everything* was a colossal bluff from here. Most of it on his shoulders, at least until Dan got her team into place.

"Reply via text with the minimum package, Ms. Hudaibirdi," Sterling said, fighting to keep his own voice calm.

Uly made it look easy, but had also taken him to one side to explain how hard he usually found it. And some of the tricks Uly used to look and sound like a proper warlord.

"Mr. Kaita, take us in on a standard orbital path like we belong here," Sterling continued. "Mr. Dovzhenko, obviously we aren't aiming at anyone, but I want a prioritized list of potential threats and targets as Ms. Hudaibirdi gets her scans processed."

One part of his screen showed that outbound wave, slowly reflecting off other ships and identifying them. Nobody his size yet. Shouldn't be any, given standard Auga practices.

At the same time, as Uly liked to remind people, shit happened. You had to be ready to immediately run or fight.

Once Dan departed, it would be fight, because there was no way in hell he was leaving her and the Congress behind.

"Main station requesting live channel communications, Conductor," Maikki said a few minutes later, as she had everything scanned and they were going in. "I'm detecting concerns that we are violating procedures."

Her voice had calmed, which helped calm him. Nobody had done this before, but he had more experience at shooting Auga than anybody here.

And swindling them, considering Nyri and Zhoralong. Or whatever you wanted to call it.

Sterling wanted to smile, but the Auga never smiled.

He had seen it occasionally with Conductor Székely. Mostly talking about his family and hoping that they didn't suffer for his cowardice, as he saw it. On duty, Anari had assured him that they were as grim and dour as one might imagine.

He focused on presenting the image of his old captain, Tevin Winter from *King Hewitt II*. Not a man he particularly liked. Nor respected. And had Uly to compare to as commanding officers.

That settled a scowl in his shoulders like a cloak.

Sterling nodded and opened the line.

Another Auga, which he had expected. On the screen, Auga-Sterling looked good enough to punch in the Third Eye.

He stared at the stranger for a long count.

"We are on a classified mission," Sterling growled quietly at the man, thinking about how he would be looking down his nose at the fellow were they in the same room.

Auga tended to run about one hundred and fifty centimeters on average. At least a head shorter than him. Probably the man weighed more than he did, though. Broad, muscular, and solid, as they had engineered themselves.

"This is highly irregular, Conductor Erdős," the man replied.

Haydar had selected Erdős, conductor of the Heavy Striker *Escorial*, a vessel their records showed from Sector Twenty-One. It would be incredibly bad luck if this fellow somehow knew him, but Sterling would deal with things as they came.

"Were the orders unclear?" Sterling asked. "And who are you to challenge them?"

"Magistrate Pichler," the man cringed ever so slightly. "I challenge them not, sir. They were unclear and we sought clarification."

Rabiu had prepared him for how bureaucracies conducted warfare verbally. Sterling made a note to thank the man later for those lessons.

Passive-aggressive. Malicious compliance. Testing boundaries.

It only worked if you showed weakness.

"Magistrate Pichler, if it becomes necessary for you to achieve clarity into my mission, I presume that it will be necessary to transport you to Ajorn along with my prisoners," Sterling shot back cruelly.

Being brought to the attention of powerful players at the capital itself because you were a pain in someone's ass was a fantastic way to screw up a career. The Khet would exile you to the worst warehouse station they could find in the corporate entity. The Auga would simply fire you and dump your silly ass on whatever planet you happened to be on, with an ugly black mark next to your name preventing you from ever being rehired.

More cringe. Fool had thought himself the social equal of a Heavy Striker Conductor. Might be, because Sterling had no intention of asking, because by putting himself on some secret mission that might involve the Imperial Court itself, he raised himself to a level where even the mere governor of Stradosha would be his inferior.

Or he could go out shooting.

"My apologies for our confusion, Conductor," Pichler replied hastily. "We have the order package in hand. Was there anything you needed from the station?"

"Clearance to deliver a transport to the surface," Sterling growled, watching himself where that Third Eye cracked just a shade, supposedly the mark of awakening anger. "The coordinates are marked. As is the destination. Notify the warden that he will have guests and to prepare certain prisoners for transport to my craft. Then order a cleared zone around my vessel."

Sterling went ahead and cut the line, rather than wait for a response. Either they bought it, or they didn't, and he wasn't close enough to any orbital station to be threatened at the moment, so he'd know if they began ordering a squadron to assemble to attack.

Minutes passed, single drops of water landing on his forehead like torture.

"Clearance from the station," Maikki finally said, relief evident in her voice.

"Everybody, as your plans run," he ordered, containing his sigh, then opened a line aft.

"Chastain."

"Dan, I think they bought it," Sterling said. "You're on."

FORTY-SEVEN

Dan cut the line and nodded to Nasrin. Today's shuttle reminded her of the escape at Vynchen, mostly because it was the exact same model as they'd stolen on that day.

Auga standard everything. Minus the bars designed to lock prisoners down in their chairs. She'd had those specifically removed.

She moved to the intercom and opened it.

"Flight deck."

"Stand by for clearance to launch," she said. "We're all strapped in here."

"Coming up, Commander."

Dan moved back to her seat and settled, hooking everything and trying not to listen for Marlowe's voice in the rear as he broke everything and freed them to escape the Auga that first time.

Suka Kuri wore a shawl over pants and a long tunic for this mission. It made her look like an old grandmother set to go for a walk on a slightly windy day. Yet more confusion.

"It'll be fine," Suka Kuri grinned at her.

Dan settled for not rolling her eyes at the woman, turning to Anari instead.

"All set here, Dan," Anari nodded.

Those two were on point. Solomon was holding the ship, like he usually did for *Nubia*, having gotten everyone and everything as prepared as that young man could.

Dan was willing to admit to being fidgety because she had nothing to do. Assuming everything went right.

She just didn't trust it. Simple as that. Too many moving pieces. Too many random elements that could cascade through the equation. But that was specifically why she'd brought one hundred and fifty extra troopers with her.

And not just troopers. The best of the best that she'd been able to recruit and train even better.

But for the shapes, they'd have been the most elite unit in the *Batyr* navy. And maybe even then anyway.

She nodded. Grimaced, but only inside.

At least she had a much better understanding of what Uly went through when she went off on her various missions, leaving him to hold the ship or the station while she was gone.

It sucked.

"It's called growing up," Nasrin offered from down the way.

Of course, she'd been tracking everything by scent. And she was right.

Dan leaned out and smiled at her.

"*Touché*," she replied, acknowledging how many times she'd said that to the young Mazhin woman over the years when Nasrin had gotten nervous about something.

"Commander, we have clearance," came the call. "Launching in thirty seconds."

Good team. The best.

And they were about to lay it all on the line for the most audacious thing anybody could remember.

So far.

FORTY-EIGHT

Anari had supervised Omid's people creating uniforms in the gold and red of the Auga for everyone to wear on this mission, up to and including the pilots who would remain behind with Dan. Everything had to look official. Be official.

Helped that there were rules and procedures for transferring high value prisoners between systems, once Uly and Haydar had been able to take apart *Vauquelin*'s systems to look.

She understood that bureaucracies caused empires to last. Dictators usually did whatever they wanted, to whoever they felt like, which was why so many of them ended up getting assassinated or overthrown.

At the same time, both Uly and Suka Kuri had made it clear that too much government was as bad as too little, leaving it as much art as science in trying to find that happy middle ground.

Uly started with a system where everybody was equal, regardless of size or shape or color. Which, near as Anari could tell, tended to be utterly at odds with the rest of the galaxy. Even the nice folks.

In-groups and out-groups. Something to be resisted.

But today, she got to take unfair advantage of existing systems. And it had to be her, because she was the only ex-Imperial soldier in a position Dan trusted. And they had rearranged teams so that she had a few

Emro, plus those Zuath and Ugotha that had rallied to Uly's banner. And met Dan's standards.

All the Khet and Ononguli would remain on this shuttle with Galli and Loh-An, available as a reaction strike force if Anari needed them.

Landing went softly. Following the Auga playbook page by page, possibly with the book itself open in their laps so that the pilots could do everything exactly as specified.

Anari unbuckled with the rest and stood, towering over everybody, including Yanouk who was her Second-in-Command today. Dan's folks remained seated, but they needed to stay out of the way for now.

Anari turned to Suka Kuri and Yeong-Suk.

"We'll slip out when everyone is busy getting you loaded onto the trucks," Suka Kuri assured her.

Anari nodded. Walked to the intercom.

"Flight deck, where are our trucks?" she asked.

"At the starport main gate now, getting clearance."

Anari turned to Yanouk.

"Open it up and let's add some confusion," Anari told her younger sister.

Yanouk grinned and moved to the hatch. Quickly, the forward team followed the woman out onto the tarmac. Cold outside today. Maybe five degrees above freezing, but at least calm. They'd dressed for it.

Anari joined Yanouk on the tarmac, then walked to one side.

"Everybody sort yourself into your teams," she yelled, loud enough to be heard at a reasonable distance.

Bodies in motion. Lots of bodies. Big. Little. All armed. Out of the corner of her eye, Anari watched Suka Kuri and Yeong-Suk slip out under the shuttle, vanishing into the shadows beyond.

They had the hard part.

She just had to keep all eyes on her.

FORTY-NINE

Suka Kuri decided that perhaps she had led a more interesting early adulthood than Haydar had, but she wasn't about to admit to some of the things she'd done as a young Adept out on her own for the first time. Folks might get the right idea about what a rabblerouser she'd been in those days.

Not that she was much better today.

Perhaps a bit more discreet about it.

Something.

She had her cane as a walking stick and Yeong-Suk along as some sort of assistant like an old, frail woman might bring when she went out shopping.

Or causing trouble.

Certainly, it made her appear nonthreatening, as she made her way from the landing field to the terminal, crossed inward with a bit of a faked limp, and out the front to locate a taxi. Folks watched her, but only in the context of a giant, elderly Emro woman, walking with a purple-furred Guezal. Both were species known in the Empire, though she had no idea how common they might be on Stradosha.

Didn't really matter, as her paperwork was either sufficient if challenged, or it wasn't and the two of them would be calling for help.

Their driver was Narni, which she recognized by description, never having actually met one. Erect biped between Auga and Human for size, with leathery skin and scales protecting their heads and joints. Usually yellowish, this one was verging over onto a golden orange, though she wasn't sure if it was natural, makeup, or a biological component related to the seasons, like the Ancyn did it.

She gave him an address, then settled back and watched the drive with Yeong-Suk beside her doing the same.

They weren't going to the prison itself, but to a place around a corner. The taxi went right by the target's front door, then turned and let her out. She paid and smiled to herself as the Narni drove away, headed the wrong direction to be of any further involvement with what was coming.

Everything she did from here was designed specifically and entirely to generate chaos. And add several layers of confusion later, when somebody was tasked with interviewing witnesses and attempting to assemble any sort of coherent monologue covering today's events.

Unlikely, but possible.

"Come," she told Yeong-Suk, locating a nearby tea house that looked promising.

There was a precise timing involved at this point. And a message from Anari that would light a metaphorical fuse to burning.

But there was time to pause.

To fade into the scenery for a moment.

Before she got out of hand.

FIFTY

Suka Kuri put away her comm, having seen the single word message from Yanouk indicating that they had five minutes until the trucks carrying Anari and her people arrived.

She needed to be inside the compound at that moment, where she could dissipate any organization she came across before it could crystallize.

Yeong-Suk nodded as they rose and carried their mugs and pot to the front counter with a smile as they departed, went around the corner, and walked right up to the front door of the local prison.

Two guards eyeballed her nervously as she approached, using the loud ticking of her cane on the concrete almost offensively to get inside their minds. The scowl on her face was probably a bit frightful too, but better too much than not enough at this stage.

At least that had been her assumption going in. What fool broke INTO a prison, after all?

A pair of Zuath guards. One of the more common species out in the direction of the Khet and Spinward Reaches, so she was familiar with them. Obviously loyal servants of the *Auga Empire*, but she wouldn't hold that against them, as this planet was a considerable distance from any imperial border.

She still towered over them and scowled *down*.

"Where is my son?" she demanded angrily, digging deep into some theater work she'd done an impossible number of years ago.

"Ma'am?" the one on the right asked nervously.

Both were nervous. That was good. There had been a concern on her part that she might run into bullies. Possibly, anyone smaller might have, but she had mass, height, and apparently anger on her side.

"My son," she snapped. "They told me he was here. Where is he?"

"Uh, ma'am, we're a prison...?"

"I know that!" Suka Kuri snapped. "That's why I'm here!"

"Grandma, they might not know," Yeong-Suk said, as if on cue, then pivoted to them. "Who can we talk to about a prisoner?"

Bad cop. Good cop. Psychological assault, but it worked. The one speaking turned to an intercom set in the wall beside him and pushed the button.

"What's going on?" a bored male voice came from the speaker.

"Woman here claims that we have her son in prison and wants to see him, sir."

"Can it wait until tomorrow?" the voice asked. "We've got a fire drill going on shortly."

"No, it cannot wait," Suka Kuri answered, loud enough that the nice folks at the tea house around the corner might have heard her. "WHERE IS HE?"

Hell, any car driving down the street might have heard, had they had their windows down. Both guards flinched away from her.

There was a pause as she considered exactly where to place a foot, if she needed to grab both guards and slam their heads together. Neither of them was looking at her, that intercom holding all their attention.

"Crap," the man said. "I'll send someone to get her. Hang tight."

The two men painted fragile smiles on their faces and looked up at her. Suka Kuri dialed herself down to a mild smolder and nodded, as if partly assuaged.

Anything to get her inside the building, knowing that Anari was bringing up the smaller force and Dan could drop more trouble if she had to.

Hopefully, not.

A few moments passed and the big steel door behind the men beeped and opened.

An Auga bureaucrat stood there, watching her with his Third Eye at least partly open.

Suka Kuri focused pure rage on the man, aware that he could pick it up at this range. And that he could detect the apprehension coming off Yeong-Suk.

But for all the wrong reasons.

"Mistress?" he asked nervously, looking up.

"I am told that my son has been thrown into your prison," she snarled. "I demand to see him. To speak to someone who can explain to me what you think he's done."

The man actually took a half-step backwards in the face of her emotional barrage, but she didn't allow a hint of a smile into her being.

Angry mother, though she'd never actually had children of her own. Of the flesh, anyway.

She'd helped raise up more than most people could probably imagine, once she'd found them.

This mood would be like what she would feel if they'd somehow captured Dan or Uly.

She let the fury embrace all of them like a flaming hurricane.

He shivered for a moment, then nodded.

"If you'll follow me, mistress, we can try to sort this out," he said, attempting to placate her. "There are no Emro in this facility, so I'm not entirely certain what you were told."

"Here," she snapped. "No other explanation. Just that I would find him here."

He shrugged, palms coming up.

"I don't know," he said. "But come."

Inside, the space was reasonably well lit, but she supposed that prisoners came and went via the loading docks, and Suka Kuri had been told by Galli what those were like. Ugly, dirty, and dark.

He led her to an area that was a bit nicer than an office might be, but not much.

Generic. A waiting room, with an unoccupied desk along one wall, protecting a door to somewhere Suka Kuri assumed was the interesting spot. Sofas for medium-sized species. Chairs, too. Art so bad she'd have burned it as an offering, though she wasn't sure to whom.

The Auga gestured to the couches.

"If you can wait here a bit, we can circle back and have a better conversation," he offered. "At the moment, the facility is a bit busy."

"I was told he was here." Suka Kuri ground out the words like she carried millstones. "I have yet to have anyone explain to me WHY."

More rage. More intense. That Third Eye snapped open, then closed.

Short-range empathic powers were only useful if someone didn't know how to take advantage of them.

"Mistress, there are no male Emro at this facility," he replied. "Who told you this place?"

"A magistrate on Eln," she snapped, letting her voice turn to vinegar and vitriol now.

"This facility?"

"Stradosha," she nodded. "Uryuon. This exact address. Said he was some sort of political prisoner, which I have an impossible time believing, as he was merely an artist."

In her mind, she visualized Hiko as he might have been in other circumstances, leaving off the bit where any good art was necessarily political.

"I will need to confirm, but I am not aware of any male Emro, mistress," he repeated, obviously attempting to calm her.

To placate here.

"Where is your supervisor?" she demanded in a shrill voice that managed to rattle the pictures on the walls, even as Yeong-Suk placed a hand on her elbow.

Rather masterfully done, too. The Guezal woman was obviously an actress, among her many other talents. Con artists had to be.

The Auga withered under her assault.

"If you'll wait here, I'll ask the warden if he has a moment to talk." And then he was backing away, passing through that mysterious door to someplace else.

Someplace Suka Kuri obviously needed to be.
She nodded to Yeong-Suk and they waited.
Everything proceeding to plan.

FIFTY-ONE

Anari had fifty troopers with her, plus Nasrin and Yanouk, with Dan leading the other hundred from the shuttle if things got out of hand.

Uryuon wasn't an especially fortified city. Nothing at the starport had hinted at any sort of defenses beyond what the local police might have on hand, so they could only overwhelm her on numbers if they got serious. They had enough numbers for that.

It would be in orbit that she and Dan had any sort of advantage.

Her job, then, was to get everyone there.

The vehicle Anari rode in was something of a bus, with space for sixteen prisoners and perhaps ten guards riding up front, outside of the cage. She was next to the driver, watching the roads themselves as the convoy swung around a high-walled corner and approached an open gate.

Inside, the space turned into a circular drive, with a guard shack in the center and a massive hatch to the interior, plus barred windows up both sides that she presumed were reserved as rewards for the less pain-in-the-ass prisoners. The troublemakers would be inside solid boxes with lights. Or underground.

She'd never gone down that path in her training, though Anari supposed that a Sabre School enlistee might have found themselves there. Maybe Moss hadn't been the worst idea? It had put her in the motor pool and aboard Uly's ship when he stole it, instead of being a guard at a prison like this.

Lead truck pulled up and stopped. Anari led her group out, then waited as the others joined her, fifty folks pretending to be Auga goons and having something of a staring context with the outnumbered local goons.

Handful of Emro on both sides, so it looked roughly balanced by mass, save that she and Yanouk could probably take them all by themselves. Hell, most of her people could probably take an Emro guard one-on-one, if they weren't facing Sabre Adepts.

She smiled that at the guards, then focused on the one peon who looked like he wanted to be in charge today. Zuath, but older. Possibly dignified, if you could use that term for a prison manager.

"Are my prisoners ready?" she snapped, stepping right up to the smaller birdman and TOWERING over him.

"They are currently being processed," he replied, tone somewhere between diffident and nervous.

"Take me there," she ordered brusquely. "Now."

Dan had reminded her that Auga tended to be assholes, especially to those they viewed as lesser species. And Anari could feel some of that pecking order bullshit coming back as this mission progressed.

She'd use it today as a club, then work with Suka Kuri later to pack it back up and stuff it in a closet.

Uly had no space for that crap. You did your job as well as you could, looking to your supervisors for direction and training then inspiring those behind you to get better.

The Zuath cringed a little, but that was probably her invading his personal space and dropping a whole bunch of attitude on him.

As intended.

FIFTY-TWO

Sterling had kept his stolen Auga Heavy Striker at a specific distance from the main stations in orbit. On a screen, everything looked close to one another, but the physical separation was still thousands of kilometers.

It was the social spacing he wanted to focus on. The orders he was supposedly operating under—according to what he'd sent to the main station—meant that he didn't have time for anything social at all. No station calls, because he would be departing as soon as he picked up his prisoners, and the locals didn't need to know any more than that.

Officially.

Still, this was probably a once in a lifetime opportunity, so he rose from his station and walked around to stand next to Maikki Hudaibirdi, causing her to look up with a bit of a jolt.

"Sir?"

"What does the Auga regulation manual say about how a ship should scan local orbit?" he asked her. "Even on arrival or after sitting here for a few hours, such as we've done."

She blinked. Processed. Nodded.

"Excellent question, sir," she replied. "Let me check."

He nodded back and waited as she pulled up various screens and quick-read through them. Sterling couldn't remember anything that jumped out, but it hadn't been a question he'd really asked himself. Or anyone else.

"I'm not seeing anything beyond the standard notes about maintaining appropriate clearance from other ships and flying with transponders and other systems for proper navigation, Conductor," she finally replied. "What were you looking for?"

"How much reaction we'll get if we hard-pinged everyone in orbit," Sterling smiled. "Turning your transmitters up to a level that might be rude, if someone were to point it at you instead."

She paused, whiskers flickering.

"You had an idea?" he asked.

She hadn't been with him long enough to relax like Drew or Haydar were around Uly.

And, he supposed, he'd been doing this a little too professionally up until now, but that was mostly because almost everybody under his command was older than he was. And all of them were extremely competent at what they did.

They just didn't have Uly's trust yet. Or his.

That would come.

"If we adjusted our orbital path to move to Stradosha's northern pole, we would be able to scan almost every craft and station in orbit, since they mostly maintain an equatorial placement, sir," Maikki replied. "Not sure how the local authorities would respond, though."

"I like it. Let them think we're assholes from Sector One, pissed at having to go deal with the backwoods folks in Sector Three," he replied, grinning. "Take charge and make it happen."

Two blinks. One because she wanted to ask a stupid question. The second one because he could almost see the words *Pop Quiz* float across her mind. Because a well-trained crew was ready to respond when circumstances got weird.

"Aye, sir," Maikki responded crisply. "Our shuttle has landed and remains at the starport. Jatau, swing us up and over, to polar coordinates zero/zero and hold there. Bring your facing around and down until we are nose-on with the main station. I'll trigger the scan at that point, review the findings, and then we'll probably return to this exact location, relative to everyone else, presuming that they don't throw a fit or attack us."

Sterling nodded. It would give them a perfect view of everybody, which would let them compare local layouts to something later, if he ever found a reason to return to Stradosha.

Anything was possible.

And it would keep eyes focused on *Vauquelin*, instead of letting minds wander to what was happening on the surface.

FIFTY-THREE

Anari had followed the Zuath into the facility. Half of her people had followed automatically, the other half standing around outside like they were relaxed, while plotting the location and movement of every single guard they had seen.

She knew exactly how keyed up her people were. No one else would. Her group might be outnumbered overall, but were all ready to charge into battle as Dan needed them.

Both sides of a long room had been sectioned off behind floor-to-ceiling wire fencing sufficient to hold the average prisoner. An Emro could probably do damage barehanded, but the guards she saw were all armed with stun weapons of various capacities, from wands up to pistols.

Nobody would be getting out without help.

Twenty or so Ancyn on her right as the Zuath led her to a workstation with two others seated and watching screens. Anari moved around to see both camera images and text.

"What seems to be the holdup?" she demanded.

One of the seated guards glanced at her, then his boss.

"The list you provided is out of date," he said quietly, hunching in like he expected a blow.

From where she was standing, Anari could drop all three before they could react. Her troops could get the rest, even with Nasrin and Yanouk outside keeping order in the courtyard.

"Out of date?" she asked in a hard, cold, superior tone. Right up there with a predator suddenly seeing a lamed rabbit on a game trail.

"Four of the men listed are deceased," the Zuath said, reaching to touch his screen and show status. "Two others were released and are no longer in my system."

Normally, she'd say something funny and rude right now, having been part of this same bureaucracy at one time.

Anari recalibrated her persona to relax one notch.

"Somebody sent the wrong list to my ship?" she asked, being more friendly now.

Like maybe it wasn't their fault and it could all be resolved without Important People™ having to get involved?

The main Zuath saw the opening and lunged into it.

"That's my read," he said. "Your list almost dates back to...shit."

"What?" Anari asked, measuring where she would throw punches.

"There was an escape, maybe five years ago?"

"Four, sir," the silent-until-now guard mentioned. "I'd just gotten out of training."

"Four, then," the leader said. "Most of the female Ancyn prisoners escaped, but none of the males."

"Most?" Anari asked, curiosity piqued.

Galli had brought all her political prisoners, but might have missed a few. Or thought they'd been captured or failed to escape with the men. And they needed more Ancyn if they wanted to build a proper colony that far from home.

The guard typed and the screen changed.

"These forty-seven men have all been here since before then," he said. "You've requisitioned them, but like I said, I have names marked unavailable. Dead or released. Then these six women. Oh, I take it back. All of them are from after the escape. Looks like hostages got taken."

"Hostages?" Anari asked, still watching the room.

A block of about twenty Ancyn men scowling mightily back at her, but separated by the wire. And the guards. And her people watching everyone.

"Relatives of the escaped women, from the way it reads here," he said, touching a letter code that meant nothing to her.

"Bring them, too," she announced.

"What?" the leader asked.

"We came to clear out all the Ancyn," Anari scowled at him. "To haul them all to Ajorn. If these women are somehow related to the men we're taking, we might as well save everyone the effort of bringing the ship back later. Or sending another one. And it makes your life easier."

"I don't know," the leader said. "The orders that were transmitted were for a specific list of politicals."

"And it's out of date," she reminded him. "Do we gotta do it the hard way, or can you do me a favor?"

"That's above my paygrade," he replied nervously.

Anari tensed for violence.

"Suggestions?" she asked.

"If I don't want to get fired, it needs to be approved by my people," the leader said.

Anari took a deep breath. There had been no counter message to her original one, so the plan was hopefully still running forward.

"Call the warden and ask him," she told the fool.

FIFTY-FOUR

Suka Kuri had hoped that she'd be allowed to see the warden of the prison in all the confusion. Let the man take a long moment to get rid of her before going down to deal with the problem that Anari presented.

Alas, she was stuck in the outer waiting area. The Auga who had greeted her had stuck his head out long enough to hint that they were still working on her problem, then closed the door again.

She'd heard the thunk as the lock engaged, so there was no quiet way to get through. Kicking it in wasn't yet her recourse.

Then the door opened and two Auga men walked through. The one she knew. A second, older one who was a stranger.

Again, she was reminded of how they had fully engineered their entire species at one point, aiming for health, longevity, and beauty. Strength, too, at least compared to most species as they were half her size and probably only two-thirds as strong.

The one she knew paused directly in front of her as she rose, with the one she took to be the warden two steps back. A man in a hurry.

"Mistress," the man said apologetically. "There have been some complications at our end and we will be unable to address your questions and concerns today. The warden asks if you could return tomorrow, when he will be able to better understand."

"Warden?" Suka Kuri asked, looking at the man.

He nodded silently, obviously trying not to give much offense.

She turned her attention to the magistrate.

"I suppose that will have to do, sir," she said, voice carrying deflation and acknowledgment, even as she held out her hand. "Yeong-Suk?"

Suka Kuri stepped forward and shoved the magistrate to her left with her cane, flowing through his bouncing mass to step right up to the warden.

Dan had taught her that was the rudest thing you could ever do in a bar fight, and Suka Kuri found it an exceptional opening gambit as the man's eyes grew confused.

Before he could reach *concerned*, she slapped him, though not all that hard. Open palm ringing like a steel bar breaking. Then did it again, just as quickly, with the other hand as she dropped the cane.

Suka Kuri stepped in and caught the Auga with her right hand around his throat. Not squeezing hard enough to knock him out instantly. Nor crushing anything and killing him slowly.

No, she braced her feet and got under that elbow. The Auga weighed too much to actually lift off the ground, though Anari and Yanouk could probably manage, but it did get his *undivided* attention.

Then she walked him stumbling backwards into the nearby counter, slamming him into place with solid thunk as fear began to replace every other emotion in all three of his eyes.

"Yeong-Suk?" she asked.

"Not as elegant," her partner replied.

Suka Kuri took a quick glance and noted that Yeong-Suk had laid the man out cold on the carpet. That quickly.

But Dan and the Combat Team trained daily in the deadliest arts of close combat that a dozen species had been able to assemble and polish.

Suka Kuri turned her attention back to the warden.

"I'd rather not have to kill you," she informed him simply. "You decide if you live through the day. Simple?"

His eyes were a little bugged out. Stress and panic.

Yet another fool who'd looked at her as an old woman and forgotten that she might actually be dangerous.

"Speak quietly or I will crush your throat and kill you," she instructed him. "Where were you headed just now?"

"To deal with prisoners on the loading dock," he murmured around her fingers.

"What was the problem?" she asked, aware that Yeong-Suk would be facing anyone else who entered.

"A request to remove all of the Ancyn prisoners, rather than the original list transmitted," he offered, still deeply aware of how angry she was.

An empath could hardly miss it. These were Galli's people being held.

And, if the request was framed like that, it was Anari's doing, most likely.

Suka Kuri quick-scanned the room, noting the space just behind the Auga where a receptionist would normally have sat. And a handcom.

"What is the extension for the holding pens?" she asked, flexing her fingers exactly enough to echo through his skull.

She had his undivided attention already. Suka Kuri wanted his cooperation.

If he felt like surviving this. No doubt, he could read that, too.

She hadn't killed anyone in decades. That wasn't the same thing as *never*.

"Twenty-three," he gurgled.

She dialed, then put him on speaker, leaning close to whisper in one ear.

"Behave and live," she said. "Vex me and die."

He tried to nod. She got enough of the movement to nod back.

"Aft Station," a male voice came. Sounded Zuath.

"It's Warden Gáspár," her prisoner said. "What is the hold up?"

"They're asking to take another group of prisoners that aren't on their list, sir," the voice said. "Plus, their list contains a few that we don't have. Old list. Possibly a bureaucratic issue."

Suka Kuri leaned in until they were touching noses.

"Release them all," she whispered, breathing angrily on him.

He flinched, then realized that she outweighed him. And was stronger. And had him pinned. And was extremely angry. And was about to crush his throat.

Mental empathy did have drawbacks.

"Go ahead and release the extra prisoners," he said, even sounding moderately relaxed and comfortable. "Mark it under my authority."

His eyes were pleading. She relented just enough that he could breathe more easily. Without letting go.

"If you say so, sir," the voice said.

"I do!"

Suka Kuri nodded and cut the line. She smiled at him.

"Thank you," she said. "This could have been so much more difficult."

An Adept of the Sabre School had taught her a thing once. A particular grip that caused mild blood flow issues. She did it and the Warden went unconscious between heartbeats.

Yeong-Suk was there a moment later with plastic binders that would be sufficient even for an Auga's superior strength. Suka Kuri dragged both unconscious men around behind the counter where they were hard to spot, then snapped the wires to the handcom and stuffed them in a pocket.

"Out the way we came?" Yeong-Suk asked, handing her the cane.

Suka Kuri took a moment to adjust everything that had gotten a little askew in her excitement.

"I think that would be a fabulous idea," she replied. "Best we be a little gone before all this can get sorted out."

She turned and made her way back whence she'd come.

FIFTY-FIVE

Anari sighed when the release came through, but only on the inside. Outside, she remained a gruff prison guard going through the motions. A nod to her team and they all relaxed a notch as well.

Might still go sideways, but they had the boss supposedly giving them the go. Anari wondered if the situation had just made it easier to send them off, but Suka Kuri was involved, so anything was possible.

"How long?" she asked the helpful goon.

"Maybe ten minutes?" he shrugged.

"Faster would be better," she replied, suggesting that they'd all be out of his feathers quicker.

Folks were in motion. She stood around, looking tougher than everybody else.

And sent a message to Nasrin and Yanouk updating them. Plus saw a message from Suka Kuri indicating success there. Whatever that meant.

Several Ancyn women got delivered from a different hatch and put in opposite the extra men being brought. Anari had no idea who they were, but if they were hostages taken to ensure good behavior, Galli would want them free.

Hell, Galli would want all of them free, but there were limits to what Anari and her friends could accomplish on this mission.

Maybe next time.

She noted that all the prisoners wore a type of binding that hooked wrists to waist. Ancyn had longer legs and shorter arms, relative to most biped species. Thighs instead of shoulders. Probably would develop some interesting kicking forms for martial arts, if they went in for that sort of thing. Galli hadn't known any, but she'd been a politician. Loh-An had been much younger, though also more on the intellectual side of things.

"That's all of them," the leader finally sighed.

"First batch of sixteen," Anari ordered. "I want the one named Coelomedon. Where are you?"

A beak and headcrest snapped up at her. Older male. Feisty-looking fellow, though.

"You," Anari pointed, then split the men into two groups with her hands. "Let's load up."

All of her people and the local guards were armed and primed for violence, so the prisoners followed Coelomedon to the end, then got onto the first bus. Anari made sure that every one of them was firmly latched down, like prisoners normally were, then paused when only her people were still on the bus.

She leaned in close to the wire separating her from Coelomedon and smiled.

"Galli sent us to rescue you," she said so quietly that he looked at her confusedly for a moment. "All of you."

Then that head bounce again. Eyes big. Then narrow as he studied her closer. Wary, but she figured that the local goons had been assholes to the prisoners for a long time.

And these men had likely given up all hope by now.

Anari nodded and stepped outside the bus.

Time to load the next bus.

FIFTY-SIX

Dan had a comm tracking the few messages going back and forth, all of them in plain language that was still cryptic enough to be meaningless to anyone reading them. Or going back later to understand what had happened.

Suka Kuri and Yeong-Suk successful and returning via black cab. Anari loading prisoners onto several buses for transportation to the starport.

All of her remaining folks had stayed inside the shuttle, most of them still in their seats in case they had to make a sudden lift-off.

Time passed.

Yanouk sent a note that the buses had gotten fully loaded and were in motion. It had taken longer than she'd hoped to get to this point, but nobody had said why, so all she could do was stay sharp.

"Dan, we've just gotten an emergency alert signal," the pilot called. "All-points-warning of a jail break. All police forces being mobilized and every militia member ordered to arms."

There it was. That other shoe she'd worried about. Expected.

"Stand by to launch," Dan replied.

She keyed the button that put the entire Combat Team into circuit, including that silly old woman who had insisted.

"This is Dan," she said simply. "Whatever you were doing, break cover right now. Call me with your status."

The jailbreak had just turned hot.

FIFTY-SEVEN

Suka Kuri had turned down the volume on her comm, but was able to read the message when it vibrated at her.

"Driver," she called, waving to get the young woman's attention. "Can you pull over here and drop us off? I saw a shop we want to visit. You can go on from there, because we'll probably be a while and I'll call someone later."

"Are you sure, Mistress?" the driver asked.

"I am," Suka Kuri said, calmer than a beautiful ocean.

Quickly, they got to the curb and exited. Suka Kuri watched the vehicle disappear before starting to walk.

"What's next?" Yeong-Suk asked.

"The port will lock down," Suka Kuri replied, opening her comm fully. "Trying to get there will be folly at present. Dan, I presume we'll need pickup, since you likely cannot complete the mission from there?"

"I have your coordinates on screen," Dan replied. "Not sure how quickly we'll get to you. There is a park a few blocks to your west. Make your way there."

"Understood," Suka Kuri replied, closing the unit and nodding to Yeong-Suk. "Two friends, out for a walk."

She moved to the mouth of an alley as they went, slipping off her cloak and dropping it and the cane just inside.

Any description probably started with that blue cloth and the cane, so it would confuse people. She considered sending Yeong-Suk ahead, then switched things up.

"You follow half a block back," Suka Kuri said. "Keeping watch and flanking, since an old Emro woman might be the most they have to go on at present. Well, several Emro women, but only in retrospect."

"Got you covered," Yeong-Suk said, immediately turning to look in a shop window as Suka Kuri set off at a pace that would get distance quickly.

Dan would have to either come get them, or leave them behind. Suka Kuri could find her own way up and out. Emro and Guezal were Imperial citizens, so they wouldn't stand out as much as Humans or Ononguli.

Worse come to worst, she could hide out here until the heat died down after *Vauquelin* left, though that might be measured in months.

Still, she knew a few tricks. And had learned more from Dan and the others.

She could manage.

FIFTY-EIGHT

Sterling jolted when the alert came.

"It's Dan. We've been uncovered down here. Go to combat footing."

Nothing more, but he didn't need more. They had a scan of every ship and station currently in the system, generally complete with build specifications to a level that made him smile.

No other warships. Nothing but local defense forces generally intended to resist some crazy pirate in an Ultra-Bomber or something equally small.

Not an Auga Heavy Striker on alert.

"Maikki, hard ping everyone one last time, then start tracking blue-shift for trouble and feed that to Dovzhenko," Sterling said. "Pilot, keep us at this location, but be prepared to maneuver if someone decides to come out and threaten us. All hands, take it up one notch, as we are expecting combat to break out at any time."

He settled into his station and pulled up Maikki's list, grouping things into locations, in case they did attack later. Three stations he needed to worry about, given that they could possibly get themselves organized enough to threaten the shuttle as it lifted and climbed out.

Still, he'd chosen this location and vector for a reason.
Now, he just had to hold it against all corners.
And get Dan and her team home.

FIFTY-NINE

Anari grabbed the Zuath driver and pulled the man right out of his seat.

"Somebody, take over," she ordered. "Keep us moving."

The bus started to drift, but one of her people had already been moving and got the vehicle under control before they even left the lane.

Anari turned to her driver and smiled at him.

"Don't tempt me," she said simply, sitting him in the chair that had opened. "Somebody tie him up."

She grabbed her comm and opened it.

"Everybody check in," Anari ordered.

"I'm going to get a ticket for hit and run back here," Nasrin replied. "Clipped a couple of parked cars."

"We're good here," Yanouk replied from the rear of the convoy. "All vehicles still in motion."

Anari nodded.

"Dan, I assume trouble at this end," she said into the comm. "We'll need to be extracted at this point, because I don't feel like trying to bust through starport security with stolen buses."

"Understood," Dan replied, sending her a set of coordinates. "Meet us there and get everyone ready for lift-off."

"See you shortly," Anari said, cutting the line.

She turned to the driver.

"Hang a right at the next intersection and don't let anyone stop you," she ordered. "Push other vehicles out of the way or drive into oncoming traffic or up onto sidewalks if you have to."

The man glanced back at her, a bit wide-eyed for a moment, then nodded and hunched his shoulders forward.

Times like this, a flying truck would have been nice, but those required a lot more effort and could be overridden from a central authority by air traffic control. Better that they add car theft to the list of other things today.

Like getting away.

Quickly, they made it to what turned out to be a parking lot next to some sort of nature trail park. More trees than open spaces, which would work to her advantage at the moment.

Later, the bad guys would be better able to sneak up on them, but she had a mass of armed troopers handy, so they'd have to exercise care first.

"Park there, but don't disable the vehicle in case we need it later," she ordered, then turned back to the prisoners in the cells.

Anari produced a key as she opened the cage holding the prisoners.

"Give me your wrists," she ordered the closest man.

His hands came up and she got him unshackled quickly, then handed him the keys.

"Get the others free then join us outside," Anari said. "I need to set our perimeters."

Though, looking outside, Yanouk had already gotten things in motion.

SIXTY

Yanouk had unlocked all her prisoners as soon as they left the facility, though they had remained in the back for now. The cage was already open and she was out as soon as they stopped moving, her troops flowing around her like a rising tide.

"Get the corners nailed down," Yanouk ordered. "Work with Nasrin's team and push out a perimeter we can hold for the shuttle to land. Move it!"

Forty troopers got things done quickly. Sixty-odd Ancyn sat in the middle of that box, still a lot confused at the state of things.

One of the men trailed Anari as she got close, nodded, and kept moving towards a set of four picnic tables that were already being turned onto their sides and rested against anything handy to provide cover against cops and rain, though the day was dry.

More troops were behind trees or stretched out flat on the backside of various rises. Bushes had eyes.

The Ancyn male stepped close, waiting for her to stop issuing orders as Anari and Nasrin took over. Yanouk supposed that she had the mobile reserve by default, so she knelt and gestured all the Ancyn to join her.

"You really are here to rescue us?" he asked.

"We are," Yanouk nodded. "Galli Fyodon and her women were prisoners of a group of pirates. We rescued them several months ago. Once we heard her story, my bosses decided to rescue all of you as well."

"So they made it?" he asked. "Where?"

"We found them clear out on the inner edge of Imperial Sector Thirty-Two," Yanouk replied. "Our normal base is in Sector Fourteen, but we're allied with the Khet in Fifteen and the Ononguli in Twenty-One."

"Allied?" he asked. "Someone yet resists the *Auga Empire* with strength?"

"The Corsac Fox," Yanouk explained. "He is Human, as is the woman in command of this operation, Dan Chastain. They come from Sector Seventeen, but the Corsac Fox has decreed that the *Auga Empire* must be stopped. He is rallying many nations to join him."

"We are not a nation," the man said simply.

"There are just over one hundred Ancyn, when we get you to your mates," Yanouk replied. "That is the seed from which a nation will grow. The Humans number less than twenty, but the Corsac Fox is building a thing that will stop the Auga eventually."

Yanouk ignored the sounds of disbelief from the folks around her. They would learn to believe in Uly. She had, transforming from the shy teenager she had been into the warrior/scholar she was today. Younger than Anari and perhaps not generally as aggressive, but no less competent.

No less dangerous.

Movement drew her eye. Locals had generally been moving away, no doubt warned by the authorities to return home for their safety as a group of dangerous prisoners attempted an escape. Most of them had only gone a certain distance. Not enough to protect them if the authorities started a firefight, but having them there bought Yanouk and the others time, because those same cops would hopefully move people to a safe distance before causing trouble.

At least, she hoped so.

The movement was an Emro, towering above the vast majority of other pedestrians. Yanouk found her comm.

"Is that you, Elder?" she asked, waving.

The figure waved back.

"Indeed, it is," Suka Kuri replied. "I take it we were successful?"

"So far," Yanouk said, then muted the line in order to yell. "Friendly forces on the southwest corner! Someone bring them in!"

Didn't matter who did it. It would happen. Figures emerged from brush and gathered Suka Kuri and Yeong-Suk.

Farther away, a single police flyer landed and two figures got out, but wisely kept their distance.

"Anari, first response forces have arrived," Yanouk yelled, pointing.

Anari turned around from what she had been doing, nodded, then ignored her again.

They all knew what they were doing. And had trained for any number of eventualities. Most of their scenarios had involved a situation where they got stopped short of the starport. Solomon had gone deep into his planning.

Yanouk had confidence.

"And just like that, we will escape?" the man asked, drawing her attention again.

She studied him. Older, she thought. Gray plumage like Galli, but with red fading down to purples. Fierce eyes.

"At this moment, while the police are attempting to sort themselves out, our shuttle should be lifting off to fly over and land there," she pointed. "At that point, we board it and run. In orbit, we have a stolen Heavy Striker, and I am not aware of any other warships in this system powerful enough to stop us at present, though we will be hunted later."

He did not seem convinced, but again, Yanouk wasn't surprised. She had to remind herself occasionally that she had been there. Had seen many of these things.

Had done them with her own two hands. Or a cannon.

A sound drew her head around. A shuttle, flying low. Dan.

At least she hoped it was Dan, and not a police gunship of some sort.

SIXTY-ONE

Dan had taken up a spot on the flight deck, but out of the way of the two pilots, one a Zuath male named Freleng, the other Min Choe, one of Yeong-Suk's "cousins" who'd gotten a gig as the co-pilot.

"We are lifting off in five seconds," Freleng announced. "Everyone strap in for maneuvering."

Dan had a solid grip on a bar and her feet braced. Freleng nodded to himself as he worked, that cockatrice crest bobbing and flopping as the shuttle started to roar, then lifting as smoothly as an elevator.

"Commander, forty-five seconds to destination, coming in low and wide, then circling," Freleng yelled. "Map shows a space to land, but we might have to knock some trees over to manage."

"I'll steal you a better shuttle later," Dan answered. "As long as you get us back to *Vauquelin*."

"Deal, sir," he laughed. "Min Choe, you watch the landing gear and don't deploy it until I know how much damage I need to do to trees."

Dan settled and watched. The shuttle didn't get very high, riding on thrusters and noise over an Auga city. They didn't like tall buildings as much as Humans did, so it tended to be spread out more. Lots of green spaces and walkways connecting things, rather than a grid that was efficient.

"Callsign Two-Five-Five-Three-One, I am about to fly through your corridor," Freleng announced. "You can get out of my way, or I'll ram you and you will crash. MOVE IT!"

Dan saw a glint of sunlight on metal up ahead. Saw a much smaller craft waver for a moment, then suddenly dart madly off to the left as Freleng and Min Choe laughed.

Whales, chasing off guppies.

As long as it worked.

They continued forward, low enough that other vehicles were either landing or flying lateral as the cops got over being freaked out and started ordering things into motion.

The Auga did not deal with surprises well, but had a tremendous bureaucracy for handling any number of chores. She was reminded of a gigantic rock, poised on a slope. Took a lot of effort to get it into motion, but once it was, it would roll for a long time.

If she was really lucky, Dan figured that she could haul a significant amount of their fleet into a blind chase down every dead-end alley in the galaxy looking for her.

It might be years before things settled down again. The *Auga Empire* thought in centuries anyway, so they cared a lot less if they lost a decade here and there, but she and Uly really only had thirty years, give or take, to really build something, if they wanted it to last.

To stop the Auga. Even if that didn't happen until she was gone.

Still needed to be done.

"Commander, we're there," Freleng called. "Circling now. Don't see anybody in a position to threaten us on the ground."

"Watch the skies," Dan reminded them. "They aren't supposed to have anything that can shoot us down. At least, not this fast, as they should have to scramble the pilots, get authorization for force, then make it happen. They might still react fast enough."

"Nothing headed our way in the sky," Min Choe replied. "Starport control has ordered everyone to get clear of the area, but I have not heard an order to ground, which I would expect if they were sending someone to shoot us down."

"Stay on it," Dan ordered.

Over their shoulder, Dan could see the park. Shuttle was low and tilted slightly to port as Freleng circled.

"Headed in now," he finally said, apparently satisfied.

Dan held on as the ship shuddered to a hovering stop and started down.

Now, the hard part.

SIXTY-TWO

Nasrin had her flank covered. Gendarmes had arrived, but only a handful at present, all gathered up over there behind their vehicles and a little uncertain from their body language.

It was the Auga. Chaos was utterly anathema to their entire way of life. Of governing.

Civilians and interested citizens—or bored onlookers—were also gathered. Or watching out windows or from sidewalk cafes across the street.

Overhead, their chariot was coming in, landing in the larger part of the park where she presumed they played some sort of organized team sport that involved a field roughly eighty meters wide by twice that long.

Auga were all about team sports instead of individual competition. Singular glory was apparently anti-social somehow, in ways she had never really cared enough to research deeper.

Might be a worthwhile afternoon at some point, though, if they were going to be spending more time inside the Empire being hooligans.

It would let her express the occasional anti-social tendencies that she was supposed to have outgrown by now.

Or maybe it was the juvenile delinquency. Nasrin was never sure.

Right now, those police looked like they were prepared to do something organized. She couldn't imagine them actually stomping over here and ordering everyone to surrender, but Nasrin supposed that someone in charge might be that stupid.

Or that callous with lives.

The pity was that she'd had to leave her Omnibow on the ship, because guards supervising a prisoner transfer weren't supposed to have that level of firepower handy. Might make people nervous.

Yup. Cops getting organized. Walking around the nearest vehicle like they were here to read her the act about this being a riot and everyone needing to disperse immediately. Or surrender and go back into their cages.

How about *No*?

She looked at the men and women closest. Scout Three under the current classification.

Scouts tended to be the crazy ones. Or the ones that hadn't outgrown their juvenile delinquency.

"Scout Three, stand by to charge the closing enemy element, screaming wildly and howling like wild animals that have come for their souls," she said to the group. "Stun only, because we're not mean, but we might as well induce a level of panic as the shuttle lands. On three, two, one, CHARGE!"

She was up and running. Mazhin weren't particularly built for ground speed. Not like Zuath with those backwards-hinged legs like chickens. She was with one Emro male and two Ugotha as they fell behind the three lunatics up front.

Still, her team suddenly charging did the trick. Cops over there had a moment of uncertainty that quickly turned to dread. Didn't help when Nasrin opened fire and Scout Three joined in. Not that the beams were loud. And hardly visible on a bright day.

It was her charging like a fool at armed servants of the Auga who had never faced something like this in their lives.

Those same civil servants paused, backtracked, then started hauling ass every which way. The civilians took a little longer to catch on, then the infection hit them and they started flooding the other direction.

Gods, what she'd give for a couple of Painspheres right now.

"Hold here," she announced as they got to the edge of the park at the boulevard that circled.

Parked land vehicles provided adequate coverage both directions, but Nasrin hadn't wanted to try to hold a perimeter that large. Not with a force this small.

She couldn't even do anything more than chase off the cops. At the same time, she didn't need to do more, either.

Just get them going the other direction so she could withdraw her people and get the hell off this planet before the locals figured out how to stop her.

If they could.

SIXTY-THREE

Yanouk watched the shuttle settle and started walking at a deliberate pace as it did, waving the mass of Ancyn to follow her.

Off to one side, Nasrin started running and hollering. She seemed to be using psychological warfare on the local gendarme and didn't need Yanouk to grab all her people and charge in to help.

The rest of the team was holding stable, so Yanouk walked at her normal slow speed at the head of her convoy. All the nervous Ancyn followed.

Dan was visible at the top of the ramp when they got close. Galli stood next to her.

Coelomedon suddenly cried out when he saw them and surged past her, running. More of the Ancyn joined him as Yanouk walked and watched.

Yanouk stopped at the bottom of the ramp and turned back, counting bodies flowing past her and into the shuttle.

"Anari, I'm loaded," she called as the last one got inside.

"You get aboard now," Anari replied. "I'll follow. Nasrin, you bring in the last group once you have the police cowed."

Yanouk went up the ramp and found Galli and Coelomedon

tangled up and necking pretty heavily. The rest of the Ancyn clustered around Loh-An, peppering her with questions.

"Everyone to your seats," Yanouk yelled, reaching out and gently herding bodies towards the seats in back.

The Khet and Ononguli who had been prepared to assault the park had instead flowed backwards, opening space. Yanouk got people moving, nodding to Dan over Galli's head. Those two might have to be physically picked up and carried.

Yanouk had never really faced that level of loss, though she found herself missing Uly. But she had all the rest of her sisters. Dan might be the worst off when they got home, but Galli and Coelomedon had been separated from one another for years.

She left them alone for now.

Suka Kuri and Yeong-Suk entered next, right ahead of Anari and Scout One. Yanouk counted bodies and confirmed that everyone was doing well.

There was a gap, so Yanouk stuck her head out the hatch.

"Nasrin, they've had enough!" she yelled, reminding Three that they needed to get off this planet, rather than frighten the locals.

Bodies separated from cover and started backwards at a dead run. Yanouk watched beyond them, but nobody felt like racing after an armed mob. She was still ready to fire over heads if anybody got reckless over there.

Feet pounded up the ramp and inside, not breaking stride.

Yanouk glanced over, realized that Dan was busy getting the love-birds towards a seat, so she took charge.

Anyone could do it. That was the secret of the Combat Team. Everybody could cover one another. Halyna was out of sight, while Katya was supervising the Ancyn as they settled. Suka Kuri and Yeong-Suk got involved, answering questions.

Nasrin came up the ramp at a jog, laughing maniacally. Yanouk shook her head and slammed a palm on the controls, bringing the ramp in and closing the hatch behind her.

"Flight Deck, give us ten seconds and lift," Yanouk called over the voices. "When you do, keep it soft until we're ready."

"Roger that, boss," someone replied.

Yanouk got back to where Anari and the other Emro had their seats, taking the closest one and grabbing the crash harness.

She was down and clicking things as the noise tripled and down started moving around.

They'd done the impossible with Solomon's help.

Now, it was up to Sterling.

SIXTY-FOUR

Sterling saw the message on his board when Dan lifted the second time. Everyone safe.

So far.

Time for him to bring them home.

"Maikki, what's Station Three doing?" he asked, toggling through images and lists to make sure nothing had changed in the last five minutes.

"Shields at full power and all weapons appear to be powering up, sir," she replied. "Weapons neutral has shifted and I'm getting turrets rotating to track on us. Nothing larger than 12dm, with most ranging 4–6dm as defensive weapons. We are out of range of the station and I've added a safe perimeter with a margin outside that for maneuvering."

He nodded to her and turned to Jatau Kaita.

"Pilot, start dropping us down lower," he ordered. "Not enough to matter on the edge of atmosphere itself, but I'm fine if someone decides they want to get up over us and shoot down. We've got several options going sideways."

"Conductor, I'm getting preparations for a mass launch command from the primary station," Maikki announced. "They've ordered all ships in orbit to withdraw from orbit, either landing on the surface or docking with one of the armed stations to clear space. They've designated a command channel and are currently communicating encrypted."

"Can you crack it?" Sterling asked, fully aware of what Haydar had sent along with them.

And that man's usual complaints that he and Roshan had *forgotten* more about signals encryption than the Auga ever knew.

Hopefully, it was more than comet gas.

"Working on it now," she replied. "Even given the volume of traffic, it will take a while, sir."

"Keep the systems processing," he said. "Jatau, you have several courses already plotted for our escape?"

"Affirmative, sir," Jatau replied. "Saved all of them and Drew required that I be able to commit jazz on the fly in order to fly for you."

Sterling laughed, imaging how that conversation must have gone.

"Maikki, throw the navigation computer at it for the extra processing power," he said. "I'd rather listen in on their chatter now."

"On it, sir."

He leaned back and closed his mouth as the folks around him buckled down and got to work.

Everything that everybody had planned for was coming together now.

A message from Aibek caused him to pause and open.

** *If we set course initially for Tlani on departure, that should draw the pursuit forces lateral,* Aibek wrote. *That gives Jatau space to come around and slingshot out the bottom when we're done here.* **

Sterling brought up the map Aibek had attached, wondering what his Isann First Officer had seen, then spotting it. A fox, drawing the hounds in his wake, like perhaps they were frightened of being captured.

Everything they'd planned had been left a little underdone to this point, with no way to be certain what they would find when they got to Stradosha.

He sent Aibek a note, thanking him. Sterling knew he would have come up with something on the fly, but this added at least one more layer of planned misdirection on top of that. His team was coming together nicely.

Sterling forwarded the message to Jatau with a note to add it to the list of escape and evasion patterns.

"Update!" Maikki called. "Main Station is launching a wing of snubfighters. Also detecting similar patterns from the other three."

"Pilot, stand by to come around and accelerate. If we let them gang up on us, we're in trouble, so we have to take the war to them," Sterling ordered. "Maikki, I need you to crack that encryption code."

"Working on it, sir."

SIXTY-FIVE

Maikki set her scanners to automatically ping everything in orbit. Then she cranked up all manner of electronic warfare tools that the Humans and Mazhin had added to the vessel during reconstruction and refit. Nothing the Auga normally did, and her previous experience had barely prepared her for what was coming.

Things were about to get crazy.

She hoped that she was prepared.

If anyone could be.

Vauquelin was broadcasting static, crap, even random snippets of music and spoken poetry on every channel that she'd heard used over the last several hours, just in case the local defense forces ended up trying to use those channels later.

She checked the nav computer and studied the output. Then added a few commands to help refine the search.

Every ship or station that was broadcasting led with their identification. Even with frequency hopping, they stayed within ten channels, so her systems could stay with it. Slowly, she began teasing out numbers and names as Auga defense squadrons began flying.

Ten per station, flying in two wings of five each, like birds headed north for the winter in a large V shape. Four stations. Forty signals. A few smaller ships that looked like patrol or rescue vessels, though from this range she wasn't sure if they were armed.

Maikki went ahead and assigned them a threat rating anyway, on the assumption that any fool charging a Heavy Striker in this situation had to have something. Even Neutron Omnipulsars mattered because they could be used to degrade a wavebolt before impact.

She considered it and put them third in priority, behind the tips of those eight flight wings. The commanders would be important to damage or destroy.

Maikki felt her face grimace briefly. Whiskers flexed and ears back.

"Maikki, everything okay?" Commander Huff asked.

"Getting over myself, sir," she replied. "There is no challenge or sport to this."

"Understood, Hudaibirdi," he said. "Not like when Kalev came to Bastion and challenged for honor. This is war."

"Understood, sir," she replied. "All my training wants to throw a bolt at them anyway, just so we do not lower ourselves to their level. As I said, getting over myself."

"No, that's a good idea, Lieutenant," Sterling told her, causing her to flinch and look over her shoulder.

At least she finally appreciated why he was going to rip this entire bridge space out later and make it better. His face was deadly serious with intent when she looked.

"Gunner, send one 12dm at the primary station," Sterling ordered. "I appreciate that it will hit like a kitten, even if they ignored it entirely. Honor must be served."

In that moment, as he spoke, Maikki found one of the missing keys to understanding Humans. According to Eskil, they might be viewed as dorthargion back home. Pack hunters known for some level of crafty intelligence, but dangerous beasts.

Sterling was fully prepared to go entirely rabid on the Auga and their servants, because that was the most efficient way to win here. Or anywhere.

Focused destruction, aimed at a single target. Crush it, move on.

Eskil had warned her, though, that Uly and Dan were more. And had trained Sterling Huff. Honed him like a blade.

Once she'd reminded him of honor, he'd accepted the idea, rotated his plans to challenge the Auga station, then went right back to preparing to maul and rend.

And honor would be served. Even in war, one cannot allow the situation to drag you away from that.

Maikki felt her ears come forward again and nearly laughed to herself.

Honor would be served.

She focused a pair of emitters on the station that was Huff's target. Locked them on and turned up their broadcast power as far as it would go without risking burnout over the next hour. They had brought replacement parts that could be installed after they escaped.

And if it helped blind Auga's gunners against the incoming threat, that would just make it worse for them.

They had, after all, chosen the Corsac Fox as an enemy.

SIXTY-SIX

Halyna had stationed herself on the bridge once they landed in the park, allowing Dan to handle the hatch and Katya to deal with escapees.

She probably had the best understanding of Auga culture of all the Congress, mostly a result of entertainment media disseminated widely by the Empire as a means of extending soft power. Make people forget that the *Auga Empire* was **coming** for you eventually.

The Ononguli never forgot that, having lost half of their worlds since they had first encountered Imperial scouts. At the same time, they did study their foes.

At least she did. Bondarenko, and someone who had fully intended to rise in the clan at some point, though not this quickly as nobody could have predicted Uly.

Worse, she looked at other Ononguli men these days and found them wanting. Her cousin Maks and his friend Lukyan had been the first to see the light and attempt to live different lives, but there was an entire culture that Halyna found she needed to change.

Fortunately, she was in the right place. And had the right lever.

She studied the airborne scans and interpreted signals.

"Is that a news flitter or something more dangerous?" she asked, leaning over Min Choe's shoulder and tapping his screen.

"Stand by," he said, typing furiously.

A video image came up, grainy with distance and nose-on perspective.

"Standard model, according to my records," Min Choe replied. "Used by both civilian and police, though a police version would have a weapon in that turret underneath instead of cameras."

"Anything that could hurt this craft?" she asked, already calculating what orders needed to follow.

"Negative on ship," he said. "Personnel on the ground would be at risk, though."

She looked over Freleng's screens, watching bodies flood towards her like a drain in a bath.

"Flight Deck, give us ten seconds and lift," Yanouk said on the intercom as Nasrin's group raced aboard. "When you do, keep it soft until we're ready."

"Roger that, boss," Min Choe replied.

Halyna grabbed a bar rather than sit. She'd flown with pirates right out of school, and learned all those hard lessons then.

"Freleng, I want a jousting pass at that news flitter," she ordered. "High speed, but obviously missing and prepared to get crazy if he somehow ends up with enough armaments to damage this craft. Fly crazy if you have to, because we've got medics to deal with shipboard injuries."

"Understood," Freleng said, hands flickering across controls with deadly certainty.

The thrusters came up with a rising note like a guitar. Lights changed colors.

"Lifting," Freleng announced quietly. "Min, watch the skies."

"Nobody else on your flight vector," Min Choe replied. "Got you a path taking him down our port side."

"Locked in," Freleng said. "Boss, getting crazy."

Halyna confirmed her grip on the post and leaned in, then wrapped a calf around it as well, just in case.

The shuttle lifted smoothly, but started forward like a race horse almost immediately. They might even clip a few trees on the way out, but she knew how tough this model was. Short of hitting a building, it could take the abuse.

Louder as they settled at less than two hundred meters relative elevation. Lower than the news flitter, who had stopped moving entirely and discovered uncertainty as Halyna's team started a charge.

It wasn't that they were cowards. The Auga and their people could be terrible warriors. Expert sailors.

But Stradosha was far behind any front lines. Clear back in Sector Three, where not even pirates were a threat.

Normally.

The locals were emotionally unequipped for a pirate raid.

Given that every Ononguli world had to be prepared for such a thing at any time, Halyna found her rage rising. Auga and their servants were allowed to live normal lives, never beset by any significant threat.

That was a thing that was almost entirely alien to her. And all of her people.

This then—here and now—was what Uly meant when he demanded that the Auga change. Either they stopped being a threat to the rest of the galaxy, or Uly would do the thing that probably did the most psychological damage possible to Auga civilization.

He would rob them of their peace of mind.

Everyone on Stradosha would be talking about a pirate raid for years, though it hadn't been a true danger to most of them.

It could have been.

Halyna paused to wonder if it **should** have been. If she should make a more forceful argument next time for bringing weapons to blow that news flitter into flaming wreckage. Or bomb the starport's control systems.

Inflict fear on the people who had inflicted such a thing on others, but never suffered it themselves.

Fat and lazy, when the Ononguli had been fighting for their lives, their culture, and their civilization for too many centuries.

She drew a breath and held it as they blasted past the news flitter, already approaching the speed of sound and the booming shockwave that would result.

"All hands, grab something," Freleng called from every speaker.

Two seconds later, he pulled back on his yoke and the shuttle took off at an eighty-degree attack angle.

Nobody else was a threat to them down here.

Halyna still wasn't sure if that should change next time.

SIXTY-SEVEN

Sterling had to stick with his screens. The forward view was pretty but everything was too far away to be distinguishable, and his officers were circled around the room instead of lined up where he could stand behind them all at once, looking over shoulders at their screens as they worked.

Nubia was a better design.

He'd fix *Vauquelin* for whoever took over later. Possibly Aibek, for now relegated aft to a secondary command space.

Today, he had a battle to fight.

"Sensors, status on our first bolt?" he asked.

"Surprised the hell out of them, sir," Maikki replied. "Almost got an impact before they remembered to kill it."

He liked the smile he heard in her voice. Eskil had said that she had the right instincts for this job, stepping entirely outside of anything the *Illuminated Solidarity* had done before Uly and Bastion then embracing a thing that was more like Human warfare.

With honor. Always making honorable choices. She reminded him of Nyri, just watching her ears, and he knew she would have made the same choices he had.

Sterling smiled.

"Gunner, you've confirmed Maikki's targeting priorities?" he asked, turning his head.

Andrii Dovzhenko. Ononguli. A bit heavier than most. Almost Human-sized that way. Still a pirate at heart.

"Aye, sir," Andrii nodded. "Kill the command fighter in any given wing as a way to route them."

"They do everything as a team with a top-down command structure," Sterling reminded him. "The person with seniority makes decisions and everyone else executes them. I doubt that any of these forces have ever had the sorts of pop quizzes that I have put all of you through constantly. Today, I will show you why."

"Aye, sir."

Sterling studied his plot. Eight arrowheads charging towards him in four groups of ten. He had nine 12dm launchers, plus the smaller stuff he could use defensively as they got close. Except that they would swarm him with forty or eighty 1dm wavebolts if he let them.

Ergo, don't let them.

"Gunner, one heavy wavebolt each at all of Group One, ignoring one of the flankmost fighters," Sterling ordered. "Pilot, as soon as he has tracking confirmed, bring us about on gyros and thrusters and aim at Group Three for a second salvo."

Rude. Brutal, even, as the best they could do at this range would be to fire all of their wavebolts defensively at the last, possible moment, hoping to do as much damage as feasible to the incoming death.

Wavebolts lost cohesion and strength as they traveled. 12s would be reasonably weak at this distance, but still should be enough to overcome a pair of defensive 1s.

Nine bolts went downrange in quarter-second beats, then the screen began to slew around as the gyroscopes bit and twisted the ship. Sterling might not have tried this sort of hard maneuvering with any ship that hadn't just come out of a major refit. Too many things might break, but he had to start scoring kills while those fighters were still at a distance.

"Reloading," Andrii announced. "Stand by for next salvo. Groups Two and Four are moving to protect one another."

"As I expected," Sterling replied. "That's why we're going after the softer kills first. Put your third salvo into Group Two, understanding that you likely don't get any kills here."

"I'll strip them of 1s," Andrii laughed. "Then we can come back for more."

Sterling nodded but kept his comments to himself.

Maikki had reminded him of honor. It would skate along a thin line to hunt these fighters down like frightened mice and annihilate them, as they had already made several strategic mistakes that would cripple them tactically. Spread out and facing a Heavy Striker deep in their zone, where he could turn and engage any side from range, while they had to venture into the teeth of a wavebolt blizzard.

The next salvo launched like a team of archers putting on a show. Boom boom boom.

The first salvo was getting close. Sterling switched his view to Maikki's scanners and watched that group cut loose with Neutron Omnipulsars and then a pair of 1s each. Because he could only shoot with nine tubes, one of the fighters in each larger group was ignored and free to put their pair into a wavebolt targeting someone else.

He watched five impacts score kills anyway. Pretty good shooting. At this range, the debris field would be a mass of junk and expanding plasma, so he had no idea if the pilots had been smart enough to eject before impact.

Or if their own honor demanded that they die in a battle to which they were so badly outclassed. Not that he would take prisoners, but anyone in a suit here would have time to be rescued by someone after he left.

Because *Vauquelin* was gone as soon as that shuttle was aboard.

Group Three suffered the same fate as Group One. Six kills in ten, but the remaining four were functionally disarmed.

"Conductor, the remaining two groups have just come about and appear to be going bow-down," Maikki called, confused.

"Pilot, maximum acceleration," Sterling called sharply. "Intercept course. Gunner, start hammering them. Put 6s into play as well as we close, holding the smaller bolts for defensive fire."

"Sir?" Andrii asked, but his fingers were dancing across his controls.

"They are going after the shuttle," Sterling explained. "Warn Freleng to go evasive right now. And stay low where those bolts will degrade on atmospheric friction as he runs away. We can stay with him and protect him, but we have to clear his skies overhead first."

"Roger that, sir."

Sterling watched as it became something of a chase. He was on an oblique flank, and those fighters could get lower than he could because they were designed to land on the ground.

He had 12s.

Would it be enough?

SIXTY-EIGHT

Halyna was gripping her pole tight when Freleng squawked and suddenly dove again. Or leveled off. And accelerated.

"What's going on?" she asked, aware that they had headsets to talk to the ship.

"Bunch of fighters just decided to ignore the Striker and come after us instead," Min Choe replied. "Commander ordered us to run like hell."

Yes, fleeing would be good. The news flitter had been unarmed. These ships were not. They might shoot the transport down. Or at least force them to land.

And be forced to shoot the ship down when Halyna and Dan refused.

Halyna started digging up old memories of orbital geometry calculations. Ononguli ships occasionally raided orbits, but hardly ever attacked the surface of any world. Wavebolts didn't travel far in atmosphere.

Except that those fighters were above them, coming lower, their bolts more or less falling out of the sky.

"Maximum acceleration for now," she ordered, understanding that she was Senior Officer present, at least until Dan arrived from aft.

"Ignore maneuvering for pure distance. Then prepare to dive and flair once they commit to a launch."

"Understood," Freleng replied. "Already pushing. Min, cut the cooling blowers aft and route that power into the engines instead. Folks can deal with stripping layers off for now."

"Coming up," Min Choe nodded.

Halyna thought that she heard a change in engine tone, but that might have been wishful thinking. Anything to get farther away from a death they could do nothing to prevent at this point.

She also took the moment to slide into a spare jumpseat and strap herself down, understanding that the torque she might order Freleng to generate would be more than she could keep her grip against.

And Dan would be trapped aft as well, unable to risk coming forward and trusting that Halyna had it all under control.

She better have it under control.

"Getting launch signals from the flagship," Min called. "He's targeting our hawks with the big guns. Same problem they have, but they are higher and those suckers are tough enough to hurt. SHIT!"

"What?" Halyna demanded.

"Somebody was sandbagging up there," Min answered. "Waited until Commander Huff launched, then put two bolts after us, even as they are turning away to defend themselves."

"Going for low-level flight," Freleng called. "Pity we don't have a tour guide with us, because we'll be low enough that my shockwave will be knocking people over as I go by."

Halyna gulped and nodded. Nape-of-the-planet flying. Somewhere under three hundred meters relative elevation, where you were at risk of hitting a building at faster than the speed of sound.

She blinked and chewed on her lips for a moment as an idea hit her.

Ludicrous. Rude, even.

"Freleng, find me the closest major city," Halyna ordered. "One with a tower. I want a high-speed pass as those bolts close, then the sort of jink that might cause them to impact a building instead of us. Questions?"

She watched his shoulders relax for a moment, as if in confusion, then hunch in again.

"Min, where is that one place we saw?" he asked. "Uryuon is an outlying suburb, sort of. It's close to the towers she needs."

"Come around one-oh-five," Min replied. "Get into your dive then flatten it out at whatever height you intend, before coming around another forty degrees. That should have them on our asses as we go."

"Hang on!"

She did, feeling her stomach rise as the ship was suddenly in a three-g dive. At something like twice the speed of sound. Then he flattened out at six Gs for a moment, driving her into her seat so hard it creaked. Halyna wondered if it might break under the stress, in which case she'd be commanding from her ass on the deck.

Whatever it took.

Looking out the window, the trees were still below her. Not all that much below her either, but enough.

It was the sudden city ahead that caught her eye. Several towers clustered around a downtown in such a way that the view of the surrounding countryside was probably fantastic on a nice day. Everything crammed in close, then farms and wilderness starting quickly beyond that.

And Freleng hauling ass down the centerline of a highway from low enough that his wind probably buffeted larger transport trucks and might be enough to push lighter ones around.

Whatever it took.

"One bolt looks like it lost us in the turns," Min called. "No longer maneuvering or tracking. Impact on the ground somewhere."

One down. One to go. She hoped.

"All hands, stand by for crazy!" Freleng announced.

Given what he'd been doing before this, Halyna grabbed on to nearby bars as hard as she could. Smart idea, too, as her insane pilot stood the shuttle on one wing, perfectly vertical at ludicrous speed, shooting the gap between buildings that all looked down on that highway.

Everything was a blur at these speeds, then he flattened out and sideslipped hard once, racing fast enough that she heard wind screaming on the hull itself.

"Impact!" Min Choe yelled. "Got one of the buildings at the end of the run. Don't think it had enough energy left to collapse it, though."

Halyna nodded as much as she could given the speeds and pressure involved. Earlier, she'd wondered if she should have brought some sort of weapons to threaten the Auga and their servants.

Something to make a statement.

Looking past Min's shoulder at his screen, she could see smoke billowing out of a tower already. Innocents, to be sure, but orbital forces had fired that shot, and would likely have to answer to someone for the damage done and deaths inflicted.

And the people on the ground would be both scared for the next raid, and furious for what had happened here.

She simply made a note to never try a stunt like this again in a ship that wasn't armed.

This was war, and things were dangerous.

SIXTY-NINE

Maikki had a feed from the transport, so she could see what they saw. And how crazy it had gotten with that one wavebolt that had slipped past everything Commander Huff had been able to do to stop it.

He had, in retaliation, destroyed the squadron that launched it, pouring three salvos of heavier bolts into the mass, even as they broke and scattered like pigeons when a hawk arrived.

A few pilots had managed to eject, based on her scanners. For a moment, she hadn't been sure whether or not Huff would go after them as well, but he'd growled, shook his head, and blown out a heavy breath.

"Hudaibirdi, are there any other hostile vessels in scanning range?" he asked in a hard, ugly voice.

Automatically, she highlighted three ships that had not fired wavebolts, but had been armed with Neutron Omnipulsars and used them to break up attacks.

Hadn't done them much good, but they had tried.

Maikki wondered if she was in the process of signing their death warrants.

"I'm only seeing red shift here, Maikki," he replied in response to her image feed. "Confirm that."

She took a moment to make sure. All three running away as fast as they could, rather than challenge a successful warship big enough to carry each of them in a flight bay.

"All red shift, sir," she replied crisply.

Still inside the range of a 12, because she'd marked that sphere early and maintained it as they flew around.

"Gunner, if they slow down, goad them with one bolt," Huff ordered angrily. "I want them running. As long as they comply, they survive. Anyone coming to rest is a threat. Questions?"

Maikki held her breath. She'd flown on Samuur warships. Engaged a few pirates flying fairly primitive craft when she'd been First Officer of *Ahonen.*

Vauquelin could destroy anything in orbit today save for those four largest platforms. And maybe those as well, if Huff worked at it. She'd read about station assaults he'd commanded.

"Fire if they slow down, aye, sir," Andrii replied evenly.

But then, the Ononguli had a much longer history with the *Auga Empire.* An unfriendly one, at that, while the Samuur had had the amazing luck to meet Uly first.

Maikki focused on her boards again. Watched as the shuttle ascended into clear skies, evading pieces of shattered fighters falling out of the sky nearby.

More pings to track everyone in orbit, but nobody was blue-shifting at this point. Stations in geosynchronous orbit tracking both high and low elevation, but those were simply mountains to maneuver around safely. Every ship that could had either gone to warp, moved close to a station, or landed hot.

Vauquelin owned the space above Stradosha.

And now the chase would begin.

SEVENTY

Dan had ended up next to Galli, with her husband beyond that and Suka Kuri next to him. Those two held hands and necked a lot in spite of the maneuvering, though Freleng had announced that they were safely inserting into orbit now and would be docking shortly.

Hell of an afternoon.

A clearing of a throat caused her to turn the other way. Van-Liem Mai. Male. One of the other Ancyn leaders with Coelomedon. Husband of Hue-Vinh Mai, who had remained behind at Bastion.

"We're really free?" he asked, gesturing to the lovebirds.

"As soon as Sterling and his crew can get you home," she nodded.

"But not you?" Van-Liem asked.

"This was the first part of a mission," she reminded him. "I'm taking a group to a Human colony on the far side of the Empire to recruit people."

"It makes no more sense now than it did on the ground, Commander Chastain," he said earnestly. "Why do you not take a warship?"

"Because we'll be sneaking in and out," she replied. "And I am taking ground troops with me. We must maintain an extremely low profile."

"Would you welcome our assistance?" he asked. "You have just done us a major favor and it feels wrong to leave the scales unbalanced."

"You getting home to Hue-Vinh and starting a new life is the balance that would please me," Dan smiled at him. "Later, I will ask your help when we need to slip in and visit another Ancyn colony some-where, so we can recruit a larger tribal bloodpool for your people to join us, assuming that Galli and Coelomedon chose to stay. Your new tribe may decide to emigrate elsewhere once all of the excitement is settled."

"I doubt that we would be as welcomed anywhere as at Bastion," Van-Liem nodded. "And we would never be safe anywhere inside the Empire, once someone started asking questions. Still, it feels wrong to abandon you immediately after you saved us."

She shrugged. This had been done partly to help Galli and her people. But only partly. Another part had been a deep raid into Auga to disturb the Empire. Rock it to its very core. And to visit a Human world, where she might find mates for the men that had accompanied her and Uly into the deep wilderness of the Spinward Reaches.

Many were getting accustomed to the possibility of alien wives, but Dan knew that Humans—and the Yarikh didn't count there—would need to be represented in future generations of Bastion, after she and Uly built it up and were gone.

She watched the Ancyn man turn and look back at the group that had been rescued.

"Anh-Huy, you're single," he called. "Would you accompany Commander Chastain on her next mission?"

"Only if you find me a girlfriend to come home to while I'm gone," one of the Ancyn men cat-called back. "All cousins here."

Laughter greeted the comment, so Dan relaxed. Most of the men had wives that she and Uly had rescued. A few older Ancyn women as hostages, which must be who Anh-Huy was referring to.

"No promises," Van-Liem replied. "The whole point of this mission was getting back all the husbands that never escaped. There might be widows, but we'll see what we can do."

He turned back to look at her, dropping his voice.

"Would it be possible to stop at a place where Ancyn exist in large enough numbers?" he asked her.

"Maybe, but I make no promises," Dan said. "Plus, we do not demand that married couples all belong to one species."

"No?" he asked, as confused as most were when encountering the topic.

Dan pointed to Anari.

"See the Emro woman there?" she asked, waiting for him to nod. "She will marry the Human commander of the warship we're flying to."

"But children?"

"They may adopt," Dan cut him off. "Or foster. Or perhaps make arrangements such that Anari has an Emro child or Sterling fathers a Human one with a colonist we're going to recruit."

She watched his eyes cross in confusion. Big eyes. Prominent. Utterly lost right now.

Dan nodded. It would take time to get them around to such a radical idea, but they would come.

Or they wouldn't. Husbands and wives within a species was only necessary for breeding purposes, after all. Uly had his many wives as his primary advisors. Granted, her doing, but all had expressed surprise at the happiness they had discovered in being with Uly.

As she had expected. The man was a unicorn, after all. One who listened. Who looked past the color of her skin. Past her enlisted rank. Past her upbringing.

And trusted her. Relied on her. Needed her.

Craved her.

Already, being away from him was a chore, but she was made of stern enough stuff to endure it. The mountains would give way first.

Van-Liem seemed to find some point of mental stability.

"As you say," he muttered. "Having rescued us from life in prison, it becomes our duty to learn."

"And to make it home to your wives," Dan reminded him. "Hue-Vinh would have my ass if I took you with me instead of sending you home with Sterling and the ship."

He paused and nodded. Leaned out and looked at Galli and Coelomedon, still busy necking and murmuring to one another.

"So, Commander Chastain, it appears we have time." He smiled with eyes and headcrest. "Tell me more about this Corsac Fox."

SEVENTY-ONE

Sterling surveyed the monumental wreckage he had left in orbit of Stradosha. And on the ground, though that had been on them instead of him. He'd made sure that that specific command fighter had exploded into a billion flaming pieces.

Things were quiet. Oh sure, he had no doubts that local authorities were screaming all sorts of demands and insults on various channels at him, but Maikki had said she was still jamming everything and ignoring most of the rest.

Nobody out there had anything to say that he wanted to hear.

"Maikki, any changes to status?" he asked quietly.

"Negative, sir," she replied. "Red shift anywhere that matters. Transport has docked and locked down for flight. Local authorities in orbit and on the ground still trash talking. No threats detected."

Sterling nodded.

"I believe that honor has been served," he announced to the group around him. Samuur, Khet, Ononguli, Human. He found a pleasing symmetry to it. "Jatau, set course for Tlani and begin acceleration. We'll run a bit longer than normal before transitioning to warp, to give them time to mistake where we're headed next, but keep a running calculation just in case we need to adjust on the fly."

"Roger that, sir," the Pilot replied.

Sterling keyed a line aft.

"Secondary bridge," Aibek replied.

"Sterling here," he said. "Anything with Damage Control that you can't supervise from up here?"

"Nope," Aibek replied. "Taija has it all under control and is ahead of schedule."

Sterling nodded. Maikki's sister was as good as she was. Merely younger and lower in seniority. No less capable.

"You head up here to take command," Sterling told him. "We'll transit while you're walking, then secure from action stations and start the next phase of things."

"See you shortly, Sterling," Aibek replied.

It was good. They had done a thing. Not an impossible thing, but a hugely damaging thing to the weak spot he wanted. A reminder to the Auga that there really were no places safe behind the lines if the crazy, warlike Humans decided to strike.

To come for you.

If nothing else, that would cause them to rearrange significant fleet assets backwards, possibly permanently, protecting places they had thought were safe yesterday.

He wasn't sure what he could do next to cause them grief and strife, but once he got Dan and that team dropped off, he could circle back and maybe scan a couple of other places on his way home. Maybe pull another Zhoralong, as long as he did a little scouting from the edges first, rather than dropping out and being in range to open fire immediately.

"Ready to go to warp, sir," Jatau announced after a few minutes.

"Take us out," Sterling said. "Maikki, secure the ship from action stations, then you take command until Aibek arrives, at which point you go off duty and we'll start our usual watch rotations. Questions?"

She looked at him with a bit of surprise, but they'd won and there hadn't been anybody in a position to chase them. Probably wouldn't be for a few days, if the folks at Stradosha had to send to the nearest naval base for help.

And that was the only place they'd find it.

He'd be long gone by then. And not in the direction of Tlani, though they would send folks there to stop him from...something.

Sterling nodded to the woman and rose, heading towards the exit.

He and Dan needed to plan out the next step of this crazy mission.

PART NINE

RAYZIAN

SEVENTY-TWO

Inari Johansson wasn't entirely certain, but was leaning more and more into the belief that she'd been swindled, somehow.

From being on the Paramount's personal bodyguard team to a transfer that saw her temporarily leading the Corsac Fox's personal bodyguard as they'd departed Saari on a diplomatic mission to the Ononguli Sphere, she had turned into something like Third-in-Command overall, behind Aliisa Sekam as Ground Commander and Tyyni Salo as Team One Commander.

Inari Johansson, Bodyguard Commander. She was pretty sure it was a promotion. At least on paper. And had read about the Combat Team that Commander Chastain had created, where all the members were female and most of them were directly married to Uly.

After spending a few weeks in his direct company with her new team, getting used to guarding someone so much smaller and more valuable than the Paramount, Inari also understood why everyone listened to the Human.

He listened. Had ideas, but happily discarded them if someone had a better idea. Admitted ignorance and asked experts for advice.

But man, was he dangerous, just listening to some of the ideas he discussed.

Inari was single. Idly, she wondered what it might take to catch the eye of Commander Chastain when she got back. Ground combat was already something she was expert at, though the two Human males, Emil and Gennady, had shown her several new dance forms that Dan and the others practiced.

She still wondered if she'd been swindled.

Today, they had arrived at the Ononguli capital world. And taken an armed transport to the ground because both Inari and Aliisa had put their size twenty-one feet down and *required* Uly be able to shoot back if someone caused any grief.

And he'd only rolled his eyes once, then grinned at her before acceding to her objections. Bodyguards were normally silent and invisible, but good ones had to shape their principal's day for maximum security.

As they walked through the corridors of the *Vatazhko*'s Government Hall, Inari watched the Ononguli watch her. She was used to people like Governor Maks and a few experts who had originally gone to Bastion with him to build Uly's station.

Today, there were an excess of closed-minded punks scowling back at her. Hotheads, Uly had called them. Still angry that the Horde couldn't do it all themselves, and required outside—*ALIEN!*—assistance to fight the Auga.

Fortunately, none of their horns came up to her nose. And had thighs about as big around as her arms. And she led seventeen more killers, all armed and grumpy, scowling back.

The *Vatazhko*, when they entered the final chamber, was obvious, even though Inari had only seen pictures of the woman.

Anna Shevchenko owned the room. Reminded Inari of Commander Chastain that way. Or Uly, but he was a male, and there was a subtle gender difference there.

Ononguli women tended to be a shade smaller than the men, which Inari found bizarre. The *Vatazhko* was the same general size and mass as Lukyan Chayka. Or Dan and Uly.

Teeny.

She kept her grin inside and focused on the Ononguli bodyguards that had accompanied the woman. All looked tough and professional. Competent.

Someone in this building had still cast aside all honor to warn the *Auga Empire* that Uly was going to Zhoralong. Such dishonor stained all of the Ononguli, until that person could be located, identified, and *purged*.

Half of Inari's team had remained with the shuttle, under Aava Kinnunen's command. The rest spread out behind Uly and Haydar at the table, facing the *Vatazhko* and Chayka.

"It is good to see you, Uly," the woman nodded.

Inari had ordered her women to watch the other guards exclusively, so that Inari was free to watch the negotiators. Not that she expected betrayal, but because she had no doubts that Haldur and the Paramount would demand an extensive debriefing later.

The Ononguli were allies and neighbors, but both conditions were brand new and everyone was still attempting to frame things cleanly. Inari had known a few Zuath and Ugotha and Thogin growing up. One Emro merchant that had left a lasting impression.

Then the Samuur had discovered the rest of the galaxy. So many interesting people to meet.

"I'm happy to come, Anna," Uly replied. "Lukyan brought you up to date with what Maks and I have been up to?"

"He did, but I have concerns," the woman said. "You expect the Auga to strike your Silk Road at some point?"

"Years from now," Uly nodded. "After Ixtin, I expect that they need time to send out spies to understand what has happened to their grand plan. Then time to coalesce that data into information. Then and only then will someone high in their government be able to make decisions that have offensive, strategic implications. Moving at the speed of bureaucracies."

That seemed to assuage the woman.

"Should we strike first?" the *Vatazhko* asked.

"Absolutely not," Haydar intruded sharply, drawing eyes to his tentacles.

Mazhin could hold complete conversations with them. Inari still found the entire concept equally bizarre and interesting.

"No?"

"The raid into Auga Sector Three will deeply disturb them," Haydar continued. "As intended. They will hunt Sterling, but because he is in a Heavy Striker, they will have to assemble squadrons large enough to be a threat. Where will those ships come from?"

Inari controlled her automatic nod to stillness instead, lest she draw attention to herself. Always a bad idea for a bodyguard.

Lukyan nodded for her.

"They will come from border fleets," he agreed. "Those might be fleets directly facing the Horde, and they might not, but someone will have to organize that. Then rearrange things."

"I expect that initially they will be local forces," Uly said. "Later, when those fail, they will stretch their net wider, which will require that they range laterally across their entire frontier for bodies and ships. At the same time, they must have discussions about reinforcing worlds deep behind those frontiers against more raids. Those squadrons have to come from somewhere as well, and they will not be able to suddenly redouble the speed of their ship-building. Bureaucracies don't work that way, under anything less than emergencies and wartime conditions."

"And if we don't do anything here, maybe they stop looking." The woman suddenly saw it. "Can we really lull them to sleep?"

"We can cause them to lower the priority of threat they assign to the Ononguli Sphere," Uly said. "Hold back raids. Not bother them as much as you can stop your people for perhaps a year. If we could convince them that you needed to retrench as well, they might even fall for it. I honestly think you have a year to build, train, and prepare."

"Then another strike somewhere?" Chayka asked.

"That depends on what your scouts find," Haydar offered.

"Scouts?" Shevchenko asked, looking a bit confused.

Inari understood, but the Samuur looked at things differently. They didn't all want to grow up to be pirates, after all.

"Small ships, designed for long range work," Uly said. "Seeker-scale, but generally configured as Probes. Defensive armaments only. Good sensors. Smart conductors who can slip into an enemy system quietly, look around, then slip out again without rousing any suspicion."

The *Vatazhko* was still confused. Inari must have moved wrong, because the woman looked up and locked eyes with her across the space.

"You understand him?" the woman asked.

It was a hard voice, but not an angry one. A woman experienced at supreme command. A Paramount, ruling perhaps five hundred times as many worlds and people.

And demanding a response.

"Surprise is the best way to win a battle later," Inari quoted the legendary Yrjö Savolainen in his tome on tactics and strategy. "Know the ground. Know the people. Know their fears and exploit them from a blind angle. Attack weakness with strength. Resist hard with soft."

Uly aimed a smile at her and Inari blushed with her ears. Haydar's tentacles laughed. The two Ononguli had to close their mouths. Inari shrugged and went back to immobility.

It took a moment for the room to recover.

"A pirate raid to count coup, if you will," Haydar offered into the stretching silence. "Never fire unless you make a mistake, but learn the exact layout of a system's defenses ahead of time. Or several times so you can watch it evolve as the Auga rearrange their strategic thinking. Find a soft spot, then you *slam* a knife into it."

Inari had heard stories about Haydar's youth, but only because Haldur had mentioned it. Now, she saw it in grim detail.

Middle-aged didn't make him less deadly. More, perhaps, by layering experience on top.

"What does that look like?" Chayka asked.

Inari settled in and listened as four top minds roughed out a campaign that might take decades to unfold.

SEVENTY-THREE

Lukyan had gotten Anna off alone. He didn't call it a date night, but that was kinda what it was. Harald had been designated to answer if any emergencies came up, so he could drag her to a private room at her favorite restaurant and relax.

"What's really bothering you?" he asked as they finished their desserts. "Uly's here. Maks keeps up a regular courier run from Saari. The Auga have gone weirdly silent and that's only going to get worse if Uly's right."

"And only a fool bets against Uly," she completed his second favorite saying.

Lukyan smiled at her. He could see the stress, but she was still an amazingly beautiful woman. He might have to remind her of that later.

Anna put her spoon down and sighed. Lukyan watched carefully, aware that she had finally learned to trust him. To loosen up around him.

"Everything is about to turn inside out," she pronounced like some oracle from a story.

"Oh?" he asked.

"Uly sent Dan and Halyna and the rest on a mission," she replied. "So he stopped by Saari and acquired an entire new ground force made up exclusively of Samuur women. It likely could have just as easily been Isann women, I suspect. Or maybe Ononguli, if he'd been going some-place like Z'Gosza."

Lukyan nodded. Anybody who spent any time around Uly felt that charisma envelop them eventually. Even his enemies, given what Lyra had said about that one Auga conductor they'd captured while stealing his ship out from under him.

"And?" Lukyan prompted her carefully.

She was still the supreme boss around here. The Lord of the Endless Plains herself.

"I have spent most of my adult life preparing for that next war with the *Auga Empire*," she admitted. "Looking at maps and trying to figure out which worlds we would lose this time, because they would bring overwhelming force. Where we could settle newly homeless popula-tions. Every *Vatazhko* before me who has lasted more than a few years has faced similar difficulties."

He remained silent and attentive. Listening to her vent was a signifi-cant portion of his job these days. Especially with Chervonya off with Maks at Saari, charming their new neighbors and allies.

Anna chuckled quietly.

"There is a whole series of notebooks that every *Vatazhko* inherits from their predecessors," she continued. "All of them detailing what they did. And how. And why. Nothing ever shared outside the office, even with their closest advisors, because being *Vatazhko* is its own issue. I read what they had to say about all the previous wars over the last several centuries."

She paused and studied him.

"I am on the verge of having to throw all that accumulated wisdom and advice out the airlock, because everything has changed, or is about to."

Lukyan nodded. He'd felt that the first time he had encountered a Human on a screen, sitting in Adrian's ship and about to start ending piracy in Sector Fifteen.

Tuesdays.

And it had only gotten weirder since.

"How do we take advantage of it?" he asked.

Wasn't a Tuesday. Except in his mind. They occasionally snuck up on folks anyway.

"Do we need to follow up Dan's mission by sending a few ships out ourselves to locate and recruit her more Humans later?" Anna asked.

Lukyan pondered. That topic had come up more than once, though never with any seriousness.

Too far away, clear across the width of the *Auga Empire*.

And yet...

A thought struck him. Lukyan blinked as he processed. Anna suddenly shifted to combat mode on him, but he waved it away.

"Imperial Sectors Twenty-Two and Twenty-Three," he mused aloud.

"What about them?" she asked.

"Who's out there?" he asked back. "Nobody really knows, because we've always been defensive, being slowly pushed back from the inner borders of Twenty-One. If we aren't, can we look to scout and expand that way?"

He watched her eyes unfocus, studying some documents or maps he knew were the personal property of the various *Vatazhko*s down history.

"The Yousses come from Sector Twenty-Five," she said quietly. "Almost exactly opposite Z'Gosza on a map and about that far out the other direction. There are notes about Mazhin ships originating in either Twenty-Three or Twenty-Four, but nobody was sure and nobody cared, either."

"Not at the time, no," he agreed. "Might matter these days."

"Extend Uly's Silk Road the other direction?" she smiled.

"Build a really deep moat," Lukyan proposed. "Never kept us out when we were mounted on a zeonx and raiding cities, but it works as a psychological tool. Especially if the Auga start seeing the walls around them, even if only in their minds."

"I feel like I need to order several warships back out of commission," she said abruptly. "Then dig up Probes and send them every which way. We really do not know what's out there. And we need to. Possibly almost immediately."

"Do we have Mazhin tradeships anywhere that we could hire to carry messages?" he asked, starting to feel some of the excitement he could see in her eyes.

"Yes, but I'd need to check the latest intelligence reports to know where they are," she nodded. "I'll do that tomorrow after lunch."

"After lunch?" he asked.

She stood abruptly, so he matched her.

"It's my night off," she reminded him. "I might have a whole new campaign to prepare, but I'm planning on sleeping in late tomorrow after being up half the night. Assuming you're up for it."

She said that last with the kind of leer that he'd only seen occasionally from her, but Lukyan felt a smile rise to match hers.

"Let's go find out," he said.

Tomorrow was coming.

And it looked like it might be even better than today.

SEVENTY-FOUR

Uly listened as Anna explained her new plan, with Lukyan occasionally offering expansions and Haydar answering a few questions about the Mazhin. Eventually, everyone fell to silence, watching him.

For a long moment, Uly felt the weight of the entire galaxy on his shoulders, but that was merely the expectations of the two Ononguli that he would offer some pithy advice to their proposal.

"I like it," he replied simply. "It builds on everything we've been doing for several years now. It extends the Horde the other direction, where hopefully you'll be able to find more allies in that gap before the Auga decide to get moving again. If I knew where and when Sterling would emerge, I'd have you sit down with him and talk stellar cartography. I will send messages to various places, but he might need to drydock the ship again after that long of a sail and whatever happens. If nothing else, he will expect your conductors to build up better maps than you have today."

He turned to Haydar next.

"How do we locate the Speaker of the Mazhin Convocation herself and convince her to travel to Rayzian?" he asked.

Haydar's tentacles nearly knotted themselves, which made Uly grin.

"I'll put together a package for all the Ononguli conductors going out," Haydar finally offered. "Explaining the what and the where. I have no idea who might be in charge these days, as I've been out of touch for close to eighteen years now, dealing with Human affairs in various iterations."

Uly nodded. Captured by *Danumash* and held as a slave. A *Technical* in their parlance, researching better technology in trade for better circumstances than working on an agricultural latifundia or something equally gross.

Then rescued by *Batyr*, only to be captured by other pirates. Then the whole adventure of the Corsac Fox.

"Good enough," Uly agreed. "Getting them to talk to the Ononguli and whoever else on that flank helps everyone. Eventually, we want to invite them to Bastion as well, understanding that to be an exceptionally long sail, even by Mazhin standards if they are from Twenty-Two or Twenty-Three."

"Is it the right thing?" Anna asked.

"Absolutely," Uly turned back to face her. "It means that the Ononguli Sphere might have even more allies on that far side to help hold the line and eventually push the Auga back. To make them behave better. And perhaps be less assholes to everyone else, such that we can start trading across the whole galaxy as equals. I have no idea if they can be changed that far, but I intend to try, just as you are doing here. I bought myself time to build up Bastion by hammering Nyri and then Zhoralong. Stradosha maybe buys you a year or more to do the same to your flanks, while trading more with Saari, Isann, and anybody you might find closer to the galactic core when you also send Probes that direction."

"Inward?" Lukyan asked.

"Absolutely," Uly repeated himself. "We crossed briefly into Thirty-Two, but didn't explore. You should. If everything we're doing today fails, the Horde will eventually be pushed that direction, so you need to know if you have space to expand, or will be crushed between the Auga and someone else nobody knows about yet."

"A suggestion?" Haydar offered. "Long-range Probes should be sent out with the smallest crews you think are safe, to let them travel a greater circle. We can't assume that they will find folks willing to trade, so food will likely be the limiting factor on mission length. Especially since you aren't sending pirates who can resupply themselves from their victims."

"That will require a bit of a mind-shift from our people," Lukyan grimaced.

"Understood," Uly accepted. "I'd offer to send some Samuur or Isann sailors with you, if you thought that might improve things. Possibly not, though, unless you have the right set of conductors already in mind."

"I might ask for some full crews that I could send out in our hulls," Anna countered. "Assuming they'd be willing to go."

"*Karaŋgılıkka*," Uly told her, as if that covered it all.

For the Isann, it did. Oh, how it did.

He turned in place to smile at Inari, trying to be invisible behind him.

"Think I could convince Eskil and Aarne to ship a few crews here to help?" he asked her.

She nodded. One up and down. Nothing more. Nothing more really needed saying. He'd come to understand how smart the woman was. Just usually quiet about things unless specifically asked a direct question.

If the *Vatazhko* asked for assistance, Uly would offer. As would the Paramount. And the Chief of Chiefs.

Uly grinned at them.

"We should ask Maks if he has plans for ultra-long-range Probes that they might turn out," Uly continued. "I know Kit has been working on improving life support systems, and there are a few Yarikh engineers involved now that might enjoy such a challenge. Since I need to talk to Sterling, I'll head that direction shortly and start them on a process. The usual couriers can carry messages back and forth, so you'll know as soon as I do and can start sending ships from here when you get things organized."

"What about Dan's mission?" Anna asked.

"By now, I presume that part one is complete and they should be onto part two," he said. "And that she'll be home eventually."

PART TEN
FREE TRADER POLAT

SEVENTY-FIVE

Rabiu had largely settled into this command thing, what little his small crew actually needed of him, understanding that Dan and Sterling would be along soon enough and that she would take charge at that point.

Still, it had been eye-opening, watching his new people work and learning from them. And figuring out how to make ships like this more efficient. Usually, the trade-off was comfort for efficiency. More space for cargo meant crews crammed into smaller volumes. Bigger engines did the same.

Conversely, if you made things spacious for the personnel, you lost cargo volume or generators or something, following a fairly predictable pattern that Rabiu felt he could reduce to a mathematical formula.

Worse, he'd been tinkering one night and figured that formula out. At least in the roughest phase. Then refined it. And added a couple of really interesting starting variables, based on the average physical volume of a crewmember by species.

Thogin like Ethir and the cousins could build a much smaller ship. Or build extra decks into an existing hull and have a lot more personal space for the same mass. At the other end, Emro and Samuur needed more volume for bigger bodies. Khet, Humans, and Ononguli in the middle were generally the basis upon which ships were built, except that everyone tended to build decks tall enough for Emro to move around, and vault ceilings in places.

When he got home, Rabiu would dump it all on Piruz and Ethir and let them poke holes in his findings. He hadn't been able to as yet, but they had to be there. Right?

"Rabiu, we got company coming in," Yalwa Emeghara said over the intercom.

Yalwa was nominally First Officer, but he was also the sailing expert who generally handled things, once he'd taught Rabiu how to give useful orders. Uly and Drew and Sterling had already done that to a certain extent, but Rabiu hadn't had final authority ever before this.

"Ship on alert?" Rabiu asked immediately.

The siren came up at the same instant, so Rabiu nodded, cut the line, and headed aft to the bridge. From the outside, *Polat* looked like a cargo transport, but it was a weird design where most of the control spaces were in the aft quarter above the engines and such.

The front two-thirds had been built in a long time ago and turned into a slightly-better-than-expected troop transport. Or a cheap cruise ship. Something to haul a lot of people in decent-enough comfort over long distances.

Which was what had gotten him onto efficiency in the first place. Hopefully, all the new Humans would be like the ones he already knew, so this ship would meet their needs.

Because getting home to Bastion was two months or more, depending on how well they could connect with resupply ships along the way, including a couple already closer to Human space.

"*Vauquelin* off our starboard flank," Yalwa announced as Rabiu got to the bridge.

His ship wasn't all that well armed. A pair of 1dm wavebolts and a single Omnipulsar for defense. Any pirate coming along was a threat, because the ship was almost empty of crew at the moment.

That would change quickly with Dan here.

"Hail them?" he asked, taking his formal station.

"Coordinating with Huff's people for docking," Yalwa confirmed.

"Excellent," Rabiu replied. "As long as you make me look good on the quarterly reports."

Yalwa laughed. They both understood that Yalwa could have done all this without Rabiu, but having him there meant that it added a certain panache to things.

That would matter later, when Yalwa was up for command of his own ship somewhere.

Rabiu found the comm line he wanted and sent a message. Dan appeared on his personal screen quickly.

"All good?" he asked her.

"Successful at Stradosha," she nodded. "Rescued a mass of prisoners and Sterling put the fear of God into the locals."

Rabiu shuddered at that thought, understanding the implications of Sterling and *Vauquelin frightening* people.

"We're ready for you here," he told her. "Yalwa is bringing up life support forward, though it might be a bit chilly when folks take their bunks. I've got a course already plotted here to meet up with *Free Trader Trinity Khitan* for next resupply outbound."

"We're in good shape for consumables," Dan said. "But that's the margin of error we baked in at the top. And the expectation that we can resupply at our final target. Failing that, we might be raiding or trading more than I hoped."

"We'll see it done," Rabiu nodded. "See you aboard in a bit."

He looked at Yalwa as he cut the line.

"All technical stuff at this point?" he asked.

"Far as I know," Yalwa replied.

"Good, you handle it," Rabiu rose. "I'll go play Cruise Director forward."

Because honestly, that was going to be a chunk of his job from here on. Dan would take overall command. And she had all of her Combat Team. He knew the ship and small crew Yalwa had assembled.

Then, off to the next grand adventure.

SEVENTY-SIX

Dan studied the training gym she'd claimed when they had first selected this ship for the mission. Most of the troops had a larger space on the bow, but she had wanted someplace private where she could work with her Team and not have to deal with outsiders.

That was going to matter more if and when she managed to recruit Humans to travel to the far ends of known space with her, possibly never to return. Oh, and to meet a whole raft of alien species that none of them had ever heard of.

She'd been in the business long before she'd met Uly, and had only known of a few, after all.

"You seem glum," Katya announced as she entered, walking close with a bag of personal weapons she started unloading onto a rack of similar ones.

"Long ways from home," Dan replied, thinking about it for a moment then moving to stand next to the Ononguli pirate who had gone legitimate. Or something.

"I thought you were getting closer to home?" Katya asked, looking up from her task.

"Bastion is home these days," Dan said, feeling the honesty of it. "I'm going back to places I never really expected to see again."

"Like visiting your hometown all these years later and running into folks who never traveled more than fifty kilometers away, even on vacation," Katya nodded. "Might be a reason I signed up with Adrian's crew originally. Dumb move at the time, but I like how it turned out for me."

"Are the Zehlennko getting used to having clan-by-marriage to Uly?" Dan asked.

Katya's grin was rude in response.

"Only sort of, considering how much money they could make," she chuckled. "Then they realized how close that drew them to the *Vatazhko*. Folks freaked out a little about that and somebody offered a motion in clan council to exorcise me. Calmer heads prevailed when someone else told them how quickly that would make enemies of some of the biggest players in the Sector. I expect cousins and kin to start looking more seriously at Bastion soon, but most of them never leave M'Ilar, except to maybe take a big vacation to Rayzian once in their lifetime."

"Same with a lot of my people," Dan agreed. "I just went a lot farther away."

"At least the boys might have a better chance at having normalish families," Katya said. "Not necessarily anything I ever planned, but none of this was on any scanner I had."

Dan nodded. She had Uly. Sterling had Anari, but they couldn't have children together without all manner of potential complications in adopting or donations. Same with Kit and Melpomeni, though Dan didn't think that woman was young enough anyway. Or even the same species. However, a couple hundred Humans intent on a grand adventure, halfway across the galaxy, that might shake things up.

"How often are we likely to run a mission like this?" Katya asked as she finished putting swords and sticks away.

"Clear to Human space?" Dan asked, surprised.

"And maybe an Ancyn world somewhere," Katya nodded, grinning. "Or finding some Thogin girlfriends for the cousins. Never thought I'd grow up to be some sort of pimp, truth be told."

"Me, neither," Dan laughed with her. "But with the Ancyn and Thogin, we can at least advertise for folks willing to relocate to Sector Fourteen to start new lives. I don't dare do that with Humans. Not yet, anyway. Too big a risk of them deciding to really start exploring beyond those dead zones that have protected *Danumash* from the Auga up until now. At the same time, you're probably right that we'll end up doing this again at some point. Maybe a different world next time, after we talk to some of these recruits and get leads from them."

"Any chance we can walk around on the ground of a Human colony?" Katya asked, eyes glittering with excitement.

"I doubt it, but anything is possible," Dan replied. "Depends on a lot of things that happen after I walk around there first."

Katya shrugged, then nodded. Dan watched her walk to the center of the floor and start practicing forms.

Could she take the ladies down to the surface when they visited? She wasn't sure if Iethert or Masym would be a better starting point. Gorge was too much vacation spot, though that also meant that many folks were just visiting anyway, and might be open to greater travel.

Elias and Dionysia could walk around with few questions, but they appeared nothing more than dark-skinned humans to the average folks.

But aliens...

Too many questions today, and none that she could answer.

None that she needed to answer.

In a few weeks, they would be back in Human space. That was when things would get really interesting.

SEVENTY-SEVEN

Uly had smiled when *Nubia* dropped out of warp at the edge of Saari's navigation zone. The first ship to challenge them had been *Nikodemus Lindberg*, under the command of Eskil Haldur running a shakedown cruise.

The ship was a Light Striker by mass and armaments. And still twice the size and power of *Tiikeri*. Nikodemus Lindberg the person, from what he remembered, had been a founding-type hero, a fighting explorer in the Samuur's earliest star travel days, just as they broke out of Saari proper and started building their first out-system colony, with the most primitive Variable Pulse Spatial Generators anyone could remember.

How far they had come.

After a round of meetings with Eskil and Aarne, as well as Maks and others, Uly had invited Melpomeni aboard *Nubia* to talk. Just the two of them in his outer chamber, where they could be alone without being overheard.

Because it would be one of those conversations.

"No, I do not know who might be found in what you call Sector Thirty-Two, Uly," she said when he finished his explanation. "Nor in the regions beyond the Ononguli Sphere. Of course, our records are extremely out of date, even accounting for those things we salvaged from pirates who tried to attack Traiffe."

He nodded. It had been worth a try.

"How much of Yarikh history are you and Nomiki prepared to share with the rest of us?" he asked.

Melpomeni turned cagey. It was in the eyes, though he supposed that you needed to be Human to see it.

"What do you mean, Uly?" she asked, voice just the slightest bit *off*.

"I know from Sterling's records and Kit's theories that you are not native to Traiffe," he replied evenly. "That you withdrew there from several other worlds in Sector Fourteen when you decided to vanish from galactic history. And Blair is firmly convinced that we did both originate from the same species, before the Yarikh upgraded themselves during that dark period, so we appear to have come from the same base stock. The same worlds. And those are not the worlds that make up *Danumash* or *Batyr* today."

She grew a bit more uncomfortable, watching him. Uly waited.

"What are you after?" she asked carefully.

"Where do Humans come from?" he asked her bluntly. "Sterling suggests hints of something in or even beyond Sector Forty-One, largely based on his analysis of the cartographical records he inherited from this ship. Something about the depth of detail and how much more he knew about places nobody around here had ever gone."

He fell silent, watching. She remained silent, watching back.

The silence grew long and uncomfortable.

Finally, she nodded.

"I warned her that you were smarter than you had any right to be, Uly," Melpomeni grinned wryly. "Nomiki might have a blind spot that we have of course upgraded our minds as well as our bodies, and must be superior."

"Of course," he replied ironically, causing her grin to turn into a smile.

"We talked about it before I left on this most recent mission," she continued. "At present, all we have are theories. Theories, mind you, because even our records show that *Nubia* was destroyed by Selene Praxis instead of being oh-so-carefully abandoned where it might be found later by some intrepid explorer."

"Meaning?" he countered.

"Elias immediately started digging into some of those oldest records, fearing that someone had altered them at some point, then nobody had caught on soon enough to fix them back," Melpomeni replied, turning serious. "He might be right."

"So you don't even know?" he asked.

"We can't be certain," she corrected him. "There are ideas. Theories. Tall tales, even. Whole mythologies. Nobody, however, can point to any book or fact and say 'Yes, this one is indisputable.' That has caused a great deal of consternation back home."

"I can imagine," Uly said. "At the same time, it doesn't really matter."

"No?" She seemed offended.

"No," he shook his head. "That was thousands of years ago, and everyone involved is long since dead. *Nubia* survived. Other ships might have as well, but I doubt it, given the precise care Selene took. Anything we might find at this point is likely a wreck on a planetary surface somewhere, useful from a purely archaeological standpoint. Should we consider doing what Anna Shevchenko is, and build up the capability to send exploration ships into the depths of Forty-One looking? It's been, as noted, millennia, but Sterling is the best cartographer and astrogator I have ever met, so he probably could narrow it down to a reasonably small sphere if I challenged him. Is it worth doing?"

More silence. He could see the calculations in her eyes. How much to tell him. How much truth to tell him. How to shade the lies.

Uly nodded gravely at her indecision.

"Can I be blunt?" she asked finally.

"Please," he said. "That's why it is just the two of us right now."

"Some of our oldest records suggest—only suggest, mind you—that we were fleeing something," she said. "Or somebody. That our distant ancestors packed up and disappeared, slipping into the deepest night they could find. To cite Aibek Sulaymanov, we went *Into Darkness*, but intentionally tried to go as far as we could in it. Possibly hiding. Again, the records in question hint at things twenty or even twenty-five thousand years ago, so they can only be stories. We've evolved ourselves into a new species, as Kit discovered and Blair confirms. I cannot fathom what those Humans might be like today. If our history is anything like theirs, the civilization we fled from has long since disintegrated and vanished, but it could have been replaced by anything."

"Or nothing," Uly reminded her.

"Or nothing, yes," she nodded. "The old Yarikh have vanished from more than a dozen worlds that Kit and Anari never visited, but which might be habitable today. So yes, it is possible that we came from somewhere beyond Imperial Sector Forty-One, but I do not think you should explore that region. Not yet."

"Why not?" he countered. "What if they might be allies?"

"Anybody might turn into an ally, Uly," she smiled tightly. "I've seen your charm at work. At the same time, it would represent a massive undertaking on your part. And, as with Traiffe, you would have to send a Human ambassador of some sort, in addition to whichever member of the Congress of Wives went. And you do not have the people. Not if you are building towards your war with the Auga. Your second war, at least."

"Second?" he asked her, intrigued.

"You started at Vynchen and Zhoralong," she noted. "Nyri and Zhoralong and Stradosha will nicely bookend it, I think. Everything I have heard about the *Auga Empire* suggests that they will spend five or perhaps ten years introspecting to understand the threat you represent. Peace, if you will, but a brittle one, broken by raids and possibly the first Auga diplomats sent to understand Bastion. They never bother with Rayzian, and Z'Gosza is too far away, but Bastion might be important enough."

"Others suggest an Auga war fleet showing up one day," he offered.

"We intend to turn Bastion Station into a fortress sufficient to hold them off," she said, turning so deadly serious all of a sudden that he nearly flinched. "It becomes necessary, if we wish to protect Traiffe."

"Fight them here instead of there?"

"Crude, but accurate, Uly," she confirmed. "New weapons comparable to *Nubia* or perhaps a little better. New war systems that will not adapt well to warships, but will make the station impregnable for now, while we determine what will be necessary to protect ourselves after you are gone."

Uly understood. The Yarikh lived up to three centuries or more, so they had a longer view. And saw him as a tool to blunt Auga's imperial intentions, which folded in well with his own plans.

At least for now.

"And adding more Humans from Forty-One threatens to unbalance that?" he asked, seeking the shape of her logic.

"Today it does, yes," she said. "Bastion and the Conclave and the Congress are as yet too amorphous to build a counterweight empire. That's coming. That's your lifetime, I think, used to create what needs doing."

"Will the Yarikh join me later, if I do go?" he asked.

"The kids that came with me here to Saari are the ones you will need to ask," she replied. "They are the adventurous ones, so you will need a few Yarikh elders to temper their new enthusiasm."

"Such as yourself?"

She shrugged, which was probably the most honest answer he could ask for. They made some small talk after that, then she left, leaving him alone.

He missed Dan. Missed her coming in to sit and lean on him. Steal his warmth. Offer him smiles or solace.

And all the other Wives had gone with her, which he approved of, except on nights like this when he found himself alone and a little lonely. So many questions he needed to get her opinion on, especially Sector Forty-One.

He couldn't even mention anything to the Khet, because they would send someone looking. It would have to remain a secret within a small group of important players.

At least for now.

One of these days, he would send a ship. Or a squadron, given the distances presumably involved.

Sailing Into Darkness.
Wondering what—or who—might be on the other side.

Read the thrilling conclusion to Part One of the Corsac Fox in Book
Seven: *In Congress Assembled*.

READ MORE

To read more of my fiction, sign up for my newsletter. You'll also get a free book!

http://www.blazeward.com/newsletter/

ABOUT THE AUTHOR

Blaze Ward writes science fiction in the Alexandria Station universe (Jessica Keller, The Science Officer, First Centurion Kosnett, etc.) as well as The Corsac Fox and several other science fiction universes. He also writes action-thriller (present day as well as historic). In addition, he's the editor and publisher of Boundary Shock Quarterly Magazine and Thrill Ride Magazine. You can find out more at his website www.blazeward.com, as well as Bluesky, Goodreads, and other places.

Blaze's works are available as ebooks, paper, and audio, and can be found at a variety of online vendors (Kobo, Amazon, and others) as well as the Knotted Road Press website directly. His newsletter comes out monthly and you can also follow his blog and his Patreon on his website. He really enjoys interacting with fans, and looks forward to any and all questions—even ones about his books!

Never miss a release!
If you'd like to be notified of new releases, sign up for my newsletter.

http://www.blazeward.com/newsletter/

Buy More!
Did you know that you can buy directly from the KRP website?

https://www.knottedroadpress.com/shop/

Connect with Blaze!

Web: www.blazeward.com
Boundary Shock Quarterly (BSQ):
https://www.boundaryshockquarterly.com/

www.ingramcontent.com/pod-product-compliance
Lightning Source LLC
Chambersburg PA
CBHW060225100726
47907CB00003B/510

ABOUT KNOTTED ROAD PRESS

Knotted Road Press publishes dynamic fiction set in exotic locations. Our authors cover a wide range of genres including science fiction, fantasy, mystery, literary, and poetry. We also have unique non-fiction voices in genres such as autobiography, business, cookbooks, and how-tos. We offer both DRM-free ebooks and print books for a global readership.

www.KnottedRoadPress.com